COME OUT – COME OUT

H. A. QURESHI

ISBN-13: 978-0578111520
ISBN-10: 0578111527

To HS

ACKNOWLEDGMENTS

All of the characters in Come Out – Come Out are fictitious, but the people who brought them to life are real. I'd like to thank the editors, who took time out of their busy schedules, for giving life to each character. A special thanks to John Richman. John encouraged me to publish Come Out – Come Out, and offered to edit it as well. An offer I couldn't refuse. I did entice him with a couple of cigars. Thanks to my brother, BQ, who spent countless hours after his busy work day to edit the novel as well. He put up with my late night phone calls and emails without a single complaint. For that I am grateful. I'd also like to thank Zuul Q. who offered valuable suggestions.

Thanks to my dear friend, Dennis Sheil, who offered to help market the novel and gave me valuable guidance on other fronts as well. Dennis, I've always valued your advice.

A very special thanks to Michael Walters for providing guidance and being a mentor. You've been an integral part of my journey.

Special mention must be made of James Patterson. Though we've never met, he inspired me to write Come Out – Come Out. I was first introduced to his novels while I was an employee of J. Walter Thompson. Coincidently, Mr. Patterson worked at JWT at the same time I was there.

When my wife, Nadia, read Come Out – Come Out, I prayed she'd forgive me for its graphic content. "Honey, it's only fiction," I told her. I think she fell for it. Nadia, thank you for putting up with me. I will always love you.

1

She heard the sound of a car, and thought it was her father. She adored him. He was coming home that night from a business trip. Her mother was in the kitchen preparing dinner for the family. It was going to be special.

The Christmas lights surrounding the house illuminated the pure snow as it fell briskly from the night sky above. She looked up for a brief moment. Her lips glistened as each snowflake carefully settled on her porcelain-like face. She looked like a princess standing in the middle of a snow globe.

The station wagon was parked in the driveway

with its headlights glaring. The little girl struggled to look inside the car. She raised her tiny hands to her forehead to block the bright light. She wondered why her father was still sitting inside the car. She waved towards him, and said, "Daddy!"

There was no response from the idling car. She inched closer, and again said, "Daddy!" in a bubbly voice; a voice which could never be duplicated. She jumped up and down, and clapped her hands out of excitement. She was certain he had brought a Barbie Doll for her.

The driver-side window rolled down. The man inside stuck his arm out, and waved a doll. It was too much for the little girl to bear. She ran toward the car, reassured. She was too excited to notice it wasn't her father's car. As she grabbed the doll, she was startled. She tilted up her head slightly, much like a puppy, to look at the man sitting behind the wheel. It was too dark to see his face clearly. It all happened too quickly. The man grabbed her by the wrist, and pulled her close. Before she could scream there was a white cloth over her nose. She became unconscious.

The man took a leisurely step out of the car. He opened the back door of the station wagon, picked up the little girl, and laid her down on the seat. He paused to look at her face. He couldn't wait to play with her. He could barely contain his excitement. "Oh, how much fun I'm going to have with you," said the man aloud.

The little girl's mother didn't hear her leave the house. The radio was turned up loud, and the faucet was running as well.

The man walked up to the front of the house. The door was unlocked. He stepped inside the living room without making a sound. He had done this before. Something on top of the fireplace caught his eye. It was a framed photograph. He picked it up and studied it. He was in no rush. He positioned the frame back in its exact place, turned around, and walked towards the kitchen.

He watched as she swayed her body to the music which was playing on the stereo mounted under a cabinet over the granite countertop. She had striking blond hair tied up in a pony tail revealing the back of her neck. She was wearing a

8

tight dress with a flower pattern. The dress expressed every curve on her body. She danced as she moved her hips, side to side, ever so slightly. She was too occupied with the cooking to notice she wasn't alone.

The man placed his left hand over his crotch, and felt himself getting aroused. He would enjoy what he was about to do. He wanted to hear her scream. He wanted to hear her call out for help. He got off on that sort of thing. He pulled out a knife from his jacket.

He felt something he had never felt before. He couldn't describe it. It angered him. He felt enraged. He wasn't an emotional man. He was a calculating and methodical killer. He wanted to be inside her. She would love him, he thought. He had never fucked a woman before - that's not what he did. He liked to play with little girls. They were his "little dolls."

He walked up behind her like a ghost, and said, "Don't turn around. I have your daughter. If you make a sound I'll kill her. Trust me."

The tears dripped down her cheeks as she

compliantly nodded. He wrapped his right arm around her waist, and placed his left hand over her face. He put his nose near the back of her neck, took a deep breath, and exhaled. He wanted her to feel the warm air come out of his mouth. She was shivering. He could smell her perfume. Or was it her fear? Whatever it was, he liked it.

"We are going to have fun," he whispered in her ear. "Oh, we are going to have so much fun."

He spun her around. She was almost as tall as him. They stood face-to-face, inches apart. She stared at him blankly.

"Please don't hurt her, please don't hurt my daughter," she begged. She rolled up her lower lip between her teeth, and bit down.

"Do exactly as I say, and everything will be just fine," said the man.

He began to undress her while kissing her softly; first on the cheek, then on the neck. He took pleasure in the feel of her soft skin against his parched lips. She struggled to stop him. He shook his head slowly as he stuck out his tongue, and ran it between his lips to wet them.

"Now, now, let's play nice if we want to have fun. Nice. Nice," he said.

She stood facing him with her body inert. He pulled down her dress. She wasn't wearing a bra - only black panties. She felt exposed. She was exposed.

He shoved his left hand inside her panties, and tenderly caressed her crotch. He fondled her breasts with his right hand. She turned her head to the side, and closed her eyes. She groaned as he pushed his middle finger deep inside her pussy. The pain was unbearable.

He pulled out his finger from inside her, and his hand from her panties. He placed the finger under his nose, and took a deep breath to smell her.

"You smell sweet," said the man as though he expected her to thank him for the compliment. He looked disappointed!

"Please don't. Please stop," she pleaded.

"It's going to be okay. You'll see how much fun we're going to have," he said with a smile.

She felt a sudden surge in her body. She attempted to break free. He grabbed her arm, and

slapped her across the face. She fell to the floor.

"Don't do that again, bitch!" he said angrily.

He knelt down to his knees, and pulled off her panties. She was terrified. She lay on the floor, naked, staring up at the ceiling. She sat up with her legs straight out, but he pushed her back down.

He looked at her, shook his head, and said, "No. No."

She was afraid if she didn't go along he would hurt her daughter. He spread her legs slightly apart, and shoved two fingers inside her pussy. She groaned louder than before. He went down on her.

"You see how much fun we are having? I told you it would be fun," he mumbled as he looked up from between her legs.

With his fingers still inside her, he moved up her body, and began suckling her breast; first the right, then the left. He was ready to erupt. He loosened his belt, unbuttoned the fly, and took off his pants.

She was absolutely helpless. She prayed her husband would come storming through the door, and save them. Her life was flashing before her

eyes.

She felt a piercing pain as he penetrated her with his penis. She felt the dead weight of the man on top of her moving back and forth, in and out. That's all she felt. It seemed like an eternity.

He kept repeating, "You see how much fun we are having. You see how much fun we are having...."

Just as he was about to ejaculate inside her, with the knife, he slit her throat. Her body shook violently. She gasped for air; blood spurted out of her neck as her body became limp. He lay on top of her, with his face covered in blood, looking in to her lost confused eyes. All along, he maintained a constant smile.

"You see how much fun we had," he said as he pulled out his penis from inside her.

2

Jake Burke called the house for the third time. His wife usually picked up on the second ring. He knew she would be home. He was out of town, and was due to be back by 9 o'clock that evening.

Jake spent the majority of his time traveling. The Agency sent him out as frequently as they could. He was one of their best agents.

He had hoped to spend more time with his wife and daughter. But turmoil around the world kept him, and the other good guys busy. Hell, sometimes they caused the turmoil. Jake

understood that was the world of politics. It was sometimes necessary to stir up chaos, before a prolonged calm. At least that's what they told him during training. He trusted that they were right.

Jake had missed the connecting flight to New York. He decided to spend the night at a no frills hotel. He was in the habit of making himself at home as soon as he would check in to a hotel. It gave him a sense of peace. Since he was scheduled to leave early in the morning, he did not unpack.

It was a clear night. Jake knew it would be difficult to fall asleep. He poured a drink, and decided to sit out on the balcony. The room he was staying in was as small as a sardine can. Budget cuts at the Agency came at the expense of its agents.

Jake sat down, and put his drink on the plastic table. He lit a cigar, and took a deep drag.

"Jesus Christ, that feels good," said Jake.

He was smoking a Cuban. His wife didn't mind him smoking cigars. She even let him light up inside the house on occasion. He had hit the jackpot with her.

Jake called her for the fourth time. Again, there was no response. It wasn't like her not to pick up. He tried to convince himself that there must be a good reason why she wasn't answering the phone. Maybe she's having an affair - no, that couldn't be, thought Jake. She loved him too much.

He finished the first three drinks rather quickly. The last two had been difficult. He stood up, and dragged himself to the bed. He was out cold within a matter of seconds. It had been a rough day. The five drinks he chugged in the last ninety minutes didn't help the situation either.

Jake had been asleep for only an hour when he was awakened by a loud ringing sound. It was his phone. He looked at the caller ID. The number was blocked. He didn't pick up, and dosed off. A few seconds later the phone rang again. This time he answered without looking at the caller ID.

"Hello," said Jake.

"Jake, this is Paul."

Paul was Jake's neighbor. He was a little bit of a nosy body. He and his wife, Tulip, were always in other people's business. Paul always seemed to

be out on his lawn, doing yard work. Tulip mostly stayed inside the house. She was a recluse. The couple yelled at each other all day. The entire neighborhood could hear them. The problem with Paul was that he didn't know how to be quiet. If he saw a neighbor he would run up to them, and start random conversations. This habit irked the neighbors. They tried their best to avoid making eye contact with him.

Paul was handy. If there was ever a problem in Jake's house or with his car, Paul would volunteer to help. He wouldn't take no for an answer. He just wanted to stay busy, and get away from his crazy wife.

The strange thing about the call was that it was the first time Paul had ever called him. Jake wasn't sure how he got his number. He didn't remember giving it to him.

"Paul, what's the matter?" asked Jake.

"There are police cars, and ambulances all around your house," said Paul nervously.

"What? What's going on? What are you talking about?"

"It would be better if you spoke to the police…Jake…Jake?"

Jake ended the phone call. He wasn't thinking straight. He couldn't. He looked around the room, and tried to sort things out. He grabbed his things, and stumbled out of the room.

Jake walked up to the concierge desk, and requested a taxi to the airport. Everything seemed a blur to him. He needed to get home to his wife and daughter. The thought that something terrible had happened to either of them, was something he couldn't stomach.

A taxi pulled up in front of the hotel. Jake opened the back door, threw in his bags, and stepped inside. He instructed the driver to take him to the airport. The driver looked back at Jake through the rearview mirror and nodded. He stepped on the accelerator, and pulled out on to the street.

"Faster!" yelled Jake.

"Who's going to pay the speeding ticket?" asked the taxi driver in an accent Jake couldn't place.

"Don't worry about the goddamn ticket. Just get me to the airport." Jake pulled out his CIA identification, leaned forward, and shoved it in the driver's face.

The taxi driver didn't seem to be impressed by Jake's occupation. He continued at the same speed. Jake was prepared to kill the driver. He thought about putting his hands around the driver's neck, and choking him to death. He knew that wouldn't help his cause. He sat back quietly.

He called his wife again, but there was no response. If there were police officers at the house, why weren't they answering the phone? Thought Jake. A myriad of thoughts were flooding his mind – none of which made sense.

It was 3 o'clock in the morning. The roads were clear of traffic. The ten minute drive from the hotel to the airport felt like an eternity.

As soon as Jake stepped out of the taxi, he ran inside the airport to the American Airlines counter. "I need a flight to New York."

The heavy set woman sitting behind the counter punched keys at a mile-a-minute pace. She had

long fingernails that generated a lot of noise as she banged on the keyboard. She glanced at Jake, and noticed the desperate look on his face.

"The next flight to New York leaves at 9 a.m., sir," said the woman.

"Listen, I need to get back to New York City immediately. Please help me," pleaded Jake.

"Sir, you can check with another airline."

Jake looked around desperately for help. The airport was quiet. He looked back at the woman behind the counter. She noticed the anxiety in his eyes.

"Look, there is a plane leaving for Washington DC in 30 minutes. If you want, I can put you on that flight. Maybe you'll be able to get a flight to New York City from there."

"That would be great. Thank you."

She began typing once again at a feverish pace. It was amazing to witness the speed at which she was able to type despite, what appeared to be, three inch long fingernails. A few seconds later she handed Jake the boarding pass. He thanked her once again, and ran to the gate.

3

The cab pulled up to Jake's house. He saw four marked police cars parked outside. There was no ambulance. Paul was standing outside.

"Ja…Jake," stammered Paul.

"What's going on? Where are Nadine and Jenny?"

"Jake," said Paul as he grabbed Jake's arm. A sinking feeling overcame Jake. He freed himself from Paul's grip.

"Where are my wife and daughter?"

Paul was lost for words. This was a guy who

looked for any opportunity to talk. He could talk for hours about a subject no one cared about.

Jake looked around, and saw several of his other neighbors standing in front of their houses. They looked frozen. None of them had the courage to walk up to Jake.

It was a particularly cold night, twenty below zero with the wind chill. Jake's suit was drenched in sweat. His shirt was stuck to his body as though he had just walked out of torrential rain.

Paul was wearing an open winter coat. The pajamas he had on underneath the coat weren't appropriate for a person his age. They had Spiderman characters printed all over them.

"It would be best if you spoke to the police," suggested Paul.

"Okay," said Jake. He didn't know what else to say.

Paul was trying to be as supportive as possible. He was the most helpful guy Jake knew. He took pleasure in helping people, even complete strangers.

There was yellow tape around Jake's house. Written on the tape in block letters was, "POLICE

LINE DO NOT CROSS."

Jake walked towards his house. The door was open. As he stepped inside, he was greeted by an African American police detective. He appeared to be around the same age as Jake. He was built like a brick house. Jake was six-one and weighed two hundred-twenty pounds. The detective was four inches taller than him, and had at least eighty pounds on Jake. The detective wore a tailored blue suit that could barely contain his shoulders. His eyes were hidden behind sunglasses. He took off the shades when he saw Jake approach him.

The detective had a friendly face. He looked vaguely familiar. He resembled a guy who had played college basketball for either, Arkansas or Illinois, pondered Jake.

"My name is Jake Burke. This is my house."

"Mr. Burke, I'm Detective Jones," said the detective as he extended his arm for a handshake, "and this is my partner Detective O'Brian."

Jake shook hands with Detective O'Brian. Compared to his partner O'Brian was a small man. He was five-ten, and looked to be around a

hundred-seventy pounds. O'Brian's hands were small, but he had a firm handshake. To Jake, it felt as though he shook hands with a midget.

"Where are my wife and daughter?" asked Jake.

Detective Jones hesitated briefly, and looked at his partner for help. Whatever he had to say wasn't good, and Jones didn't want to be the one to deliver the bad news.

Jake began to feel a fury rising in him. He didn't know why, but he did. He was a focused man, and knew how to compose himself in any situation. However, this wasn't just any situation; this was his house, his wife and his daughter. This was his life.

"We have some bad news Mr. Burke," said Detective O'Brian.

"What?" Jake didn't want them to beat around the bush. He wanted the detectives to get to the point.

"Please sit down, sir."

Jake sat down on the couch. To him, it was the most comfortable couch in the world. He

remembered when his wife bought it. She was so excited. It was their first purchase for the new house after they had gotten married. She had made a big deal out of it. She was like that. She made a big deal out of the smallest things. Everything in the house was special to her. Jake thought about the first time they made love on that couch. She was nervous. She kept telling him to be careful.

"Your wife was attacked last night."

"Is she okay? Where is she? Is she at the hospital?" Jake asked everything that would indicate his wife was alive. He couldn't imagine anything else, even though he feared the worst.

"She…your wife…she didn't make it, sir" said Detective O'Brian.

"That's not right. You're wrong. Fuck. No." Jake was slurring. He looked around the living room. It was spinning. He couldn't make it stop.

He looked at everything in the room. It was all just as he had left it when he went away. "Why did I go? I shouldn't have gone," said Jake. He was talking to himself. Nadine had asked him to quit on numerous occasions. She wanted him to find

another line of work. She had told him that he would make a great banker or a lawyer. She was always concerned for his safety. He could never tell her where he was going. The only reason she knew he worked for the CIA was because that is where they had met. She worked there as a secretary. It was love at first sight. Jake knew when he saw her for the first time that she was the woman he was going to spend the rest of his life with.

Everyone who met Nadine fell in love with her. She had that effect on people. She quit her job soon after she found out that they were going to have a baby. She wanted to be home, and get settled before the baby came.

"...And we did not find your daughter in the house? Sir, do you know where she could be?" asked Detective Jones.

"No, you're wrong. My wife, Nadine, she - she's alive. I'd like to see her." Jake became hysterical.

"We'll need for you to come to the station with us, sir"

Jake stood up, and stumbled towards the

kitchen. This felt like a nightmare, but it was real. This was worse than a nightmare. As he walked into the kitchen he was greeted by two uniformed police officers, both in their twenties.

"I'd like a glass of water," said Jake.

"I'll get that for you," said one of the officers.

He couldn't remember the officer's name. A lot of things which happened that night seemed like a blur to Jake. The CIA had trained him to memorize everything he saw. This wasn't difficult for him as he had photographic memory. The shock of what happened that night hindered his ability to think straight.

Jake saw the blood. It was spread all over the floor in front of the stove. He saw Nadine's dress and panties there too. They were soaked in blood. He remembered when she bought that dress. They were on vacation in Miami. She saw it hanging in a store window, and said she had to have it. He thought about when they went inside the store, and she tried it on. She wanted to show it to him. He remembered how beautiful she looked.

Nadine loved to try on clothes before she

bought them. She would model them for Jake to seek his approval. She looked stunning in everything she wore.

Jake tried to guess what she was cooking. It smelled like Indian food. Nadine loved to watch cooking shows, and read cookbooks. She made something new for him every time he came back from a trip. She would guess where he was coming from, and cook something from that part of the world. This time she must have thought he was in India or Pakistan. He missed her. He wanted to go to the stove, and taste whatever she had made. The officers wouldn't allow him to step further inside the kitchen. It was understandable. They were trying to keep him from contaminating the crime scene.

"Here you go sir," said the officer as he handed Jake a glass of water.

"Thanks."

The water tore at Jake's throat. He stared at the floor. As hard as he tried, he couldn't stop, but to think of his wife laying there in a pool of blood. He felt powerless. This wasn't supposed to happen to

my family, thought Jake. What kind of a monster would do this?

Jake hadn't seen any signs of forced entry at the front or the rear doors. The windows on the main floor of the house were shut. Whoever it was had walked in through the door without being noticed.

Nadine made sure both doors were always locked. Jenny, on occasion, would open the front door to greet Jake when he came home from work.

"Please God, please let her be safe," prayed Jake.

They lived in a small town called North Hills located in Nassau County. Forbes Magazine had listed it as one of the top ten places to live in the country. Nadine and Jake had selected it carefully. They wanted to be certain they lived in a place where it would be safe to raise a family. It was a house that was well beyond their means. They were pulling it all together to make it work. Things were supposed to get easier.

Detective Jones walked up behind Jake, and put his hand on his shoulder.

"Sir, are you ready?"

"Yes," replied Jake.

"We'll need you to identify the body."

Jake was afraid of asking Jones about his daughter again. The detective had asked him if he knew where she was. Jake didn't. The possibility that she wasn't in the house when it happened, gave him some comfort. He had no idea where she could have been. Nadine never let her out of sight.

Jenny was five years old. She was the spitting image of her mother. She had her mother's blue eyes, blond hair, beautiful cheek bones, and soft lips. She looked like a doll.

Jake had to find her. He had to find his baby.

4

Jake's neighbors, friends, most of his family, including two older brothers and a younger sister, everyone other than his parents thought he was a normal run of the mill pencil pusher. They believed he led an average life as an accountant.

Jake cherished the time he spent with his daughter. He would often take her to the park. He enjoyed watching her as she ran around and got dirty playing in the grass. This became quite a routine. A routine he treasured.

Jake was always observant. After he joined the

Agency he had become increasingly paranoid. He always knew what, and who was around him. As a medical student believes he or she has every conceivable disease while in medical school, since joining the CIA Jake believed he was constantly being watched or followed. It came with the job.

When Jenny played with other kids in the park, she would give an occasional glance back at her father, and wave cheerfully. Jake would wave back to her. He did his best to provide for her everything which he didn't have when he was growing up.

Jake's father was stern. He didn't like it when the kids ran around. He concentrated on teaching those values which he felt were important. Running around "foolishly" as he called it wasn't one of them.

Jake got along with other parents at the park. He did his best to seem normal. Frequently, people would ask him tax or accounting questions that concerned their personal or business matters. That is the thing he dreaded most. He had taken two accounting courses while in college, and done some extra reading on the subject to appear to know as

much as was necessary to get by when asked random questions. When he didn't know the answer he would respond by saying it wasn't his area of expertise. Mostly, people left him alone. He was just fine with that.

On one particular day, while at the park with Jenny, Jake felt he was being watched by someone. He looked around the park to put himself at ease. When he didn't see anyone, he dismissed it as paranoia.

Jenny was a beautiful girl. Jake realized he would have a tough time keeping boys away from his precious little angel. He dreaded that thought. He was prepared to answer the doorbell, with a shotgun in hand, when boys would come to see her. He was protective of her now, and that would only get worse as she grew older. Even now he scared off little boys who tried to kiss her on the cheek. They were only four or five years old, but he looked at them as adults. Every time one of them attempted to kiss her, he would yell "Jenny!" This usually did the job as she would run towards him and jump into his arms.

Jenny adored Jake. She had a constant smile on her face when she was with him. He was her hero. She loved introducing him to her little friends. "This is my daddy, and I love him very much," she would say. This always brought Jake to tears. It never got old.

"Daddy, can we get ice cream?" asked Jenny

"Yes, of course sweetheart. You can have anything you want," replied the proud father.

There was an ice cream shop a few blocks from the park. Jenny held her father's hand, and skipped as she walked alongside him.

"Are you tired? I can pick you up if you'd like"

"Yes, daddy, I'm tired. Pick me up…pick me up…pick me up" replied Jenny with a giggle as she threw up her little arms with the palms of her tiny hands facing the sky.

Jenny loved it when Jake picked her up. She felt tall. She would put her arms around his neck, and rest her head on his shoulder.

"Don't fall asleep now darling."

Jenny wouldn't answer him. She would

pretend to be asleep. It was a game to her. She was having fun.

They arrived at the ice cream store. Jake stood by as Jenny picked the ice cream she wanted. She pointed to the chocolate flavor one, and said, "That one daddy."

Jake asked the teenager behind the counter for two cones. As the kid bent down to scoop out the ice cream, Jake noticed a reflection of a man in the glass behind the counter. He quickly turned around to see who it was. There was no one there. He had that same feeling in his gut as he did when he was at the park. He was certain that he was being followed. Or was he just being paranoid, he couldn't figure it out.

Jake paid for the ice cream, picked up Jenny, and left the shop. He walked to his car which was parked two blocks away. As he turned the corner, a man bumped into him. He dropped the ice cream cone. Jake's instincts let his right hand fall to his right hip. That is where the gun was hidden under his jacket.

"Watch where you are going!" said the man.

Jake ignored him. Jenny began to cry. "It's okay honey. It's all right, everything's fine," said Jake as he comforted her.

Jake turned around and looked at the man who had bumped into him as he walked away. The man didn't look back. He turned at the corner and disappeared.

Jake walked up to a car, and opened the rear door. He had a BMW. He wanted to buy a Porsche, but those dreams were put on hold when Jenny was born. He promised himself, as soon as the stars were aligned, he would get one.

Jenny hated sitting in the baby seat. She wanted to sit up front, and feel like an adult. She tried her best to convince her father to let her sit next to him. This included throwing a tantrum, but Jake would never allow it. He tried not to reason with her as that only made the situation worse.

When Jake pulled out of the parking spot, he glanced in the rearview mirror to see if Jenny had settled down. His attention was diverted to a man who was leaning against a tree and smoking a cigarette. He thought this was the same man whose

reflection he had seen at the ice cream shop. He reversed the car back in the parking spot, and quickly stepped out.

As Jake approached the man leaning against the tree, a woman and a young boy walked up to him. The man tossed the cigarette, kissed the woman, and picked up the boy.

Jake's paranoia was getting worse. He had to learn to relax. He took a deep breath and jogged back to his car.

5

Craig Nealis had put a lot of thought into the plan. He had been watching the Burkes for some time. He became obsessed with the perfect family; the beautiful mother, the well dressed preppy father, and their perfect little daughter. He had done this before, but it never took this long. He was having trouble with the father's schedule. He would have to wait for the perfect moment to execute his plan.

Nealis got a job as a stock boy at the local grocery store. This was the ideal place for him to find his next target. He had built up quite a resume

as he had done similar work at grocery stores across the northeast. If he wanted to he could have applied for a job as a shipping and receiving manager, and would have gotten it. He spoke well and was intelligent. He didn't fit the profile of a stock boy. The store managers were more than happy to have him as an employee. He was dependable. He always showed up on time. He didn't require training. He was familiar with the products, and knew where they needed to be stocked. He was worth much more than the minimum wage he was paid for doing the work. Nealis only had one request which was more like a demand: he refused to work the graveyard shift. After all, if he worked at night he couldn't stalk his prey. He was a predator.

When Nealis first laid eyes on Jenny, he knew she was the one he needed to add to his collection. It was his second week working at the grocery store when first saw them. It was early afternoon on a clear summer day. Nadine was wearing blue jeans and a white t-shirt. Jenny was wearing a princess dress. As the mother and daughter walked the

aisles, Nealis followed them. He kept a safe distance. Nadine didn't pay attention to him.

Jenny held on to one of the belt loops on her mother's jeans as she walked with her through the aisles. She was lost in her little world. She didn't bother her mother as other kids did when they went shopping with their parents. She didn't make requests to buy random things which she would throw away the second she got home. Jenny enjoyed skipping along next to Nadine, and humming songs she had heard on the Disney Chanel and Nickelodeon.

"Are you having fun, sweetie?" asked Nadine

"Yes, mommy, I'm having fun…tons of fun," replied Jenny with a smile, and a skip.

"That's good."

Nealis could hear their conversation. He smiled along with Jenny. He mimicked her, "Yes, mommy, I'm having fun…tons of fun." This made him giggle.

"Is daddy going to bring a Barbie Doll for me?" asked Jenny as she looked up at Nadine.

"I'm sure he will sweetheart."

Nadine rolled the shopping cart to an available cash register. She emptied out its contents on the conveyer belt. Jenny helped her mother as much as she could. She was barely tall enough to reach the top of the counter. She picked up whatever she could with her tiny hands, and placed it on the belt. The cashier and Nadine looked at each other, and smiled.

"She's beautiful," the cashier complimented.

"Thank you," said Nadine.

Nadine wasn't much of a conversationalist. From the look on the cashier's face, she expected Nadine to say something else, but she didn't say anything. The cashier told her the amount due. Nadine pulled out the cash from her purse, and handed it to the cashier.

"Have a great day," said the cashier.

"Thanks, and you too," said Nadine.

Nealis walked up to the store manager, and told him that he was leaving early. He said that he wasn't feeling well. The store manager obliged. He told his star employee to take the next day off as well if he still wasn't feeling a hundred percent.

Nealis did the work of four people single handedly. The store manager recognized that, and knew if this arrangement was going to continue he needed Nealis to be healthy. He was even thinking of promoting Nealis to a managerial role.

Nealis thanked the store manager, and went to the locker-room to pick up his stuff. He was excited. He grabbed his belongings, and walked out to his car.

Nadine unloaded the bags from the shopping cart, and placed them in the trunk of her car. She picked up Jenny, and sat her down in the baby seat. Jenny didn't throw a tantrum. She only did that when she was with her father. She was daddy's little girl, and behaved differently with him than she did when she was with her mother.

As Nadine pulled out of the parking space, and drove onto the street, Nealis followed her. He kept a safe distance. From time to time, he allowed other cars to cut in front of him to avoid being noticed by his unsuspecting victim as he followed her.

He was driving a dark grey station wagon. The car had several small dents on each side. The inside

of the car was worn out. There was a front passenger seat, and a bench style back seat. There was some rope, and rolls of duct tape on the floor of the car. The rear windows were tinted black. Nealis had paid cash for the car. It was registered under a foreign corporation. He preferred to buy American as he thought of himself as a true patriot.

At one point when Nadine stopped at a red light, Nealis drove up beside her car. He made sure to stay in her blind spot. She glanced over her shoulder, but couldn't see the driver. Jenny was able to see Nealis clearly. She saw him and waved. He smiled at her and waved back.

"I'll see you soon little princess," said Nealis.

The traffic light turned green, and Nadine stepped on the accelerator. Nealis was a safe distance behind her once again. As the traffic began to thin out, he increased the distance between them. He was keeping mental notes of the neighborhood. He would be back again, and know the area like the back of his hand. He did not like to takes notes on paper. It was just another precaution.

When he had applied for the job at the

supermarket, he told the store manager he would come back with the application. He preferred to use a computer to fill it out. The store manager thought it was an odd request. Most people applying for a job at a supermarket preferred to handwrite their information as it was simply easier. The store manager knew he had a winner.

Nadine turned the car in to a driveway. Nealis pressed the brake, and waited for a few seconds before driving off. He watched as she took out the shopping bags from the trunk of her car.

Nadine looked up, and noticed the station wagon. She thought she recognized the driver, but couldn't be sure. She didn't make anything of it.

6

The precinct wasn't much to look at. It was a typical Nassau County police station. The atmosphere was exactly what it was meant to be - depressing. There were three police officers standing behind an elevated counter tending to civilians as they came in to the station. People with requests for police reports on accidents they had gotten into the night before, and others who wanted to be fingerprinted for various reasons. Even though there were two civilians on line, and three officers behind the counter, time seemed to be at stand still.

Things were moving slowly.

Jake was told to sit on a rundown chair across from a desk that wasn't in any better shape. There were police reports, and files scattered all across the desk. The top right corner of the table seemed to be especially busy with papers that appeared to have accumulated there over the years. Jake waited as patiently as he could. But there were no guarantees, he felt as though he could erupt with frustration at any moment.

Detectives Jones and O'Brian walked towards Jake with three cups of coffee. One of the cups was for Jake. He didn't remember asking for it. The detectives sat down across the table from him.

"What's going on here?" asked Jake in a frustrated voice.

"That is exactly what we would like to know," replied Jones.

"I don't follow," said Jake with a frown.

"What can you tell us? Do you know who could've done this? Did you have enemies? What do you do for a living? Do you go away on trips often? Were you jealous of your wife?" Detective

Jones started hammering Jake with questions. He wanted to confuse him, and make him say something that would make his job easier.

"What? I don't understand. You should be out there searching for my wife's killer, and looking for my daughter, rather you are sitting here asking me these asinine questions. This is really unbelievable." Jake expressed his frustration and anger by pounding his fist on the desk.

Jake had a gun under his jacket. He was seconds away from pulling it out. He knew better than to do something silly like that, he had to try to stay as calm as possible.

"Look, calm down, the quicker we can get the answers, the quicker we can move on from here," said O'Brian sympathetically. He picked up the cup of coffee off the table, and took a sip. "You live in one of the most affluent neighborhoods in the country. Shit like this doesn't happen there."

"You're telling me? That's the reason we moved there. Nadine and I thought it would be a safe place to raise our children."

Detective O'Brian was taking notes. Jake

couldn't figure out what he could possibly be writing.

Jake was tired, and sleep deprivation wasn't helping his situation either. He had been awake now for more than 24 hours. He seemed to grow more agitated with each passing second. His eyes wandered around the police station. He seemed to be searching for answers. He just didn't know what the questions were. His eyes stopped when he saw a young girl sitting alone on a chair in the corner. He knew it wasn't his daughter, but he kept picturing her as though she was. He snapped awake from the daydream when a man walked up to the girl, and took her by the hand. As the little girl stood up, and began to walk away, she turned around to look at Jake. She gave him a smile, and waved goodbye. Jake seemed to be comforted by the gesture. It was as though she was telling him everything was going to be okay.

"I was out of town on business. I'm an accountant, and have clients across the country. I love Nadine. We don't have any enemies...look this is all ridiculous. We are wasting time here."

"Are you sure you are an accountant? You don't sound like any accountant I've ever met," said O'Brian. He realized what he said sounded stupid as soon as the words came out of his mouth.

Jake couldn't tell the detectives what he actually did for a living. He would have to check with the Agency first. The chance they would be okay with him sharing his real identity with the police was slim.

"We sent officers to check on all of the addresses you provided us with. Jenny wasn't at any of them. Is there a place where she could be hiding?" asked Jones.

"No, I don't know."

Detective Jones's cell phone rang. He looked at the caller ID, and answered it immediately.

"Is there anything I can do? Can I go back home?" asked Jake.

"Your house is a crime scene. We can't allow you to go back there, at least not for another 48 hours. Is there anyone else you can stay with?"

"I'll figure something out," replied Jake.

Jones returned to the desk, and said, "Look,

you can go. Stay close to your phone. The first 48 hours are crucial. If we are going to capture who did this, and find your daughter we have to stay focused. If you can think of anything at all that can help us, call me immediately at this number." He handed his business card to Jake.

7

Jake contemplated what he would do next. He didn't have much faith in the Nassau County Police Department finding Jenny, and capturing Nadine's killer. He'd have to get involved.

Jake drove to his house. He parked the car two blocks away, and decided to walk the rest of the way. He didn't want to be noticed. He walked quickly, but not in a manner that would make his neighbors wearier than they already were of strangers in their neighborhood.

It was still daylight out. This would be of great

help to Jake. He wouldn't have trouble finding his way through the house. A flashlight or any other form of light would signal trouble, and the police would be alerted.

As Jake approached his house, he looked around to make sure there were no police officers around. The yellow tape was still wrapped around the perimeter of the house. He looked towards his neighbor Paul's house. It was a relief not to see him in the yard where he usually spent most of the day.

Jake walked up the driveway, and to the back of his house. He looked for anything that would indicate forced entry. He was sure the police had already investigated that, but he wanted to be certain. He didn't find anything that looked suspicious. He had hoped to find something.

He took out a set of keys from his pant pocket, and opened the back door. He stepped inside the house. He stood in the kitchen, and stared at the pool of blood on the floor. He was on the brink of breaking down again. He tried to stay composed. He couldn't do it. He broke down.

"I'm going to find the son-of-a-bitch who did

this. I promise you Nadine. I'm going to kill him," said Jake.

This was all too surreal for Jake. This wasn't supposed to happen to him, not to his family. Thoughts like that kept circling in his mind. He was looking for answers when there were none. He remembered stories he had read in the papers about similar crimes in poor neighborhoods around the country. Not this, not in this neighborhood. An aberration, an isolated incident to rest of the world, but to him it was his family; the only thing that mattered to him.

Jake looked for his wife's dress which he had seen earlier on the floor, but it was gone. The homicide investigators had taken it as evidence. The Indian food Nadine was cooking had been burnt.

Jake looked at the refrigerator, and saw Jenny's hand drawings taped all over the doors. He walked over to the fridge to touch them. He was comforted as he felt them.

Jake stepped in to the living room. There wasn't anything that stood out to him as out of place

or odd. Everything was the way he remembered it. He was looking for a break. He was having trouble finding it.

He went up the stairs to the master bedroom. He looked at the dresser, and imagined Nadine brushing her hair as she stood in front of the mirror. He was hallucinating.

He walked to the closet, and opened the door. He moved the clothes that were hanging inside to the left and the right. There was an ordinary wall in the back of the closet. He took out a remote control device from his pocket, and pressed a button. The wall shifted back. He pushed the right side of the wall. It rotated, revealing a room, and he stepped inside. There was an arsenal of weapons hanging on one of the three walls of the room. There were shotguns and handguns, both automatic and semi-automatic. He picked up a duffel bag off the floor, and filled it with weapons of his choice.

There was a cigar humidor on a table to the right of the room. Jake picked it up, and placed it in the duffel bag. He walked out of the room, and pressed a button on the remote control. The wall

rotated, and the room was concealed once again. He moved the clothes back to cover the wall.

Jake opened the door of another closet. He pulled out several suits, jeans, and shirts which were hanging inside. He placed them inside the second duffel bag.

Just as he was about to leave the bedroom, the phone rang. He walked over to see who was calling. It was a blocked number. He didn't pick it up. The answering machine sounded. It was his wife's voice on the machine. He thought about the day they bought it, and the number of times Nadine had recorded the message. She wanted it to be perfect.

It was Nadine's mother. She was hysterical. "Jake, please call me as soon as you get this. I don't know what to do. I've been trying to reach you since last night. Why don't you pick up? Please, oh God, please." With that she hung up the phone.

Jake pulled out a cell phone from his pocket. The phone was off. The battery had drained. He looked at the outlet next to the bed, and saw the

phone charger. He sat down on the bed to pull it out of the socket. The misery of what had happened hit him again. He put his head down on Nadine's pillow. He could smell the sweet scent of her hair. He buried his face in the pillow, and cried.

He pulled himself together, and walked out of the bedroom. The door to Jenny's room was closed. He opened it and stepped inside. The room was pink. There were pictures of little princesses painted on the walls. There were dolls and stuffed animals piled up on one side of the room. There was a small dresser in the corner. He picked up a hairbrush off the dresser, and stared at it. He walked to Jenny's bed, and sat down. He moved the palm of his hand across the pillow. To him, it felt as though she was there.

Jake picked up the two duffel bags, and walked down the stairs to the kitchen. He left the house, the way he had come in, through the back door. As he walked down the driveway, he saw Paul approach him.

"How are you holding up Jake?" asked Paul.

Jake didn't answer. He couldn't come up with

the words. How is a husband supposed to hold up after his wife has been murdered, and his daughter is missing?

"Listen, the cops have been questioning everyone in the neighborhood. From what I've been able to gather no one seems to know anything."

"Did you see anyone come to the house last night?" asked Jake.

"I heard a car drive up, but didn't pay attention to it. I thought it was you. I know you don't like it when I stop you to chat, so I stayed away."

"I'm sorry Paul," said Jake.

"Don't be."

"Did you get a look at the car?" asked Jake.

"Yes, but not a good one. I found it strange that the car was left running in the driveway. I thought you were unloading or going back out. To be honest, I didn't pay much attention to it. When, after a while, I heard the car back-out of the driveway, I looked out the window, and noticed it was a station wagon. It was a dark colored car. It could've been black, blue, or green. I just couldn't

tell for sure."

"Then what happened?"

"I know I get into other people's business, but it didn't occur to me to go out and check. I should've checked."

Jake felt Paul was about to start rambling. "What happened then?" asked Jake to get Paul's attention.

"About an hour later, after the car left, I came outside to throw out the garbage. I smelled something burning. The smell was coming from that direction." Paul pointed to Jake's house. "I decided to walk over to see if everything was okay. I rang the bell, but there was no answer. I waited for a minute before ringing the bell again. The smell had gotten stronger. I knocked on the door. Still there was no response. When I knocked a bit harder the door opened. It was unlocked. I called for Nadine and Jenny, but they didn't respond. I know I shouldn't have, but I walked inside to see if everything was okay. The TV was on, but there was no one in the living room. I walked to the kitchen. And..." Paul paused, as he searched for

the right words. He was at a loss. "I'm sorry Jake. I wish I could've done something."

"Paul, you did more than anyone else would have," said Jake as he patted his neighbor on the shoulder. "Then what happened?"

"I noticed the blood on the kitchen floor. I took a couple of steps closer, and saw Nadine with her....oh God...naked...with her neck...Jesus Christ...why would someone do that? I panicked. I didn't know what to do." Paul was once again searching for the right words to continue. He was choked up. "I ran out, and went back to my house. I called 911...that was it." Paul paused again as he looked at Jake. "I'm sorry, I'm so sorry."

Jake shook Paul's hand, but didn't say anything. Paul stood there looking at Jake as he walked away carrying the two duffel bags, one in each hand.

8

Jake checked in to a Howard Johnson's Hotel. He needed space to think clearly. He would have preferred to stay at his house, but the police wouldn't allow that. He was aware that he could have gone through certain channels to get the clearance, and keep the police off his back. At the same time, he wanted to make sure not to develop any conflicts with the local authorities. He wanted to improve the chances of finding the animal that had slaughtered his wife, and kidnapped his daughter.

The receptionist at the hotel lobby asked for Jake's identification as he checked in. The nametag on her chest read, Naomi. She was an attractive woman in her early thirties.

Naomi noticed the home address on Jake's ID, and the two duffel bags he was carrying in addition to the wedding band on his finger. Immediately she thought he had been kicked out of the house by his wife. However, the sadness on Jake's face made her sympathetic towards him.

"Are you okay, sir?" asked Naomi.

"Excuse me?" Jake was caught off guard by the question.

"Are you okay?"

"It's been a rough day, that's all. Thank you," Jake managed to say with a trying smile.

Jake wasn't in the mood for a conversation. He hadn't noticed how attractive the receptionist was until she spoke to him. He was completely faithful to Nadine ever since they first met. But that didn't mean he couldn't look at a beautiful woman, and acknowledge it. In his trips abroad, he had fought off many temptations. He had been around many

exotic and beautiful women who were difficult to resist. It was complicated especially when they all but offered themselves to him. To keep his cover, from time to time, he would require the services of paid escorts. His physical contact with them never went further than a kiss on the cheek. Sometimes a kiss on both cheeks to comply with local customs, but that was as far as it went.

Jake thanked Naomi for her hospitality. He took the room key cards from her. She looked at him, and gave him a comforting smile.

Jake took the elevator to the third floor, and found his room. It was a newly built economy hotel. On Long Island, there weren't too many hotels to choose from. He wanted to stay as close to his house as possible. Upon entering the hotel room, he walked out to the balcony. There wasn't much of a view; a Home Depot on one side, and the Long Island Expressway on the other. It was late. The main road, Jericho Turnpike, was relatively quiet. He stepped back inside the room, and closed the sliding door.

Jake opened the duffel bags. He laid out the

inventory of guns on the bed. There was enough ammunition to take out a well armed platoon. With Jake's skills and marksmanship, he could have taken out a couple of platoons. Jake rarely missed his targets. Even though it was touted by the CIA that the United States government did not execute people, it was done whenever deemed necessary. And when the time came to take out a target, it was Jake who the Agency relied upon.

Jake had not shared the particulars of his job with Nadine or his parents. It would have been too much for them to handle. He knew it would be tough for anyone to live with someone who had taken another person's life. Jake was okay with keeping the secret. He was performing a service for the country he loved. If it wasn't him it would've been someone else performing the same duty. This was a necessary evil if there is ever such a thing.

Jake tried to piece together the puzzle. He had to think about the events objectively. He was looking for a break. He hadn't found any clues that had given him any kind of indication about who he was looking for. The police hadn't been

forthcoming with information. That was either because they didn't want to share it, or they were clueless.

Jake's cell phone rang. He looked at the caller ID. He recognized the number, and immediately answered it. It was Detective Jones.

"Jake, I'd like to give you good news, but unfortunately there isn't any. We've searched our databases, cross checked all of the evidence, but have come up empty. Even though this is not reassuring, I want you to know we are doing our best. It may not seem like it to you, but most of us are married, and have children. We know what you are going through."

Jake listened silently. He didn't know what to say. He appreciated the fact that the detective was talking to him on a personal level. Thus far, everyone at the police department had come off cold and detached.

"If there is anything you can think of that may help us, please call me directly. I believe you have my number."

"Yes…yes, I do," said Jake as he looked at the

guns laid out on the bed. He became increasingly infuriated and restless with the rhetoric. He wasn't getting information that was relevant or useful.

9

A black SUV with dark tinted windows pulled up to the front door of the precinct. There were plenty of empty spaces in the parking lot. The license plate was marked "official." Both, the driver and the passenger, doors opened simultaneously.

The driver was a man in his early forties. He was dressed sharply in a black Italian suit, a white shirt, and a red tie. His sunglasses were clearly above the pay grade of a police officer. His shoes looked too expensive to be worn by someone driving a car with "official" license plates.

The passenger was a woman, a brunette, in her mid thirties. She was dressed as sharply as the driver. They looked as though they had gone to a two-for-one sale at Neiman Marcus.

There was a regular flow of police officers, and civilians entering and leaving the precinct. They all seemed to be staring at the two anomalies. A police officer walked up to the two characters. He was about to tell them to park the SUV at one of the empty parking spaces. Just as he opened his mouth to speak, the two suits flipped open their wallets to reveal their IDs. They evidently got a thrill out of doing that. It was as though they had practiced it as pitchers and catchers do their signs. They flipped their wallets shut, and placed them back inside their suit pockets.

Not only did the police officer move out of their way, he opened the door for them. They walked up the steps, and inside the precinct. They left the SUV parked where it was.

As the two FBI agents approached the front desk, the female police officer sitting behind the desk looked up at them. Detective Jones, who

happened to be standing nearby, turned around to see what had captivated everyone's attention. He walked up to the agents.

Once again the two agents pulled out and flipped open their wallets to show their ID's in unison. They obviously enjoyed doing this, and welcomed any opportunity to showcase their special skill. Jones did not seem impressed. He waited for them to speak.

"We are looking for Detective Jones," said the female agent.

She appeared to be a beautiful woman. Jones would wait for her to take off the sunglasses before making a proper assessment. The shades didn't come off. He would have to solve the mystery another time.

"You got 'em," said Jones.

"I'm Agent Samantha Clarkson, and this is Agent Richard Davis."

The three parties shook hands.

"How can I help you?" asked Jones.

"Is there a place where we can speak privately?" asked Agent Clarkson as she looked

around the precinct.

"Yes, of course."

Jones led the agents to a room. As they entered, Detective O'Brian walked in behind them. He was holding a cup of coffee in his left hand, and munching on a donut in his right.

The two agents waited for an introduction.

"This is my partner Detective O'Brian."

There was another round of handshakes. The four of them took seats around a round table.

"We are here to discuss the murder of Nadine Burke, and the disappearance of her daughter," said Agent Clarkson. She made the statement as she took off her sunglasses.

Both Jones and O'Brian were taken aback by her beauty. They were mesmerized. The woman sitting across from them was absolutely stunning; a perfect ten. She looked more like a model than a FBI agent.

Agent Davis in an attempt to break the two detectives out of their gaze, snapped, "This may not be a random case."

"Excuse me," said Jones.

"Where is Mr. Burke?" asked Agent Clarkson.

"He checked in at a hotel near his house on Long Island."

"How quickly can you get him here?

"If you are looking to question him, it's not necessary. We have already done that. He had nothing to do with what happened. He's clean," said Jones.

"We're not saying that he is involved," said Agent Clarkson calmly. "We have to bring him up to date on the situation. It would be best to have him meet us here."

"We'll send a car to pick him up," said Jones. He stood up to leave the room.

O'Brian followed his partner's lead, and stood up as well. The two detectives walked out of the room leaving the two agents alone.

"What was that all about?" asked O'Brian.

"I don't know. But whatever it is, it's big. These guys wouldn't be here if it wasn't. I'll call Jake Burke to let him know two officers are coming to get him."

O'Brian got the cue, and said, "I'll send a car to

pick him up."

Jones and O'Brian worked well together. They made a good team. They had been partners for seven years. Each could read the other's thoughts.

10

Jake was no exception, he too was taken aback by Agent Clarkson's stunning good looks. O'Brian rolled in an extra chair for Jake. The four men and the lady sat around the table.

This was the part of the job Agent Clarkson dreaded most. A person could never get used to talking to a parent, one or both, about their missing children. This was even worse as the poor man sitting across from her had lost his wife in the most brutal way. She tried to come up with the words that would convey the outrage she felt. She may

have come across as cold, but she was just as weak as anyone else in that room. The job made her tough, but she was still a human being.

"Mr. Burke, I would like to personally tell you how sorry I am about what has happened. I promise you we are doing everything we can to find your daughter, and the lunatic who murdered your wife. I can assure you we will find Jenny and the animal who took her."

"Look, I'm not sure what's going on here. What can you tell me?" asked Jake.

"The fingerprints which came from this police station matched those of a person we've been tracking for several years. We have suspicion the prints aren't actually his; instead he plants them to throw us off. This has been his pattern. He fell off the grid about a year ago, and has now resurfaced." Agent Clarkson paused, and looked at Jake. She was expecting another question or a statement from him. He was listening intently. It was as though he was taking mental notes. She seemed a bit confused. She was getting the sense that the man sitting across from her was not an accountant.

There was something about him that told her otherwise. She couldn't put her finger on it. She continued, "The man who took your daughter worked at the supermarket where your wife shopped. We believe that is where he began tracking her."

"How do you know he worked at the supermarket?" asked Jake.

"In each of the previous cases there has been a pattern of a man who gets a job at a local supermarket, and disappears after a kidnapping. We interviewed the manager of the supermarket earlier today. He confirmed everything we know about the suspect."

"How many other cases are there?" asked Jake.

Agent Clarkson looked as though she was unprepared to answer him. She always got asked that particular question by the parents of the missing children. She had stopped giving the exact number of the open cases as the list kept growing.

"I'm sorry, but that's not relevant," answered Agent Clarkson. She didn't mean to come across as cold. She wanted to remain objective.

Jake stood up, and yelled as he slapped his hand on the table, "It may not be relevant to you, but it's my daughter. There is nothing more relevant to me than her right now."

Detective Jones stood up and put his hand on Jake's shoulder to comfort him. Jake sat back down as he tried to regain his composure. He snapped back up, and once again yelled, "Don't ever say that again."

Jake was on the verge of a mental breakdown. He looked around the room at everyone to make sure he had gotten his point across. He sat back down. There was dead silence in the room for several minutes.

"Look, I hope you can understand why I'm agitated. I'm looking for answers, and when I hear something I don't like, I get frustrated. I just want to find the bastard that did this before anything happens to Jenny."

"Jake, we understand what you are going through. We are on it. That is why I wanted to speak to you directly, in person. I want you to know that there are hundreds of people working on

this case. You are one of many parents who are looking to get their hands on this son-of-a-bitch."

"What else can you tell us?" asked Jones.

"This man was driving a Grey Chevy station wagon. He used to rent cars, but then a few years ago he changed his pattern. Now, he purchases a used car every time he gets to a new town, and pays cash for it. He gives the dealer an out of state license which is counterfeit, but has a real ID number. This allows him to get temporary license plates. He registers the car under a foreign corporation. Once he's committed the crime, the corporation is dissolved without a trace. He's thorough." Agent Clarkson paused, and looked around the room to ensure she had everyone's undivided attention. This was a habit she had developed over the years. It started out as insecurity, but developed into an intimidation tactic. Being a woman, she often felt she didn't get as much respect as her male counterparts. As attractive as she was, she was intimidating twice as much. She could make a grown man wet his pants. In fact, she had done it, not once, but three times.

"There's one more thing."

Everyone in the room looked at each other quizzically to find out what Agent Clarkson was about to reveal. It was like being at the Oscars, and waiting for the winner of the Best Picture of the Year award to be named.

"This guy has not been linked to a murder of an adult before. The fact that he may have killed Mrs. Burke," Agent Clarkson avoided making eye contact with Jake when she said her last words. She could only imagine how difficult those words must have been for him to hear. She continued, "That's something which is baffling us. Why did he do that?"

That question, regardless of the answer, wasn't going to bring the love of Jake's life back. Once he got his hands on the animal who killed her, he wouldn't ask him either. Jake would make him suffer. The answer he was looking for was to the question - how they were going to hunt him down?

"Jake, there are some official matters I need to discuss with the detectives, please wait for me outside," said Agent Clarkson.

Jake wanted to stay and gather as much information as he could about the case. At least, he now had a lead. He would pursue it as soon as he left the police station. He exited the room without an argument.

Fifteen minutes later the two detectives and the two agents walked out of the room. They paused briefly to say a few words, and then shook hands. Each pair told the other they would be in touch as the case developed on either side.

Agent Clarkson approached Jake, and he stood up. "Jake, I offered to give you a ride back to your hotel. Would you mind riding with us?"

"That'll be fine," replied Jake.

Jake, along with the FBI agents, stepped out of the precinct. They walked up to the SUV. If the license plate hadn't been marked "official" it would have been towed, especially if the officials hadn't been FBI agents.

Agent Clarkson opened the rear door for Jake,

and stepped inside after him. Jake wasn't sure what this was about. Did they know who he was, and what he was planning?

There was something about Jake that Agent Clarkson couldn't quite put a finger on that made her want to get to know him better. The only way to do that was by spending time with him in an unofficial environment. She sensed he was hiding something.

"How certain are you that the man from the supermarket is the one who killed Nadine and took Jenny?" asked Jake.

"We are ninety-nine percent certain," replied Agent Clarkson suspiciously. She had a feeling that Jake was about to make that certainty one hundred percent.

"My neighbor, who spends a significant part of his day in his front yard, told me that he saw a station wagon leaving my house. The car matches the description you gave at the precinct," said Jake

"Did your neighbor mention anything else? Did he happen to get a look at the driver?"

"It was too dark for him to see inside the car.

But I'm a hundred percent certain that the man you are after is the same one I am...I mean the police are looking for."

"Jake, you seem like a nice guy, don't get involved. This is dangerous, you could be putting your life, as well as your daughter's, in jeopardy," warned Agent Clarkson. "Also, I need to know the name of your employer."

"Why?"

"It's just protocol," replied Agent Clarkson. She wanted to confirm that Jake was who he said he was. She knew the name of the company Jake worked for, but wanted to hear it from him.

Jake gave her the name of his employer. Agent Clarkson was about to write it down on a piece of paper when Jake pulled out a business card from his wallet, and handed it to her.

"My cell phone number is on the card. Please call me as soon as you have any information about Jenny. Is there a number where I can reach you?"

"Yes, sorry, I should've given it to you earlier." She pulled out a business card from her pocket, and handed it to Jake.

Agent Davis, who was driving the SUV, kept looking back at the passenger seat through the rearview mirror. He saw Jake look up at him each time. It was as though Jake could see through the agent's shades.

As Agent Davis pulled up in front of the hotel where Jake was staying, the receptionist looked through the front door. She saw Jake and a woman step out from the rear of the SUV. She was intrigued. The woman and Jake exchanged a few words before they shook hands. The receptionist appeared relieved when she didn't see them kiss. She watched as the woman stepped back inside the SUV, and the driver backed out of the driveway.

"Hi," said Naomi, as Jake entered the lobby.

Jake looked at her. The way the light hit her face, she looked even more beautiful than the first time he had seen her.

"Hello," said Jake.

He wasn't in the mood for small talk. He needed to stay focused.

11

Craig Nealis came from a well to do family. His father, Samuel Nealis, was a banker. His mother, Dorothy Nealis, had quit her job to raise him. Even though the Nealis' were wealthy, they did not live an extravagant life.

Dorothy Nealis volunteered her time at a shelter for battered women funded by her husband. She was a loving mother. She did her best to provide everything her son wanted or needed.

Craig Nealis was an avid reader. At first he read mystery novels. Then, at about the time of his

eighth birthday, he began reading stories about true crime. His mother was glad her son occupied his time reading books rather than spending it outside of the house. She enjoyed his company.

Dorothy Nealis wanted her son to remain her baby. It was only when her husband urged that she stop treating him like one, and threatened to send him away to boarding school, that she stopped. Young Nealis didn't take the sudden change well. He blamed his father for ruining his relationship with his mother.

Craig Nealis would talk to students he attended school with about their families. He asked them about their fantasies, and other intimate details about their lives. He questioned them about their relationships with their parents, in particular their mothers.

Young Nealis was mesmerized by girls. He was the only boy his age who would talk to them. The other boys thought girls were: "Yucky." He loved touching their skin. The young and easily impressionable girls welcomed the attention they received from Craig Nealis. It got to a point where

girls began getting jealous of one another. He held power over them.

Parents of the young girls were forced to get involved. They complained to the school principal about Craig Nealis. The parents felt a boy his age shouldn't spend so much time with their daughters. They felt the girls were being corrupted by him.

Craig Nealis's parents were called in to school regularly. They were advised of the complaints about their son from other parents. They were warned if the situation continued their son would be expelled from the exclusive private school.

Samuel and Dorothy Nealis were offended by what they had been told by the school. They felt their son wasn't getting the attention he deserved, and was being alienated. They decided to take him out of the private school.

Craig Nealis was upset when he learned he would have to leave the school he had grown to love. He cherished the time he spent there. After all that is where all of his friends were. He promised, assured, and reassured each of his many girlfriends, or "lady lovers" as he referred to them,

that he would always keep in touch. He told them they had nothing to worry about.

His departure became a big deal at the private school. It got to a point where a psychologist had to be called in to give counseling to the distraught girls. They were understandably devastated by Nealis's departure. He was the only boy who paid attention to them. A few girls went so far as to write messages on their Facebook walls about their desire to end their lives. They wrote there was nothing more for them to live for. Fortunately, none of them followed through with their tragic plans, but it was all quite dramatic.

Craig Nealis was enrolled at a public school. His parents felt it would be better for their son to be with normal kids, and not the over privileged ones at the private school.

Though he was a physically smaller than other boys his age, Craig Nealis was incredibly strong. He found that life in a public school was a lot different than the private school he had attended. He quickly learned that he would need to defend himself. He found himself getting bullied by boys

who were bigger than him. There were scuffles almost every day after school. Instead of running away from the fights, he began to enjoy them. He enjoyed getting hit. He would take a beating before unleashing his fury on the bullies. His reputation at the public school grew with each fight.

On one occasion a boy, who was two years older than Nealis, beat him to a point where most of his face was covered with blood. Nealis just stood there smiling. The boy who was beating him eventually gave up, and said, "You're a freak!" To this Nealis responded, "You have no idea."

The following day, Nealis waited patiently for school to end. He stood in the middle of the yard, outside the school. He was waiting for the same boy who had given him a thorough beating the day before, and bloodied his face. As the boy approached him, Nealis asked, "You are not tired, are you?"

"Stay away from me. Fucking weirdo," said the boy.

"Come on pussy. Don't be a chicken!" taunted Nealis.

A group of students gathered around the two boys, and began cheering and yelling: "FIGHT! FIGHT! FIGHT!" As the boy attempted to break free of the crowd, Nealis took out a metal rod from his book bag, and hit him in the back of his knees. The boy fell to the ground while letting out a piercing scream. Nealis began kicking the boy in his face and stomach as he lay on the ground in a fetal position. Though the same crowd had stood by to watch Nealis get beaten up the previous day, they stopped him before he killed the boy.

Nealis was in a rage. He began screaming at the crowd, "AHHHH…AHHHH…AHHHH." This was the last fight Nealis was involved in at the public school.

Students, mostly boys, started to stay as far away from Nealis as possible. They feared him. He continued to charm the girls. They thought he was a - bad boy.

Nealis continued to get good grades in school. He found out early on that if he did well in school, his parents and teachers left him alone.

He switched his preferred reading from true

crime to horror.   Nealis became obsessed with sadists and serial killers. This was the beginning of a new chapter in his life.

12

When Jenny woke up she was in a bed. She sat up, and rubbed her eyes. She called out for her mother and father, "Mommy! Daddy! Mommy! Daddy!" She looked at the clothes she was wearing. They weren't hers. These were not the clothes she was wearing when she went to sleep. Where am I? she thought. She couldn't remember.

She got off the bed, and walked to the door. She called out, "Mommy! Mommy!" There was no response. She sat down on the floor, and began to sob. She was confused about what was happening.

She stood up off the floor, walked back to bed, and crawled underneath the frame to hide. She did this whenever she was scared. She would stay there until her mother came looking for her. Before she knew it, she was asleep. The carpet below her face was soaked in tears.

The walls of the room were painted pink. The ceiling was the color of the sky with small clouds painted across. There were Care Bears floating on the clouds. The room was clean. It looked like a doll house. Jenny didn't care about any of it. She just wanted to be with her mommy and daddy.

13

Craig Nealis had brought Jenny to what he referred to as his: Adventure Land. This is where he brought all of his little dolls. This is where he played with them. This is where they would grow to love him.

The room Jenny was locked up in was one of many in the mansion located in Alpine, New Jersey. It was an affluent town, among the most prosperous in the country.

Nealis bought the mansion after he received an inheritance valued at over one hundred million

dollars. His parents had left him as the sole beneficiary of their estate.

Samuel and Dorothy Nealis had died during a boating trip. They were on their yacht. This was one of the few luxuries in their life. It was just the three of them. The family went out to sea several times a year. It had become a ritual.

Craig Nealis had recently turned eighteen years of age. He had asked his parents for a place of his own. He told his father on numerous occasions that he wanted to build a playhouse for himself. Samuel Nealis always shrugged him off. Then one day, while Craig Nealis was throwing a tantrum, his father told him the only way he would get the money to buy a place of his own was over his dead body. Nealis liked the sound of that. He smiled.

The opportunity came on that fateful excursion. Craig Nealis saw that his father was alone on the deck looking out in to the ocean. He had brought a baseball bat with him onboard. He slowly walked up behind his father, and took a major league swing. Samuel Nealis was knocked out immediately. He hunched over the railing. Craig Nealis lifted his

father's legs, and hurled him overboard. Dorothy Nealis saw this, and became hysterical. She ran towards her husband. She looked at her son, and asked "Why?" He answered swiftly. He swung the bat once again as she stood facing him. The bat hit her on the side of the head, above the right ear, cracking her skull. She fell to the deck with her eyes wide open as she stared at her beloved son.

Nealis bent down to lift her up. "Wow, Mom, you've put on a few pounds. Don't you know it's not healthy?" He said before throwing her overboard.

The boat was quickly surrounded by sharks. The water around the boat turned red as the sharks tore into the two dead bodies. Other than a few body parts, nothing was left of Samuel and Dorothy Nealis. No one would ever know the truth.

Craig Nealis cleaned the deck without leaving a trace of blood. He casually walked to the radio, and signaled for help. He was a good actor. "HELP! HELP! HELP!" he yelled.

An hour later the Coast Guard arrived at the location of the yacht. It was too late. Both, Samuel

and Dorothy Nealis' bodies had been torn to shreds. These were Craig Nealis's first murders. He was coming into his own.

An investigation was conducted. There was no sign of foul play. It was concluded Dorothy Nealis accidentally fell overboard, and Samuel Nealis jumped in the water to save her. Both, husband and wife, had been attacked by sharks, and killed.

Nealis told the authorities he was under the deck when he heard screams coming from above. When he rushed out to see what was happening, he saw both of his parents were in the water being attacked by sharks, and that is when he called for help. He kept crying throughout the questioning. The investigators felt sympathetic, and tried to comfort him the best they could.

Much of the fortune he inherited was in the form of cash. His parents had other assets, but Nealis didn't care for any of them. He sold everything he could. If his father had given him what he wanted, he would still have been alive.

Craig Nealis was going to build an adventure land. And he did.

14

He sat down on a sofa in the massive living room. He was wearing a black silk robe. He untied the belt to reveal himself. There were seven midsize television screens hanging on the wall. Those screens surrounded one large screen television. Craig Nealis picked up a remote control off the coffee table, and pressed a few buttons. The screens lit up instantly.

Each screen was hooked up to a sophisticated audio and video system. It was nothing short of a major network's studio. There were cameras

covering the inside and the outside perimeter of the house. He could zoom in on any one of the kidnapped young girls, in any room, or bring them all together on the middle screen through the central console via remote control.

Each girl was under the age of eight. Each room was decorated uniquely. Each was set up to play a fantasy that was in Nealis's deranged mind.

His attention was focused on his latest capture. He was watching Jenny. There was something special about her as she evoked nervousness in him. He had never felt this sensation before. Not being an emotional man, he wasn't sure how to handle the new feeling.

He began flipping through various news channels. After every capture he spent several days looking for media coverage on the girls he had kidnapped. He changed the channel to CNBC occasionally to check on the latest financial news as well.

Craig Nealis learned early on to use disguises when going after his victims. He wore gloves which would attach to his skin. The gloves left

false fingerprints. He would dye his hair, or shave them off altogether to reveal a perfectly bald head. He would wobble when he walked so when witnesses described him, they talked about the limp. Sometimes he grew facial hair, and yet at other times he shaved them off completely including his eyebrows. He spent significant time coming up with the disguises. He thought of himself as a genius. He had been inspired by the books he had read, and the movies he had seen when he was a young boy.

There was nothing about the latest kidnapping on the news. He wondered how they had managed to keep it quiet; especially because the murder of Jenny's mother was covered by every media outlet.

Nealis thought about his own mother when they talked about how loving a wife and mother Nadine Burke was. As he listened to the flagitious details of the crime scene, he became aroused. He began to touch himself. He closed his eyes, and thought about the rape and murder he had committed. He couldn't contain the excitement, and finished himself off quickly.

His attention was diverted when he saw his little dolls begin to awaken one by one. Nealis stood up, wiped his hands with several tissues, and tied the robe. It was going to be another fun filled day. He had to get ready.

He walked in to the dressing room, and picked out an outfit. "Who am I going to dress up as today?" said Nealis aloud. He went through the closet, but wasn't able to make up his mind. He had a new guest in his adventure land that he needed to impress. He wanted dress up as someone special. Perhaps I should dress up as Ken, he thought. After all Jenny loved Barbie Dolls. He seemed disappointed as he looked around the closet for the appropriate clothes to make up the outfit. He would have to go out, and buy new ones.

15

Jake told his superiors at the CIA about Nadine's murder, and the kidnapping of his daughter. They offered him any assistance he required. He asked for full access to the police radio, and any communication within the FBI that involved his case. This was standard operating procedure within covert operations, a simple task for the Agency.

Jake arrived at the building where the station wagon had been dumped. It was parked underneath the back parking lot of a vacant office building. The car had been burnt.

"Are there any video cameras in the vicinity? If there are I want to see the footage immediately," ordered Agent Clarkson.

Detectives Jones and O'Brian were on the scene as well. Whatever was left of the station wagon was being taken apart piece by piece.

"Nothing could survive that. Whoever this guy is, he knows what he's doing," said O'Brian. "But there must be something here. These guys always leave behind something that gives them up."

"Mr. Burke, have you been following us?" asked Agent Clarkson when she spotted him on the scene. "Please leave the investigation to us."

"This involves my family. I am going to find Jenny, and the man who took her and murdered my wife. You have been after this guy for years, your own words, but you haven't been able to get him. I will sleep a lot better if I know everything possible is being done to apprehend this sicko, and save my daughter," said Jake.

"How did you know we were here, Mr. Burke?" asked Jones.

Jake pointed to a police frequency app on his

cell phone, and said, "It wasn't very difficult."

One of the investigators taking apart the station wagon, called out for Detective Jones. "I think you should see this," said the investigator.

It was a small fireproof safe. It had been left in the glove compartment. It was charred from the outside, but was intact. It was the only thing in the car that had survived. The safe had been left unlocked.

"Call the bomb disposal unit just in case there is a surprise in there for us," ordered Jones.

Within minutes of the call there was a bomb disposal unit on the scene. The officers in the unit quickly put on their safety gear, and approached the fireproof box. They used electronic devices to listen for a potential timer. They didn't hear anything. They drilled a small hole in the safe, and inserted a camera to look for mechanical devices. They didn't find any. They proceeded to open the safe. Inside, they found a piece of paper with a typewritten note.

The note read:

Dear Samantha,

Haven't you learned by now that you are wasting your time trying to find me? Nothing you do is going to bring him back. I wish it was me who took him, but I had nothing to do with it. Boys don't interest me.

I followed that case closely as it was well covered by the media. I was pulling for you. I really was. I promise. I've been an admirer of yours since. Does that make you feel special?

On the other hand, I would like to personally let you know that the little doll who I took is safe with me. I am going to take good care of her. God, she really is beautiful...just like her mother. Don't get me wrong, she wasn't nearly as beautiful as you.

If I made a mistake somewhere, and left clues which would lead you to find me, please know that I will not spare the little angel. Don't make the mistake of testing me. I think I have already proven myself, and shown what I am capable of.

Yours truly.

Agent Clarkson had been assigned a high profile kidnapping case of the son of a professional football player. She had been given the case a year after joining the Bureau. The handling of the ransom demand had gone terribly wrong. Agent Clarkson blamed herself for what happened. The kidnapper had laid out clear instructions for the transfer of funds, and warned if there were any hitches he would kill the boy. Agent Clarkson had personally handled the money. The exchange was supposed to occur at a mall in the middle of the holiday shopping season. There would be a lot of people around which would make it easy for the kidnapper to disappear if anything went wrong. He calculated the police and the FBI would hesitate to open fire in a mall filled with holiday shoppers.

Agent Clarkson was supposed to go alone. The kidnapper had warned if he saw any other agents in the vicinity of the mall he would disappear. Agent Clarkson, as directed, took a briefcase with the ransom money in 100 dollar unmarked bills to the Starbucks kiosk located in the center of the mall.

She waited while discretely surveying the key points where undercover FBI agents had been posted. The kidnapper never showed up, and the money didn't exchange hands.

The kidnapped boy was murdered, and his body dumped near the Federal Building in downtown Manhattan. Agent Clarkson received a note from the kidnapper which stated:

"How does it feel to know you are responsible for the boy's murder? All because you failed to follow simple instructions, I hope for your sake that you'll listen the next time."

After the murder of the boy, and the guilt of feeling accountable, Agent Clarkson devoted her life to capturing kidnappers. It became an obsession.

16

Jake held the phone in his hand. He was contemplating whether or not he should let Agent Clarkson know his true identity. He needed more information than he was getting through his own channels. He realized if he went to the Agency, they would not allow him to compromise his cover regardless of the reason. But this was his daughter; he was willing to give up everything to find her. He would deal with the Agency when the time came.

He called the number on the card Agent Clarkson had given him. The phone rang several

times without an answer. It felt like an eternity to Jake. Then suddenly there was an answer.

"This is Agent Clarkson...Hello, is anyone there?"

"This is Jake Burke...I would like to speak with you..."

"Sure, what would you like to talk about?"

"Not on the phone. Is there a place we can meet?"

"We can meet at my office in the Federal Building..."

"I'd prefer to meet outside?"

"Are you okay Mr. Burke?" agent Clarkson sounded concerned.

"There is something important I'd like to discuss with you, but we can't speak at your office, or on the phone. I need to see you in person, alone."

"Sure. We can meet in Union Square by the statue."

"Which one?" asked Jake.

"The statue of Gandhi...do you know where it is?"

"Yes, I'll be there at two o'clock." Jake ended the call, and grabbed his keys off the desk.

Agent Clarkson was waiting for Jake by the statue of Gandhi as they had agreed. She was holding a cup of coffee. She had stopped by at the Starbucks on 17th Street on her way to the statue. She was dressed in blue jeans and a white t-shirt with a black sports jacket over it. Concealed under the jacket was a 9mm handgun.

Jake walked up to her. He seemed nervous. He still wasn't certain if he should share his true identity with the FBI agent. But Agent Clarkson was not just an agent anymore; they had shared grief, and a common purpose. He was dressed casually. He also had a gun strapped to his rib cage under his jacket. His eyes were red. He had barely slept since the time he had received that fateful phone call in the hotel room from his neighbor.

"Hello Jake. What was so urgent that you needed to see me in person?" asked Agent

Clarkson.

"I need to make sure that we find my daughter. I'm willing to do whatever it takes to find her. It would be better if we worked together. It would be best if we used our combined resources."

"Jake, I'm not sure I follow you. The FBI and the police department are working together on this case."

"Look, I'm not an accountant," said Jake. He waited for Agent Clarkson's reaction. He was surprised to find that she wasn't caught off guard by the revelation.

"I figured that when I first met you, Jake. I did background checks on you, but everything you said checked out. I still had my doubts. So what is it that you do?"

"I'm with the CIA." Jake took out his wallet, and showed Agent Clarkson his identification.

"Look, this is not CIA's jurisdiction…"

Jake cut her off, "You can't tell me this has anything to do with jurisdiction when my daughter has been kidnapped, and my wife murdered."

"I'm sorry. It's difficult to forget protocol. I

will help you in any way I can to find Jenny. We are at a dead end right now. We have absolutely no leads. Other than the letter which he left in the car, there isn't anything for us to go by." Agent Clarkson sounded hopeless.

She wanted to be honest with Jake. She knew that if she were in his shoes at that moment, she would want to know nothing but the truth.

"I'm starving. Why don't we grab a bite to eat?"

Jake was operating on fumes as well. "That's a good idea."

"When is the last time you slept or ate? You look as though you are about to pass out."

Jake and Agent Clarkson crossed the street, and walked in to a deli. He ordered a roast beef hero with lettuce, tomatoes, and mayo. Agent Clarkson ordered chicken salad on a whole wheat roll.

They walked back to Union Square Park, and found an unoccupied bench. They sat down together.

"What made you join the Agency?" asked Agent Clarkson.

"I was approached by them when I was at Harvard. I scored high on the SAT's, and had been awarded a full scholarship. It was my last year at Harvard when a man approached me, and told me who he was. He gave me his business card, and said he had a job waiting for me if I wanted it. After I graduated, and began looking for work, I found there wasn't anything out there that was of interest to me. I thought about getting a job on Wall Street. But that thought didn't last too long, I couldn't see myself sitting behind a desk all day. I did odd jobs here and there to stay busy, but nothing stood out. Then one day I found the card that the guy had given me, and I called him. That was it."

"Wow, that really doesn't sound very exciting," said Agent Clarkson.

They laughed aloud. This was the first time either of them had laughed in a long time. They looked relaxed.

"What led you to join the Bureau?" asked Jake.

"I guess that's only fair, I get to ask you so now it's your turn to ask me. My story isn't very exciting. My parents worked for the Bureau. They

met at work, fell in love, and got married. I've been surrounded by FBI agents my entire life. Growing up, all of my friends had parents who worked for the FBI. After graduating college most of them joined the Bureau as well. It was only fitting that I did the same. I wish I had gone into another line of work."

"Why?"

"Well, I met my husband, or rather my ex-husband at the Bureau. I guess I was looking for what my parents had, but it didn't work out quite the same way. He turned out to be a prick, and we got divorced."

Jake wanted to find out what happened, but he was interrupted by her cell phone. The phone rang, and she answered it.

"I'll be right there," said Agent Clarkson, and ended the call. "I have to head back to the office. I promise I'll keep you posted on all developments, and I expect the same from you."

That's what Jake was hoping to hear her say. They both stood up off the bench and shook hands.

17

Jenny woke up, and once again called for her parents. She was crying louder than before.

There were frames on the wall to give the appearance of windows, but there was no light coming through them inside the room. Jenny realized this when she moved one of the curtains.

She heard a noise coming from outside the room. "Hello. Who's there?" asked Jenny.

There was no response. Jenny moved along the wall until she reached one of the two doors in the room. She tried to push open the door with her

hands. She looked around the room, and saw a small chair. She dragged it to the door. She stood up on the chair to get a better grip on the knob. She turned it, but the door was locked.

"Hello. Is anybody there?" asked Jenny again.

"Don't talk so loud. He'll come, and get you if you do." The voice in the next room said. It was a voice of a little girl.

"Hi, my name is Jenny. What's your name?"

"I'm Zoey."

"Do you know where my mommy and daddy are, Zoey?" asked Jenny

"I'm sorry Jenny. I wish I did, but I don't."

"Why are we in here? Is there going to be a party?" Jenny had a lot of questions.

"I wish this was a party, but it's not. The big mean man in this house stole us from our parents. I haven't seen my mommy and daddy for a long time."

Jenny heard this, and began to cry. "I want my mommy. I want my daddy."

"Shhh...it's going to be okay. Just do what that man tells you, and you'll be fine. He doesn't

like it when you cry. So don't do it in front of him. There are other little girls here also. You will get to meet them later too."

Jenny walked back to the bed with tears running down her soft cheeks. She grabbed the blanket, and once again slid underneath the bed to hide. She covered herself with a blanket, and tried to fall asleep. She was feeling cold. She was also hungry. She prayed that when she woke up, she would be back at home with her mommy and daddy. She sobbed until she fell asleep.

18

Jake's phone rang half past midnight. It was his neighbor, Paul. He had asked Paul to call him if he detected any unusual activity around his house, or the neighborhood. His gut told him something was wrong. Paul wouldn't have called if there wasn't.

Paul could always be counted on to be the neighborhood watch. This was all new territory for him though; one of his neighbors was in trouble, and had asked him for help.

"Hello, Jake. It's Paul! Where are you? You have to come by your house!" said Paul excitedly.

"Paul, what is it? What's the matter? Calm down," said Jake as he tried to calm his neighbor down.

"There are a lot of people around your house. Most of them are wearing suits. There are at least four black cars, and five police cars outside the house. Wait," Paul had noticed something else. He wanted to confirm what it was before letting Jake know. "I just saw a helicopter. It's flying above your house with its spotlight glaring down."

"I'm on my way."

Jake couldn't end the call quickly enough. He wanted to get to his house as fast as possible. He ran down the stairs past the receptionist. She saw him running, and asked if everything was okay. Jake didn't stop to answer. He ran to his car, turned the ignition, and threw the gear in reverse. He nearly backed into the car parked behind him. He pushed the gear in drive, and stepped on the accelerator. The tires screeched as the car pulled out of the driveway on to the street. He drove as fast as his heart was beating. Jake had been searching for clues that would get him closer to

finding Jenny.

"This is it. This is it," whispered Jake.

Agent Clarkson had arrived at Jake's house just minutes earlier. She had been alerted by the police department about a dead body they had found at the house. It was a body of an eight year old girl. She had been strangled to death. She had bruises covering her petite naked body. The body temperature put the time of death three hours earlier. There was a possibility that she was alive when she was brought to the house. The forensics team gathered evidence to take back to the lab. They searched for clues that may have been left by the killer, or whoever it was that had left the body there.

The lifeless body was still on the floor when Agent Clarkson entered the house. She threw up when she saw the little girl on the floor. It made her sick. She lost her balance, and was about to fall down, when Jake leapt forward to grab her from

behind. He kept her from hitting the floor. He had entered the house just after she arrived. He helped her to the sofa.

"We have to find this son-of-a-bitch," said Agent Clarkson. "How can anyone do this to a child? What kind of an animal does this?"

"Who is she?" asked Jake. He looked at the body of the girl. The investigators had covered it. He hadn't let the thought that it could be Jenny cross his mind.

Jake walked up to Detective Jones who was the first person to arrive at the scene along with his partner. "Who is she? Why is she here?"

"We are identifying her now," replied Jones.

"Who did this?" asked Jake.

"Look Jake, you shouldn't be here. This is a police matter. You can leave on your own, or I'll have an officer escort you out."

"He's with me. I'll take responsibility if anyone comes down on you," interrupted Agent Clarkson. She struggled to stand up. She was still feeling nauseated.

Jake looked at her, and nodded. It was his way

of thanking her. He appreciated the fact that she was covering for him. He knew as well as her that the Bureau would not have approved of him being there. If the incident was reported she would have, without a doubt, received command discipline. She would've been thrown off the case, or even suspended from the Bureau.

"We don't know who did this. I received a call from a man who told me to go to your house. He said he had left a small gift for me," said Jones.

A uniformed police officer approached them. He whispered in the Jones's ear. The two of them walked away leaving Jake and Agent Clarkson alone.

"Thanks for covering my ass," said Jake.

Jones walked back towards Jake and Agent Clarkson. "The body has been identified. Her name is Zoey Seidelman. She was kidnapped three years ago from a house in Sands Point. Like your daughter, Jake, she was taken from her home. It looks like it's the same guy who kidnapped Jenny."

"Why would he bring her here?" asked Jake.

"He's getting bold. He's making a point. He

wants us to know that he's a step ahead of us. He wants to make us seem incompetent."

"What do you know about the girl?" asked Agent Clarkson.

"She was kidnapped on her fifth birthday. She was taken in front of everybody at her birthday party, but no one saw anything. The man who kidnapped her was the clown hired for the party. None of the parents were minding the kids as they played in the yard. When it came time to cut the birthday cake, they realized she was missing." Jones paused as he looked at Jake and Agent Clarkson, before continuing, "This was a very wealthy family. At first they felt there would be a ransom demand, but there was no contact made by the kidnapper. Her parents spent a fortune on private investigators to help them find their daughter, but almost all of them came up empty handed. It was as though she had vanished into thin air."

"There's something else, something you are not telling us. What do you mean by almost all of them?" asked Jake.

"Jake, I don't know how to say this," Jones hesitated as he spoke. He looked down at the floor. "Jesus Christ, I don't know how to say this."

"What is it?" Jake demanded to know.

"One of the investigators hired by her parents found a video," Jones hesitated once again.

"What was on it? God damn it, what did he see?" Jake demanded to know.

"It was a sex video…with Zoey. There was a man in the video, but his face was hidden behind a mask. Zoey looked as though she had been drugged. Her body moved around like a rag doll as the man in the video molested her. She didn't show any emotions. When the detective showed the video to Zoey's parents, her mother lost it. She became hysterical. She lost her mind. She is still institutionalized. She never recovered from seeing her daughter like that…not being able to help her."

"We have to find this motherfucker! I'm going to kill him," snapped Jake. Everyone at the house stopped what they were doing, and turned to look at him.

"I'm sorry Jake," said Agent Clarkson.

"You knew about this?" Jake asked as he turned to look at Agent Clarkson. She was speechless. "Where is the private investigator who found that video? I want to speak to him."

"He was killed in a car accident. A day before the accident he told Zoey's father that he was close to finding the clown who had taken her. The investigator didn't give him any additional details. We wish he had. We searched his home and office, but came up empty handed. It was as though everything that related to Zoey's case had been removed. There were no signs of breaking an entry at either location. All evidence, if it had existed, disappeared."

Jake looked at Jones and Agent Clarkson in disbelief. He was at a loss for words.

19

Jake rang the bell. A man in his mid-sixties, with graying hair, dressed in a blue pinstriped suit opened the door. He was the butler. He asked Jake to come inside, and led him through the living room to the study.

"Mr. Seidelman will be with you shortly. Is there anything I can get you?" asked the butler.

"I'm fine, thank you," replied Jake.

The butler excused himself, and left the room. The study was surrounded by bookshelves, floor to ceiling in length, on three sides of the room. Every

space on the shelves was occupied with books. There was a fireplace in the room, and above it were family photographs. Jake stood in front of the pictures, and studied each one. There were several photographs of Zoey with her parents, and a few in which she was posing for the camera alone. The Seidelmans appeared to be a happy family. Zoey's mother had beautiful long blond hair, blue eyes, and a million dollar smile. She looked like a movie star from the 1960s. Her father was a handsome man. In every photograph he had the same constant smile. He appeared to be thankful for being blessed with a wonderful family.

"You must be Jake Burke," said the man as he entered the study.

"Yes. Mr. Seidelman?" replied Jake as he shook the man's hand.

"Please call me Marc." He sat down on one of the two leather chairs in the middle of the room. "You said on the phone that you wanted to talk to me about my daughter." With his lower lip quivering, he continued, "I'm sure you already know they found her body. I had to go to the

morgue yesterday to identify her."

Marc's eyes wandered up towards the white ceiling, looking for a spot that didn't exist, searching for an answer to a question that hadn't been asked. He looked as though he hadn't slept for days.

"I'm very sorry for your loss," said Jake sympathetically.

"Not nearly as sorry as I am. There isn't anything in the world I wouldn't give up to have her back." Marc opened a desktop cigar humidor which was placed on the table in front of him. After contemplating for a brief moment he pulled out two cigars. He offered one to Jake.

They both cut the cigars, and lit them with cedar matches. They pulled the smoke into their mouths, held it for a few seconds, and exhaled simultaneously.

"What can I do for you, Jake?"

"I'm not sure if you are aware, but my daughter was kidnapped. The authorities believe the kidnapper may be the same man who took your daughter from you."

"I'm very sorry to hear that Jake…I'm truly very sorry," said Marc. His eyes became wet. He pulled on the cigar, and took a moment to finish his thought as he exhaled. He seemed like a man who had given up on life, on humanity. He continued, "It's a terrible world we live in. A world full of amoral, malevolent, satanic people waiting to pounce on the most innocent, defenseless: our children."

Jake looked at the beaten down and broken man as he sat there across from him smoking the cigar. Even though Marc kept his composure, he had given up on life. Jake wanted to help him as much as he wanted to do the same for himself. He wanted to catch the animal that took their daughters, and slowly torture him to the point where he wished for death.

"I understand you hired private investigators to search for Zoey, and that one of them came close before he was killed in a car accident."

"Yes, that's correct. When Frank, the investigator, said he was close to finding Zoey, he essentially put life back in Martha and me. I

remember the look on Martha's face, she was so happy. Even though our angel wasn't in front of us, the hope that she was alive made Martha come to life. That was the last time I saw her smile." Marc dug himself deeper into the chair. He took another pull from the cigar, and exhaled. He seemed as though he was trying to disappear in the cloud of the thick white smoke around him. "Frank told us about a video he found. He warned us that it would be disturbing to watch regardless of whether the girl in it was our daughter or not. We just wanted to see Zoey. We weren't thinking of anything else. What we saw on the video never crossed our wildest imaginations. Had I known about the images that were about to pass in front of our eyes, I wouldn't have let Martha see it."

"I'm sorry about what you and your wife saw on that video. Was there anything Frank told you that could possibly help in finding who did this to your daughter?"

"I've told the police and the FBI everything."

"If it's not too difficult, can you try to remember what Frank told you? I would like to

hear it from you. Perhaps the police and the FBI missed something."

"As Zoey's case was getting cold, there were no leads, Frank took on another case. A woman, I don't remember her name, hired Frank to follow her husband. She felt that her husband was cheating on her. They were an elderly couple. Frank took the case. He found it intriguing that a man in his eighties could possibly be cheating on his wife. There was an apartment in the city the old man would go to on a regular basis, but he wouldn't meet anyone there. Frank reported this to the old man's wife. She was aware of the apartment. She told him they would use it only when they went in to the city to see their grandchildren who lived in Manhattan. They didn't want to bother their children by staying with them. Frank asked her for the keys to the apartment. He let her know that he was going to install surveillance equipment in all of the rooms. The old man's wife complied, and gave him the keys to the apartment." Marc paused as he took another drag from the cigar, and exhaled a cloud of smoke. "One day the old man went in to

the city, stopped at a candy store, and went to his apartment. When he left after several hours, Frank went inside the apartment to retrieve the footage from the various cameras he had hidden."

Marc got up off his chair. He walked to a cabinet, pulled out a bottle of whiskey, and poured two drinks. He handed one glass to Jake. He walked back to his chair, and sat down.

It was clear to Jake whatever happened next was difficult for Marc to say as he was looking down at the floor searching for words. He waited patiently for Marc to continue.

"When Frank played the recording from the apartment, he saw the old man pull out a disc from a bag, and insert it into a video player. The old man took off his pants before sitting down on the couch to watch the video. He picked up the remote and hit play. It was a pornographic video. The old man began to masturbate. When Frank looked at the close-up of the television screen he noticed there was man with a mask and a young girl in the video. He thought he recognized her, and felt she may have been Zoey. He came to my house to tell me

about it, and you know the rest."

"Did the police question the old man? Which store did he get the video from?" asked Jake.

"When they showed up at the old man's house to confront him, he had a heart-attack. He died right in front of them before they could get any information from him."

"Jesus Christ!" said Jake.

Marc looked as though he had been physically beaten after he finished telling the story. It wasn't something he wanted to recall. Knowing that Jake's daughter had been kidnapped, Marc wanted to be as helpful as he could. Marc asked him to stay for lunch. Jake said he couldn't as he had to keep working on trying to find Jenny. He thanked Marc for his time, and promised him that he would find whoever was responsible for destroying their lives, and make him pay. He stood up, shook hands with Marc, and left.

Marc remained where he was. He held the glass of whiskey in one hand, with the other he continued to smoke the cigar.

20

Jenny called out to Zoey repeatedly. She was scared. She wanted to hear her friend's voice. She was too young and innocent to know the difference between good and evil. And yet she was quickly discovering how to separate the two without knowing what they meant. A feeling deep inside her heart told her that Zoey was good; that Zoey was a friend.

"Zoey! Zoey!" Jenny called out. She thought she may have been mispronouncing her friend's name. "Joey! Joey!" She tried again. There was

no response. It had been two days since she had heard anyone's voice.

Jenny had soiled her bed several times. At first she could smell the terrible odor, but now she couldn't tell the difference. It was as though it wasn't important whether the room smelled bad, or not. What was important for her was to find her mommy and daddy whom she loved more than anything in the world.

She heard footsteps outside the room. Someone was coming. Perhaps it was her daddy, she thought. She imagined hugging him. She would promise him that she would be a good girl. She would never be bad again - even though she had never been bad, she was always good.

Maybe she had been bad, thought Jenny. Maybe she was being punished for it. "I'm sorry…I'm sorry…I'll be good from now on," she whispered in a cry. "I promise I'll be good."

She heard the door being unlocked from the outside. She stepped back. She was afraid again. She peed where she stood leaving a small yellow puddle by her feet. Her legs felt warm. She looked

down and cried. She looked up, and saw the door knob turn slowly. This was it, whoever was on the other side was going to come in, and tell her everything was going to be okay.

As the door opened, a man entered. It was Craig Nealis. He stood in front of her. He was dressed like Ken. He had come to play with the little Barbie.

He looked familiar, but Jenny couldn't think where she had seen him before. She felt comforted knowing the face was familiar.

"Are you ga…going to ta…take me home to my mommy and daddy?" asked Jenny with her voice cracking. "I pa…promise I'll be a good girl."

Nealis didn't say a word. He stood still as he stared down at her with a twisted grin on his face. Jenny stepped back. He took several steps towards her then suddenly leapt forward to grab her. She stepped back further until her back was against the bed. She looked down on the floor, and cried. She fell to her hands and knees to crawl under the bed.

Nealis bent down on his knees, and looked under the bed. Jenny crawled back until she

couldn't go any further. He extended his arm and grabbed her left ankle. She kicked with all her might to break loose of his grip. She was too weak, and he was too strong. He pulled her closer, and grabbed her right ankle. He pulled her out from under the bed as she lay flat on her stomach with arms extended out trying to grab a hold of the carpet with her fingers.

Nealis lifted her upside down. She looked like a sheep that had been slaughtered, and was about to be skinned. He shook her violently as though she was a ragdoll.

"Look what a mess you've made…look what you've done. You've been a bad girl. Now, you have to be punished. You're never going home. You are never going to see your mommy and daddy again," yelled Nealis.

"Why? Why? Why?" cried Jenny. "I wanna go home…I wanna go home…I wanna go home."

"Because you've been bad, bad, bad, and your daddy doesn't want to be around a bad girl," replied Nealis. "Who's going to clean you up?"

"Mommy…my mommy will," said Jenny

reassuringly as she nodded her head.

Nealis let Jenny down before lifting her up by her shoulders. He shook her again as he looked into her eyes.

"Your mommy is dead. She doesn't love you."

"No...no...no...you're lying. You're lying. You're lying. You're a bad man, and God is going to punish you." Nadine had told Jenny that God punished bad people.

Nealis let out a loud chuckle. The sound scared Jenny even more. She felt helpless. Her body was hurting, along with her head.

"Are you going to take me back to my mommy and daddy?" asked Jenny again.

Nealis took her to the bathroom. He took off her clothes, and threw them in the garbage bin. He picked her up again, and put her down in the bathtub. Jenny stood naked in front of him as he stared at her. She kept her eyes down, staring at the floor.

Nealis turned on the shower. The water fell on Jenny as she cried. Even though the water was warm, she felt cold. Her body was shivering.

Nealis took off his clothes, and stepped into the bathtub with Jenny. He bent down to his knees to lather shampoo on her hair. He scrubbed soap on her petite body with his big hands, and long skinny fingers.

He hummed while he bathed her.

21

Jake held the Barbie Doll he had brought for Jenny. He was going to give it to her the night she was kidnapped. He couldn't help but think: what if I had returned on time that night. He blamed himself for what happened.

He took out a photograph of Jenny and Nadine from his wallet. It was just the two of them, his wife and daughter, perfect together. Jake would often look at that picture when he was away. It gave him comfort to see the two most precious people in the world were safe at home and waiting

for him. He had a reason to go back. The picture would bring a smile to his face. Now, it brought tears to his eyes.

"I'm sorry Nadine. I'm sorry," said Jake.

He was tired, and felt weak. His body was aching, pleading for rest, but his mind was racing mile-a-minute. He put his head down on the pillow to get a minute's rest. He didn't have time to sleep. He did his best to keep his eyes from shutting, and then thought perhaps closing them would make the persistent headache go away. He was asleep within seconds. He was still holding onto the picture of his family in his hand.

He dreamt about sitting in the living room of his house. He was sitting on the couch with Nadine, while Jenny sat on the floor playing with her dolls before their eyes. She looked like a little angel. Nadine kissed him as they held each other. Jenny came running off the floor to hug them both. He spread his arms to grab her, but she disappeared. He turned his head to look at Nadine, she too was gone. He was alone. Where had they gone? Why would they leave him alone? Didn't they know

how much he loved them? "Nadine," said Jake in his sleep.

His phone had been ringing and vibrating, but Jake was too far gone in the dream to hear it. The phone sat on the side table, dancing, as it vibrated. The name on the caller ID displayed: Samantha Clarkson.

Agent Clarkson dialed Jake's number for the third time. It wasn't like him not to answer her call on the first ring.

Jake picked up the phone. "Hello.

"Jesus Christ, Jake, I've been trying to get a hold of you," said Agent Clarkson.

"I'm sorry. I don't know what happened. I must have dozed off. What's going on?" asked Jake trying to get focused. His headache had subsided.

"Meet me at the candy shop where the old pervert went before going to his apartment. I'll text the address to you. I'm following up on a lead. I'll be there in an hour."

Jake had brought Agent Clarkson up to date on the story Zoey's father told him. He asked her to do a background check on the store owner, where the old man had stopped before going to the apartment, to see if there was anything that could help them in their search. He wasn't sure that is where the old man had acquired the video. It was a lead worth following up on to see if there was a connection. It was a long shot, but one worth taking.

Agent Clarkson went through the FBI database, and local police records to find everything she could on the candy store owner. The FBI file came up empty. The police files didn't show any criminal records either. The only information she found was of a complaint filed by a local resident about the store owner. There wasn't anything that had led to an arrest, or even a search warrant of the candy store. There were no follow up remarks on the file which indicated the complaint hadn't been investigated. This made Agent Clarkson furious. She wondered how many cases went unsolved simply because certain leads were ignored.

The store owner was a man in his fifties. His

name was Charles Kovian. He was an Armenian man who had immigrated to the United States twenty years earlier. He was married, and had two daughters.

Agent Clarkson had a feeling she was onto something worth exploring further. She kept digging deeper. It was as though she wanted to find something on Charles Kovian even though there was nothing there to suggest foul play.

The complaint was filed by an elderly woman. She had gone to the local police precinct, and told them she had seen Charles Kovian watching pornographic videos in the candy store.

The old lady had a habit of going to the same precinct to report everything she felt wasn't normal. The police officers from the precinct had investigated the first few complaints she filed. They didn't find anything. They came to the conclusion the old lady was just lonely, and wanted attention. They had stopped following up on her complaints years earlier.

Agent Clarkson jotted down the old woman's home address, and decided to pay her a visit. She

lived near the candy shop, on 14th Street and 5th Avenue, in Manhattan.

Agent Clarkson parked her car in front of a building on 5th Avenue between 14th and 15th Streets. A traffic cop walked up her, and said, "Hey lady, you can't park here."

Agent Clarkson ignored the traffic cop and walked in to the lobby of the building. She wasn't in the mood to get into an argument.

The traffic cop looked at her as she walked inside the building, and said, "Na-unh, she didn't just do that. I must be invisible. Excuse me ma'am, I said you can't pa'ak here."

The traffic cop pulled out a hand held ticket printer from the holster on her belt to type up a summons. As she walked to the front of the car to scan the registration sticker on the windshield, she noticed the government parking permit on the dashboard. "What'eva'," said the traffic cop. She placed the ticket printer back in the holster, and

walked away.

Agent Clarkson took out a small notepad from her pocket. She looked at the name of the old woman. "What apartment is Mrs. Sanders in?" asked Agent Clarkson as she showed her ID to the doorman.

"She's in 12-B, should I call her for you?" asked the doorman.

"No, that's okay."

Agent Clarkson took the elevator to the twelfth floor. She found the apartment and rang the bell. A minute passed, but no one answered. She pressed the bell once again followed by a knock on the door.

"I'll be right there," said a woman who sounded old. "I'm coming." She opened the door and looked at the young lady standing in front of her. "Yes, how can I help you?"

"Are you Mrs. Sanders?" asked Agent Clarkson.

"Yes, I am."

"My name is Samantha Clarkson. I am with the FBI," said Agent Clarkson as she showed the

old woman her ID. "May I come in?"

"Who let you up here? Did David send you up?" asked Mrs. Sanders.

"Yes, yes he did."

"Well, okay. If he sent you up than you can come in," said Mrs. Sanders. "This neighborhood isn't like it used to be. You can't trust anyone anymore."

The apartment was like a museum. The furniture was at least a hundred years old. The paintings on the walls belonged in a gallery, and not in a one bedroom apartment. There were some black and white photographs on a shelf. They seemed to have been taken around World War II.

"Is this you Mrs. Sanders?" asked Agent Clarkson as she pointed to one of the photographs. She wanted to make the old woman comfortable with small talk.

"Yes, that's me. And the handsome man there is my late husband," said Mrs. Sanders.

She was noticeably excited to have a beautiful young lady in her house. It had been a long time since anyone had paid her a surprise visit. She

hadn't seen her children or grandchildren for several months. Sometimes they wouldn't visit her for a year. They were always too busy with their own lives.

"Can I offer you a drink young lady?" asked Mrs. Sanders.

"No, I'm fine. Thank you very much," replied Agent Clarkson.

The old lady reminded her of her own grandmother who had died when Agent Clarkson was still in high school. They were close.

"Mrs. Sanders, I wanted to ask you a couple of questions about a complaint you had filed with the police department a couple of years ago about the candy store owner on 14th Street. Do you remember filing a complaint about him?"

"Oh, that dirty man. He's no good. Stay away from him," replied Mrs. Sanders.

"Is it okay if I ask you a few questions about him, and what you saw that day when you filed the complaint?"

"You can ask me anything you want young lady."

"What did you see Mrs. Sanders that led you to file a complaint?"

"I went to the store to buy candy for my grandchildren one day, and noticed there was no one in the store. I called for someone to help me, but there was no response. The store has a backroom, and I noticed that the door was open. I went inside to see if anyone was there who could help me. Oh God, that is when I saw him doing it."

"Doing what, Mrs. Sanders?"

"He was watching one of those dirty movies. He was sitting there in front of the television with his pants down. He had the mess all over his hand, and he was asleep. I looked at the screen, and saw a young girl with a man. Oh, God. What a terrible thing. It was disgusting. I didn't know what to do. I quickly walked out of the room, and left the store."

"What happened then?"

"What else? I went to the police like I always do, and told them what I saw. They said they would look into it. That was it. I never went back to that candy store. I don't let my grandchildren go in

there either. Oh God, that was a terrible thing to witness."

"Was that it?" asked Agent Clarkson.

"What more could there be? Isn't that terrible enough?"

"Yes, that is a terrible."

"Would you like to join me for lunch young lady?" offered Mrs. Sanders.

"Next time Mrs. Sanders. I have to go now. Thank you very much for your help," said Agent Clarkson as she stood up to leave.

"Okay young lady, okay. Stay away from that dirty man, now," warned Mrs. Sanders.

22

As Agent Clarkson arrived at the candy store, she saw Jake's car parked outside. Jake noticed her walking up the block from the rearview mirror. He opened the car door, and stepped outside to greet her.

"Your hunch may be correct; there could be a connection between the candy store and the video. There was a complaint filed against the owner of this store by a woman who lives in the neighborhood a few years ago. There is no indication the police investigated the complaint. If

they did, they don't have a record showing it," said Agent Clarkson as they walked together to the candy store.

"Is that the lead you followed up with?" asked Jake.

"Yes, I met the woman who had filed the complaint. I thought she may have forgotten about it, but she remembered it like it was yesterday."

Agent Clarkson brought Jake up to date with everything Mrs. Sanders had told her. He became increasingly enraged with every word as he heard the story.

They walked in to the candy store. There was a man sitting behind the counter. He was talking to a young girl, about fourteen years old, who was buying candy. The man immediately stopped talking to her when he noticed two people he hadn't seen before walk in to the store. The young girl paid for the candy, and left. As she walked out, Jake locked the door and flipped the sign from "Open" to "Close." There was a certificate on the wall with the man's picture on it. The man behind the counter was Charles Kovian.

"Hey, what are you doing?" said Charles Kovian. "You can't do that."

"We can play this one of two ways, easy or hard," said Jake.

"I don't know what you talking about, you leave now," ordered Charles Kovian. He had an accent and was speaking broken English.

As Jake spoke to the old man, Agent Clarkson let herself in to the back room. Mrs. Sanders had described the store in such vivid detail that she found her way around as though she had been there many times before. She began tossing boxes of candies off the shelves. She opened sealed boxes with a knife she had pulled out of her pocket. She went through the entire inventory within minutes.

"There isn't anything back here," said Agent Clarkson.

"You see, there is nothing here. Leave now. You want money? I'll give you. Just leave," offered Charles Kovian. His command of language was getting worse by the minute. He was scared, and nervous.

"Check the computer," yelled Jake loud enough

for Agent Clarkson to hear.

"It's locked, ask him for the password."

"You heard her, what is it?" asked Jake.

"I don't know," replied Charles Kovian.

"I asked you once. The next time I will beat it out of you," threatened Jake.

"I don't know."

Jake grabbed the store owner by his collar, and dragged him to the back room. He sat him down in front of the computer, and ordered him to type. Charles Kovian was shaking profusely. He couldn't control himself.

"Type!" yelled Jake.

Charles Kovian sat there without making a move. Jake slapped him across the face. "It's only going to get worse if you don't talk." He slapped him across the face again. Charles Kovian started to bleed from his nose. Jake pulled out a handkerchief from his pocket, and wiped the blood off his hand.

"I beg you. Please, stop," pleaded Kovian.

Jake pulled out a knife from his pocket. He ran the edge of it around Kovian's left cheek, an inch

below the eye socket. He began to bleed as the knife penetrated the skin.

"This is nothing compared to what I'm going to do to you, unless you don't start doing exactly what I tell you to do. I promise you. It just depends on when you want me to stop," said Jake as he glared into Kovian's eyes.

Agent Clarkson approached Jake as though she was going to stop him. He was about to cut Kovian's other cheek.

Kovian sat there bleeding, and hoping the woman would help him. He prayed she would get the crazy man to stop. She took the knife from Jake. Before Kovian could thank her, with a swift move she swung around, and the knife penetrated the skin quarter of an inch below his right eye. Kovian was bleeding from both sides of his face. She slapped him with her other hand as she swung back.

"Please. Please Stop. I don't have password. I swear," pleaded Kovian.

"I will bring your wife and daughters here, and make them watch as I tear you up. I bet they would

enjoy that," threatened Jake.

"Okay...Okay...Please leave my family out of this. I beg you," said Kovian as he began to type. His hands were shaking as he typed the password while looking down at the keyboard. When he finished typing, he looked up at the monitor, and pressed the enter key.

Agent Clarkson pushed him aside, and leaned in front of the computer. It was as though she knew exactly which files to open. She found a folder with over two hundred videos. She hesitated, and looked at Jake. He nodded his head to give his approval. She opened one of the files which were in numerical order. The first video was of a girl who looked to be no more than five years old. She was being sexually abused by a man whose back was turned to the camera.

"You sick bastard, where did you get these videos? Did you make them?" asked Jake as he restrained himself from leaping across, and strangling the dirty old man with his bare hands.

"It's not me," said Kovian.

"Who is it? Who gave you these videos?"

asked Agent Clarkson.

"I don't know. There's a private website. The videos are on it. I just download them."

"Show us the site," demanded Jake.

Kovian opened a web browser, and began typing the web address. Just as he had said a password protected website appeared on the screen. He entered a login and password in the respective fields. Instantly, thousands of videos with children appeared on the screen.

"Who buys these videos from you? I want a list of names," ordered Jake.

"I don't have a list. They just come in. I don't know them. They give me money, and I make copy of video for them. They take video, and they leave. I don't speak to them," said Kovian as he ran his fingers across his cheeks to check if he was still bleeding. He was.

Jake unplugged the CPU and picked it up. Agent Clarkson called Agent Davis and told him to come to the candy store. She didn't go into details about what she and Jake were up to.

"Bring a truck with a cage in the back."

"Who's it for?" asked Agent Davis.

"It's for an animal that needs to be locked up, and hauled away," replied Agent Clarkson.

23

Jake took the computer he had confiscated from the candy store to Agent Clarkson's apartment. It would've been quicker to go through the videos at the Federal Building, but Jake insisted they go through them alone. In case his daughter was in one of the videos, he didn't want anyone else to see it. He was furious, and trying to control his emotions. If he saw Jenny in any of the videos, he wasn't sure how would react.

Agent Clarkson set up the computer. She entered the password they had beaten out of Charles

Kovian. This brought memories of what happened at the candy store roaring back into her mind. She always followed FBI's stringent set of rules. What she had done at the candy store was anything but protocol. She had broken a long list of regulations. But she knew if Kovian had been interrogated by the Bureau, he may never have told them the password. The techies at the FBI were the best of the best. They would've eventually hacked into the hard drive, but that would have wasted valuable time.

Agent Clarkson lived in an apartment on the upper east side of Manhattan. It was a typical, 550 square foot, one bedroom apartment in New York City. The amount of things that were in there could have easily filled an apartment twice the size. She considered moving out of Manhattan to another borough for more space, but loved living in the city too much to pull the trigger.

There was a futon and a reclining chair in front of a large screen television set. A small dining table, with four chairs, sat in a corner next to the door that led in to the kitchen. The walls, other than

a cluster of family photographs, were bare.

"It's ready," said Agent Clarkson

Jake pulled out a chair from under the dining table, and placed it next to Agent Clarkson in front of the computer. She began to scroll down the videos. They would have to go through them, one at a time. They were holding tablets to take notes.

It took ten hours to go through all of the videos. They were looking for clues. There were several moments when Agent Clarkson was on the verge of tears, but composed herself. She had to be professional, but she was also human. Jake went through similar emotions. He became angrier with each video. He came close to putting his fist through the screen. He wanted to save the girls, and kill the men responsible.

None of the videos had Jenny in them. Though that was of great comfort to Jake, deep inside, he wanted some indication that she was still alive. He wondered if it would be better if she were dead than to see her in one of the videos. He wasn't sure. He couldn't sort out his feelings. He had a migraine, and couldn't think straight.

"I feel filthy having watched the videos. I'm going to take a bath," said Agent Clarkson. She stood up and headed towards the bathroom.

Jake got up off the wooden dining chair, and sat down on the futon. Within moments his head was on the armrest, and he fell asleep.

Agent Clarkson came out of the bathroom, and saw Jake passed out on the futon. He appeared peaceful as he slept. She felt sorry for him. She covered him with a blanket. She walked in to the kitchen, pulled out a bottle of red wine, and poured a drink. She walked back to the living room, and sat down on the recliner. Even though Jake was in the room, she felt eternally alone. She hoped that he would wake up. She wanted someone to speak to. The images of the little girls being molested, from the videos she had watched, were haunting her.

Her imagination was racing out of control. What did those little girls do to deserve the torture they were being put through? They were just innocent souls. Why God would let something like that happen to them while so many evil people were

walking free? There was too much injustice in the world. Would she ever be able to forget the faces of the young and innocent victims from the videos? What would she say to them if she saw them? If she told them they would grow up to have normal lives, would that be a lie? Of course it would, she thought. What if she had been one of those girls? How would she cope with it? The questions were coming at her like a speeding locomotive. She wanted to get off the train, step in front of it, and let it run over her. Would that get those images out of her head? She had to be strong. This was the time to be strong. This is why she had stayed with the Bureau. "I have to be strong," she said aloud.

She shut her eyes, and let herself go. The tears flowed out. She didn't try to stop them. Perhaps this was what she needed.

24

Craig Nealis had not heard from his Armenian friend, Charles Kovian. It wasn't like him not to email Nealis. He had made arrangements with the old pervert to exchange sex videos. Nealis was confident in the fact that there were others like him. Those who enjoyed the same luxuries in life he did, and he wanted to share his with them.

Nealis met Kovian on a trip he had taken to Brazil when he was in his early thirties. It was common for Americans and Western Europeans to fly to countries like Brazil, Columbia, and

Cambodia, and for just a few dollars be able to pick out their choice of girls, and live out their wildest fantasies. Most of the girls were under-aged. It was in Brazil that Nealis realized there was no thrill in it for him. It was too easy. He thought why should he have to travel out of the country to satisfy his desires?

Charles Kovian was on the same flight to Brazil as Nealis when they struck up a conversation. It started with simply complimenting the beautiful women of Brazil, and then quickly shifted to talking about the young girls of Rio de Janeiro. Charles Kovian told Nealis he knew of places in Brazil where any man's desires could be satisfied. The aspiring pedophile slash murderer was intrigued. He told Kovian that he would be in touch once they were in Brazil.

The night they landed in Rio de Janeiro, Nealis met Kovian at a mutually agreed upon location. It was a five star hotel in the center of the city. Kovian spoke to several people as he pointed towards Nealis.

Nealis and Kovian were asked to get into a van.

They were driven to a house in another part of town. They entered the house guarded by men holding automatic weapons. The guns the guards were holding excited Nealis. He had a gun fetish as well.

Nealis and Kovian were lead in to a large living room, and asked to be seated. Shortly after a man walked in to the room, and instructed Nealis to follow him. He eagerly followed the man in to a bedroom. The man left, and closed the door behind him. A few minutes later a middle aged woman, and two young girls, entered the bedroom. The girls looked to be no more than ten years old.

"You like?" asked the woman in a Portuguese accent.

"Yes! Yes! I like very much indeed," said Nealis as he nodded with a grin.

"You pick one," said the woman. "If you take two, I give you special price."

With a closed fist, Nealis raised two fingers. He wanted both girls.

"Ok, I give you special…fifty American dollars."

Nealis couldn't take the cash out quickly enough to pay the woman. She smiled as he pulled out a fifty dollar note from his wallet. The woman snatched the money from Nealis' hand, and pushed the two girls towards him. He put his arms around their waists, and held them close. He kissed them both on the top of their heads.

"I go now. Take it easy with them. Don't hit too hard," said the woman. She walked out of the bedroom, and left the two girls with the man who had given her fifty dollars for merchandise worth twenty-five. "Americanos estupidos," whispered the woman in Portuguese.

Nealis pulled out a video camera, and a tripod from the bag he was carrying. He set it up for recording by positioning it towards the bed. He liked to videotape himself.

The two young girls stood against the bed. They held hands to give each other comfort. They prepared the best they could emotionally for what was about to happen. Though young, they were familiar with what was expected of them.

When Craig Nealis and Charles Kovian arrived back home from Brazil, they made arrangements to exchange videos periodically. There was no money involved. Nealis got off by sharing his passion with others who were like him. Sick.

Nealis decided to visit his Armenian friend at the candy store. This is something he rarely did. As he walked past the store, he noticed it was boarded shut. There was a notice on the door which stated the store had been closed due to health violations.

For Nealis, there was no way of knowing if the Armenian had been apprehended by the police or the FBI. He was concerned about Kovian talking to the authorities about him, and their arrangement to exchange pornographic videos.

The FBI was probably already tracking him, thought Nealis. He looked around suspiciously. He had to get back home quickly, and think what he

needed to do to ensure his safety. The idea of being captured had never crossed his mind, but now he wasn't so sure of himself.

25

Jake had been checking the website regularly. Charles Kovian had told them it was updated frequently. There hadn't been any new videos posted on the site since Jake had beaten the information out of the Armenian.

At midnight Jake checked the site again. He noticed a new video had been uploaded. He hit play, and instantly felt his stomach turning. It was Jenny. She was wearing a pink dress, and tightly holding onto a Barbie Doll. She looked terrified. She was standing in the middle of a room, and

swaying side to side like a pendulum. Unlike any of the other videos Jake had seen, the man in this video was talking.

"Tell me you're happy," said the man.

Jenny stood still unable to speak. She continued to sway from side to side. She looked as though she had been drugged.

The voice of the man in the video got louder as he repeated himself, "Tell daddy you're happy."

"You are not my daddy," cried Jenny.

The man in the video walked up to Jenny with his back to the camera. He picked her up and shook her violently. "Tell me you love me."

"No. I hate you," said Jenny. "My daddy loves me. You are not my daddy."

The man in the video shook her again then dropped her to the floor. Jenny seemed to be in shock. She looked up at the camera. Jake could see her looking directly at him. He touched the screen as though he could feel her. He wanted to hold her. She was all he had left.

The man in the video began to undress Jenny. She stood in the middle of the room naked. She

held onto the Barbie Doll. The man took off his clothes. He pulled Jenny close and hugged her. She struggled to push him away. She pounded his chest with her tiny fists. He laughed.

The man in the video turned around, but his face was hidden from the camera. The video only reached up to his chest. He stretched his arm towards the camera as though to shut it off, instead he pulled it close. Only his mouth and chin were visible on the screen.

"You're never going to find me; you're never going to find me," said the man in the video. Then he screamed the words again, "YOU ARE NEVER GOING TO FIND ME!"

26

Agent Clarkson watched the video of Jenny as Jake paced the room. The hotel had a no smoking policy with a predefined monetary fine for anyone who broke it, but that wasn't Jake's main priority. He was half way through his third cigar of the morning. The room was filled with a layer of smoke. Jake walked to the window, and slid it open. The smoke blew out of the window as though it had been trapped in the room against its will.

"What do you think?" asked Jake.

"Whoever this guy is he thinks we're on to

him. We must've spooked him. It must have something to do with Kovian. We have to question him again," replied Agent Clarkson. "Kovian is hiding something."

"Let's take the motorcycle," said Jake as he handed a spare helmet to Agent Clarkson.

The Harley Davidson was parked in front of the hotel. Jake strapped on the helmet as he got on the motorcycle. Agent Clarkson put her arms around him from behind as he squeezed the clutch, and pressed the gear in first with his left foot.

The Long Island Expressway was jammed bumper to bumper. The traffic didn't seem to faze Jake. He cut through it as though he was riding a racing motorcycle. Agent Clarkson held onto him tightly. She was certain this would be the last ride of her life. Whereas this was normal for Jake, it was nothing she had experienced before. She had been a passenger on motorcycles in the past, but never when the rider was cutting through traffic like a hot knife through butter.

Jake merged onto the Grand Central Parkway as he accelerated the motorcycle past 110 miles per

hour. The traffic on the parkway was significantly lighter than the expressway. This was due to the notorious city planner Robert Mosses, who had designed the parkways of New York City and Long Island to not allow trucks and busses to drive across them.

Though it was safer than cutting through traffic, and coming within inches of getting hit by another vehicle, the speed at which Jake was riding didn't make Agent Clarkson feel any better. Her eyes were shut.

Jake took the exit for the Brooklyn Queens Expressway. He was forced to slow down. The roads of the aging highway were covered with potholes. Construction on the BQE was never ending. It was as though the city ripped apart the roads intentionally only to rebuild them. Someone was getting paid off. It had become part of life for New York City drivers.

Jake weaved in and out of traffic while trying to avoid potholes. There were a couple of potholes which he couldn't steer clear of. As he rode over them, they nearly knocked Agent Clarkson off the

back seat. She dug her fingers deep into his jacket.

They rode onto the Brooklyn Bridge. The pedestrian walkways and bike lanes on the bridge were filled with people. There were people riding bicycles while others were on their roller blades. Some were jogging while others were pushing baby strollers. It was a beautiful day.

Agent Clarkson admired the magnificent city skyline accentuated by the Empire State Building to the right of the historical bridge. To the left of the bridge the city, along with the rest of the world, had changed when it lost the Twin Towers.

27

Charles Kovian sat alone in a cell. He nearly lost it when he saw the man and the woman, who had interrogated him at the candy store, walk in to the room. He had nothing more to tell them.

Jake and Agent Clarkson sat across from the Armenian, and stared into his eyes as to scare whatever they needed to know out of him.

"I know nothing...I already tell you everything," pleaded Kovian.

Agent Clarkson produced a printout of the room Jenny was being held in by the man without a

face. When they had finished reviewing the sex videos they noticed a pattern. At least forty of the videos had several similarities. They were all filmed in rooms without real windows. Each of the rooms had been decorated in various cartoon or doll themes. Another startling similarity was the age of the girls in each of the videos; they all looked to be between 4 to 8 years old.

"Where is this house? Who is the guy in the videos who films in rooms decorated like this?" Agent Clarkson demanded to know as she pounded her fist on the table.

"I don't know…I swear, I don't know," cried Kovian.

"Your wife and kids are on their way here. Do you want me to sit them down in front of the television, and show them the videos you were distributing? They will be disgusted by you. Your wife will divorce you, and your kids will hate you," warned Agent Clarkson.

This method had worked before. The Armenian was afraid of his family seeing him like this, and finding out why he was being held by the

FBI. He believed if he told the agents what they wanted to know, he would get his life back. He really believed everything would go away, and he would go back home to his family. The pervert was delusional.

"Please leave my family out of this. Please don't tell them anything," begged Kovian.

"Then tell us what we need to know. Who is this man? Where can we find him?" shouted Jake.

"I tell you...I tell you everything I know, please," said Kovian. "I don't know him."

Kovian didn't want the agents to find out the reason for his trips to Brazil. He was certain the two agents didn't know anything about them, or they would have asked him already. He figured all he needed to do was to tell them whatever he knew about the man he had met there once, and that would be it.

"It's a man who came to my store many years ago. I don't know how he found me. But he comes in anyway. He gives me some videos, and says he wants to exchange them with me. I offer him money for his videos, but he doesn't take...he says

he doesn't need money. He just wants to exchange videos for other ones. So I give him...I give him what he wants, and he gives me his videos. That's all I know...I tell you everything. Please, I go now."

"Where does he live? What's his name? What does he look like?" asked Agent Clarkson.

"I don't know anything. He just comes in my store, take videos and leave. He had a scarf over his face, I couldn't see. And he had sunglasses, so I couldn't see his eyes," said Kovian. He was a good liar. Jake stood up off the chair. "But wait, when he left my store, I follow him. He drove a black Mercedes-Benz sedan...one of the big ones. I don't know model."

"Did you see his license plates?" asked Agent Clarkson.

"Yes, I don't remember the whole number, but they were New Jersey plates." This was the truth. "Please don't' tell my family about this...please I beg you...I swear I will stop," pleaded Kovian.

"What numbers do you remember?"

"8...that's it...that's all I know...I swear,"

replied Kovian.

Jake and Agent Clarkson would've tortured him, if they were back at the candy store, for more information. But now that the Armenian was in FBI custody, they couldn't touch him. They were being videotaped. Jake looked up at the video camera as though he was asking for permission to beat the Armenian until he told them everything he knew.

An alert was sent to the New Jersey State Police to look out for all black Mercedes-Benz sedans whose license plates had the number "8" in them. There were over fifty thousand such sedans registered in New Jersey.

The police set up road blocks across the state. They stopped and searched all cars that matched the description they had been given by the FBI. They were looking for a male in his mid-forties to mid-fifties. After careful analyses of the body type, and the shape of the jaw of the man in the video with Jenny, the forensics team at the FBI put the age

between forty-five to fifty-five years old.

The police randomly checked homes where cars matching the description had been registered. They were instructed to watch out for anything suspicious, and especially to look for homes where they saw girls between the ages of 4 to 8 who were under the care of a man. It wasn't much, but this is all they had to go on.

28

With the massive manhunt underway in New Jersey, it became impossible to keep the media in the dark. Reporters, followed by their camera crews, from network and local television stations questioned police officers about their knowledge of what was going on. The public needed to know.

Anonymous sources within the police department released information to the press. The 10 O'clock Fox News report began with the usual introduction: "It's 10 p.m., do you know where your children are?"

The press had most of the information correct. They reported the man the police were hunting was a white male in his mid-forties to mid-fifties. They also reported on the Mercedes-Benz. They left out specific information such as the license plate number, and color of the car at the urging of the police department. The press was aware that children were involved, but did not report on the exact details. They told the public they would keep them informed with Breaking News Updates as they learned more about the manhunt.

Jake was furious with the press coverage. He was afraid that any chance they had of catching the man they were after went out the window. He feared Jenny's life was in even greater danger now that the press was involved. The man who kidnapped her would get rid of all evidence. The evidence may have included any victims who were still alive.

It was close to midnight. Jake and Agent Clarkson had been on the phone with police

precincts throughout New Jersey since the time they questioned Charles Kovian. There were several leads which turned out to be nothing. There were numerous prank calls made into various police stations. This was normal in a high profile case. Each lead had to be followed up, which wasted valuable time they did not have.

"Jake, you should get some rest. You are starting to lose it. The way you've been speaking to the police officers isn't helping your cause either. They are doing their best. Many of them have children of their own. They know what you are going through. They want this guy caught just as much as you do," said Agent Clarkson.

"I know. You are right," said Jake. "If you'd like, you can ride back with me to pick up your car from the hotel."

"I don't know. I'm still counting my blessings from the thrill ride earlier."

They took the elevator to the parking lot, got on the Harley Davidson, and tied the helmets on their heads. Jake stopped at the security checkpoint, under the Federal Building, where Agent Clarkson

showed the guards her ID.

As Jake pulled out of the driveway, Agent Clarkson put her arms around him. She was at ease. She wasn't digging her fingers into him. Jake rode at normal speed. Being on the bike was his break from what was going on in his life. He wanted to feel the air hit his face. He felt cleansed by it.

It was a warm night. Other than a few clouds in the sky, it was mostly clear. The lights in New York City were too bright, not a single star in the sky could be seen. Other than the usual yellow cabs, the streets were clear of traffic. There were people hanging out in front of clubs and bars smoking cigarettes. The homeless had set up their beds made out of cardboard boxes alongside office buildings. Wherever there was scaffolding, there were at least three homeless people asleep underneath.

The financial crisis of 2008 had caused the number of homeless people in the city to increase. Crime was also on the rise. Real Estate prices continued to fall. The stock market kept rising after an initial drop. The government would eventually

have to stop pumping money it didn't have into the system. The Wall Street pundits continued to reiterate the worst was over. People on Main Street were certain that worse times were still ahead.

Jake took the same route back as he had used when he rode in to the city. The highways weren't as chaotic as they had been during the day. There were fewer cars on the road, and everyone was driving close to the posted speed limits. During the day New Yorkers drove as though they were insane.

Though it was a warm night, the cool breeze gently hit Agent Clarkson's face. She welcomed it. Perhaps she would get a motorcycle, she thought. She was beginning to understand what it was about being on two wheels that made people love riding so much. It was a drug like any other; motorcyclists lost themselves in the ride.

They arrived at the hotel within thirty minutes of leaving Manhattan.

"That was nice," said Agent Clarkson. "I'm parked right there," she pointed. As Jake stopped the motorcycle near her car, she took off the helmet and handed it to Jake.

"Would you like to come up for coffee?" asked Jake.

Agent Clarkson paused, and thought about it before she replied, "That would be nice."

The room was as Jake had left it. He had advised the hotel to only clean the room upon his request.

Jake ripped open a pouch of coffee, and poured its contents on the filter. He filled the reservoir with water, and pressed the start button. Within seconds the coffee began to brew, and filled the room with its aroma.

Agent Clarkson stood in the balcony. There wasn't much of a view other than the hotel parking lot. She leaned on the railing looking out at nothing in particular.

There was a small table with two plastic chairs on the balcony. Jake sat down, and placed two cups of coffee on the table. He cut a cigar, and lit it with a torch lighter.

Agent Clarkson turned around, and joined Jake at the table. She looked at him and smiled.

"What?"

"It's nothing," she said playfully.

"Would you like a cigar?" asked Jake.

"Sure, why not."

Jake walked back inside the hotel room. He opened the cigar humidor, and pulled out a Cuban, Romeo and Juliet. He walked back out to the balcony and gave her the cigar. She picked up the cutter off the table, and snipped the cigar before placing it between her lips. She puffed as Jake lit it with a lighter. He could tell she wasn't a novice.

"You look surprised," said Agent Clarkson.

"I didn't take you for a cigar smoker," said Jake.

"My father smoked cigars. I don't smoke every day, but when a friend offers one I can't turn it down."

Though they didn't know each other well, they enjoyed each other's company. Agent Clarkson was at ease when she was around him. Jake let his guard down as well in her presence. He had always been cautious of people, and the Agency had only made that worse. It took a long time and effort before he could trust a person. Even though he had

only known her a short while, he could sense he wanted to get to know her better.

They spoke for several hours. Jake smoked two cigars, while she had one. The smoke gave her a "little buzz" as she put it.

"I've to get back to the city," said Agent Clarkson.

They went back inside the hotel room. She wanted Jake to ask her to stay, but he had just lost his wife. The thought hadn't crossed his mind. Perhaps in a different time they would get to know each other more intimately.

Jake accompanied her to the car. As they walked to the lobby, the receptionist looked at them and smiled. Jake waved to her as he and Agent Clarkson walked out to the parking lot.

29

Craig Nealis was panicking. He told himself he had to remain calm. He had been watching the news. He was afraid the police would eventually show up at his house when they tracked the Mercedes-Benz to his address. He had parked the car in the garage, and had taken the license plates off. He considered dumping the car in a lake, but thought it would only draw more attention if the police found it.

He looked out through the living room window, and noticed a police car pass in front of the house. He quickly closed the shade and sat in the dark.

"Don't be paranoid. Don't be paranoid," repeated Nealis to himself.

He had to decide what he would do next. The thought he should let his dolls go free hadn't crossed his mind. It wasn't an option. They belonged to him. He wanted to continue playing with them. They were his little toys of joy.

Nealis never wanted to be a celebrity. He didn't like attention. He was reclusive. His neighbors rarely saw him. Whenever they could, they would try to get his attention if they saw him leave the house. He would wave at them, but avoided getting into conversations.

One of his neighbors was especially meddlesome. It seemed as though there was one in every neighborhood. She was an elderly woman. She frequently walked her Great Dane in front of Craig Nealis' house, and snooped around. The giant dog relieved himself on his lawn regularly. Nealis had asked her nicely to curb the dog. She always took this as an opportunity to start a conversation. She would hit him with a barrage of questions about his personal life. He would excuse

himself, and walk in to the house. He thought about killing her, but reconsidered as it would have drawn attention to the quiet neighborhood. Besides, he was of the policy: love thy neighbor.

Nealis became increasingly paranoid with each passing hour. He was certain the police or the FBI would knock on his door at any moment. But the question that kept ringing in his deranged mind was: why hadn't they already?

Nealis was aware that Charles Kovian did not know where he lived. However, the Armenian did know what Nealis looked like, and any half decent artist would have been able to sketch a picture with relative ease. Perhaps his friend hadn't snitched on him. If he hadn't, then it was only a matter of time before he did. The thought of what would prevent Kovian from giving him up crossed his mind.

It suddenly occurred to Nealis that it would be genius to do an exchange with the police. He would send them a message with his demands.

30

At 9 a.m. a messenger delivered an envelope marked urgent to the precinct. He left it on the front desk in a bin marked: In Box. The envelope sat unattended until 12:30 that afternoon. Checking the mail wasn't a priority at the precinct.

Detective Jones walked in to the precinct with his partner. They had been working on a homicide case from the night before. Both were exhausted and needed sleep.

As Jones walked to the front desk he started going through the unattended In Box. He was

usually the first one to touch the mail. This had become a routine over the years. He always appeared to be searching for something. Not even he knew what it was he was looking for when he went through the mail.

That day the pile seemed especially higher. Most of the mail was junk. The precinct got just as much of it as any regular business did. Half way through, Jones stopped throwing the mail in to the trashcan. He noticed a white envelope marked "URGENT." There was no return address or postage stamp on it. The envelope wasn't addressed to anyone in particular. He sliced it open with a letter opener. He dropped the rest of the mail back into the bin. There was a letter inside the envelope written in a child's handwriting with a blue crayon. He pulled it out and read it.

"What is it?" asked O'Brian.

"Oh shit," said Jones.

He walked to his desk as O'Brian followed him. He laid the letter flat on the desk. The letter stated:

To whom it may concern:

I want to do an exchange   I will give you Jenny for my Armenian friend, Charles Kovian.   I will not negotiate.   Don't waste your time or mine.   Bring him to Penn Station by the big board tonight at 5:30.   I want Jenny's father to escort him there.

Yours truly

Jones alerted Agent Clarkson about the letter. He had it faxed to her office.

"This is it. This is our break. We are going to get this son-of-a-bitch," said Agent Clarkson optimistically. She called Jake as soon as she was off the phone with Jones. It was 1:00 p.m.

Agent Clarkson began assembling a team to accompany her and Jake along with Charles Kovian to Penn Station. She didn't have much time.

It was rush hour at 5:30 p.m. There would be tens of thousands of people at the station. If there was a problem with any of the trains, which was always a possibility with the Long Island Rail Road,

the number of commuters would be three to four times the normal amount. In regards to delays, LIRR was among the worst mass transit systems in the modern world.

Jake got off the phone with Agent Clarkson, grabbed his jacket and gun, and ran down the stairs. He mounted the Harley Davidson and strapped on the helmet. He rode as fast as he could to Manhattan. If he had to drive to the city, it would have taken well over an hour. Cutting through traffic on the motorcycle got him there in thirty minutes.

As Jake stopped in front of the Federal Building, he was greeted by Agent Clarkson. There were five black SUVs with tinted windows parked in front of the intimidating structure.

"We need to get rolling. Kovian is in that one," said Agent Clarkson as she pointed to a SUV. "We will ride with him. There is strategically placed surveillance equipment in Kovian's clothing. He

doesn't know it's there. It's just a precaution."

Jake knew the drill well. Surveillance was the CIA's bread and butter. "Perfect," said Jake. "Do we know why he wants me to escort Kovian?"

"We don't know. I doubt he knows you are a CIA agent. He probably thinks you have the most riding on this exchange, and would do anything to make sure it goes as smoothly as possible. It sounds cliché, but this guy knows what he's doing."

Jake would've been comfortable in any other situation, but since his daughter was involved he was thinking like a father and not a spy. He had been involved with hostage negotiations before, and had witnessed many hostages killed when they went sour. He didn't want to think about that then. This time it was different.

Jake and Agent Clarkson got in to the SUV with Charles Kovian. The Armenian was sitting in the middle. He was trembling with fear.

"Where are we going?" asked Kovian nervously.

"It's your lucky day. You are going to do something good for once in your life."

"What am I going to do? Please tell me," pleaded the pervert. He was scared and sweating profusely.

Agent Clarkson didn't answer Kovian. She and Jake sat in the SUV quietly with their game faces on. This made Kovian even more nervous. He had a feeling he was being taken to be executed. He knew that is exactly what the authorities would have done to him if he was in his motherland, Armenia. He closed his eyes and prayed. He asked the Almighty for forgiveness.

All five SUVs began moving in unison. Each had red and blue lights flashing on the inside of the front grill. People on the street stopped and looked at them as they drove through city streets. They thought it was a politician, or even the president who was in town for a visit. The tourists took out their cameras to snap photographs.

31

At the peak of rush-hour, and as expected, Penn Station was mobbed with commuters. A track fire at Jamaica Station in Queens had added to the mayhem. Lines at ticket counters and vending machines were long.

It was mesmerizing to be a spectator, and watch the crowd as they rushed to catch their trains. While navigating the platforms people came within inches of bumping into each other. There was rarely an incident where people got into physical altercations. It had become second nature for them

to maneuver through the crowd on a daily basis. The commuters were like well trained dogs. They were obedient to the big board which indicated track numbers for trains headed out east to Queens and Long Island. As soon as the track number for a train flashed on the board, a stampede would head in the respective direction.

The alcohol vendors were busy on the platforms. They were more like bartenders. They had brief conversations, as they mixed drinks, with their regular customers who wanted to buy a beverage for the grueling ride back home after a long day at the factory.

The newsstands, the coffee shops, and the pizzerias were all busy. Penn Station was among the best spots in the city to own a retail business. Most of the stores remained open twenty-four hours a day. At the magazine stores a cluster of men could be found standing by the adult magazine section. They kept their heads down, while staring at pictures of nude girls. In their mind no one was looking in their direction, and thinking of them as perverts. They felt invisible.

The video game geeks, the digital photography nuts, and the gossip column junkies had their spots too. It was frenzy for information. The magazine shops made a killing every day. They had gotten into the food business as well by adding popcorn machines, hot dog stands, and refrigerators filled with beer, water, and soft drinks.

Starbucks was the usual meeting spot for husbands and wives, couples, and random encounters of old friends and acquaintances that hadn't seen each other in years.

Penn Station was also one of the busiest stops in the city for several subway lines including the 1, 2, 3, A, C, and E trains. Every few minutes a new swarm of commuters descended upon the crowd that had already gathered at the station.

Jake stood by the third ticket booth to the left of the big board which indicated the train schedule. He and Kovian had entered Penn Station alone. Jake looked around, but wasn't sure who or what he was looking for. He took out a piece of paper from his pocket, and held it over his head. It had a seven digit number written on it. A few seconds later

Jake's phone vibrated, he answered it immediately.

"You are doing great. Do exactly as I say, and don't ask questions," said Nealis. "Look straight ahead and you will see a garbage container...walk to it and lift the top. Inside you will find a blue bag. Take it out."

Jake did not recognize the voice. As instructed he lifted the top of the garbage container, and pulled out a blue bag. He waited for further instructions.

"Very good Jake, keep it up and you'll be with your daughter tonight. I've been taking very good care of her. She is my special little doll," said Nealis.

Jake wanted to scream at the top of his lungs. He wanted to say, "Show your face motherfucker! I will kill you as soon as I see you." He controlled himself. He had to follow orders, at least then, if he was going to save Jenny.

"Now, both of you take off your clothes, and put on the ones that are in the blue bag. I'm sure you have tracking devices on you...even if you don't, I don't care. I'm watching you. I'll be looking for anything taped to your body as well.

Do it now," ordered Nealis.

Jake hesitated as he looked around the station. Nearly everyone there was using a cell phone. Jake thought, was the man on the phone among them? And if he was at the station, where was he hiding?

Jake told Charles Kovian to undress while he did the same. He pulled out two sweat suits from the blue bag. He handed one of them to Kovian.

"I'm not taking my clothes off in front of people," said Kovian nervously. He shook his head. "No…no…no…"

"This is not a debate. Do exactly as I tell you if you want to live, and see your family again," warned Jake.

They undressed.

"I not take off my underwear," said Kovian.

Jake ordered him to do it. They took off their underwear. They were aware of the thousands of eyes staring at them. Parents covered their children's eyes, while others yelled obscenities at the two freaks. New Yorkers could tolerate a lot of things, but this was ludicrous. Even they had some moral values.

A group of high school students, both boys and girls, were enjoying the show. They giggled and pointed fingers at the two men who stood naked in middle of the busy station. They couldn't wait to get back to school the next day, and tell their friends about the maniacs. They snapped photographs with their phones, and immediately posted them on various social networks.

Jake and Kovian quickly changed into the sweat suits. Jake held the phone to his ear, and awaited further instructions.

"Very good, now, take out the two tickets that are in the outside pocket of the bag," instructed Nealis.

Jake did as he was told. The tickets were to Mineola Station on Long Island.

"The train you'll be taking is on track 22. Leave the bag and your clothes where they are. You are not going to need them."

Jake looked up at the information board. The train on track 22 was departing the station in two minute. He grabbed Kovian and ran towards the track. People moved out of the way as they saw the

two perverts run towards them.

The police at Penn Station had been alerted to stay away from Jake and Kovian. Jake had an ear piece in his left ear which Agent Clarkson had asked him to wear. This was the only way he could communicate with her and other FBI agents. Jake was forced to leave his gun behind with his clothes at the station. The gun was loaded. He hoped the police had picked it up. He was worried a homeless person would pick up the gun along the clothes. He couldn't warn Agent Clarkson. He was still on the phone with the man who was giving him instructions, and controlling him like a puppet. The only chance he would have to connect with Agent Clarkson was when the train went in to the tunnel, and he lost cell phone reception.

Jake and Kovian ran down the stairs to catch the train on track 22. They reached the train just as the doors were about to close. Jake looked around to see if he recognized anyone. People avoided making eye contact with him. They thought he was crazy. The train started to move, and within seconds it was in the tunnel. The phone connection

was dropped.

"Have you been watching us?" asked Jake.

"Yes. I'm on the train with you along with three other agents. There is no sign of Jenny," replied Agent Clarkson.

"I don't know what game this guy is playing, but it doesn't appear as though he's going to stick to his end of the deal," said Jake. "This is our only chance to get him, so let's not fuck up."

"Just keep doing what he tells you. We'll get him," said Agent Clarkson reassuringly.

The train pulled out of the tunnel after five minutes. Jake had enough time to warn Agent Clarkson about the gun he had left behind at the station. His phone vibrated again.

"Give the phone to Charles," ordered Nealis.

Before, Jake handed the phone to Charles Kovian, he whispered, "Don't say anything you'll regret. The call is being monitored."

Kovian nodded, and took the phone from Jake.

"Charles my good friend, how have they been treating you?"

"Who is this?" replied Kovian.

"That's good. Have you told them anything about me? Have you told them what I look like?" asked Nealis.

"Who is this? I don't know who you are, or what you look like. I know nothing," replied Kovian nervously.

"Good. Good. Don't worry this will all be over before you know it. You've done well. Now, give the phone back to Jake."

Kovian pulled the phone off his ear. He handed it to Jake, "He wants to talk to you."

"Now, before I forget, take the microphone out of your ear, and drop it on the floor. Don't think you're not being watched. And if the FBI agents who followed you on to the train attempt to follow you, I'll kill Jenny. I won't hesitate so don't test me. I'm sure they are listening to our conversation, and know that I mean it," warned Nealis.

Jake took out the microphone from his ear, and threw it on the floor as he had been instructed. Was the man on the phone with him on the train? Jake looked around at the passengers once again. There were several people talking on their phones.

"Hello…Hello…Are you still there? You are breaking up, hello!" Jake said frantically as he hit the end button on the phone. He watched the passengers to see if anyone would attempt to make a phone call.

Jake's phone vibrated again. None of the passengers had attempted to make a call. Whoever it was, wasn't on the train, or at least wasn't in the same car with Jake.

"Don't do that again. That's my last warning," said Nealis angrily. "When you get off the train, throw the phone in a garbage can."

The train arrived at Mineola Station forty minutes after leaving Penn Station. Surprisingly, it was on time. Jake and Charles Kovian walked off the train. Jake threw the phone in one of the garbage cans along the platform.

There was an announcement in the train, "Next stop Hicksville. Please stand clear of the closing doors." The train started to move as soon as the doors closed. The passengers who had exited the train walked off the platform. They headed either towards the commuter parking garage, or the taxi

stand. Jake and Kovian were the only two people left standing on the platform.

Jake looked around the station. He heard his name being called, "Jake, are you Jake?"

"Yes," said Jake, to a man standing by the stairs at the end of the platform.

"Okay, come with me," said the man. He was a taxi driver.

Jake and Charles Kovian walked off the platform, and followed the taxi driver to his car.

"I will take you," said the taxi driver.

"Take us where?" asked Jake.

"The man on the phone said to take you to the mall."

"Which mall?"

"Roosevelt Field," said the taxi driver.

Jake looked around for Agent Clarkson and the other agents. He didn't see them. He and Kovian stepped inside the back of the taxi. The taxi driver put the gear in drive, and pulled out of the parking lot. A few seconds later his phone rang.

"Yes, hello," said the taxi driver. "Okay." He handed the phone to Jake. "My friend, it's for you."

Jake took the phone from the taxi driver.

"You are doing great. This is all going to be over soon. By the way, Jenny wanted me to let you know she hates you, but she loves me and that she'd rather stay with me," said Nealis. He waited for Jake to respond.

Jake remained quiet, and suppressed his anger. He didn't want to entertain the man who had kidnapped his daughter and murdered his wife. The only thing Jake was going to say to him was "Fuck you!" before he put a bullet between his eyes.

"Come on now, Jake. We can be friends. Now that your wife is dead, we can both raise Jenny together," said Nealis. "By the way that wife of yours was sweet. It's not my thing, but I just had to taste her. And boy did she taste good…sweet like honey."

The taxi pulled in to the massive lot of the mall which was filled with parked cars. Jake and Kovian stepped out of the taxi.

Jake had been to the same mall with Nadine and Jenny many times before. He felt strangely comfortable in the parking lot. He felt the man on

the phone had made a miscalculation by wanting to meet there, and was going to pay for the mistake dearly.

Kovian took a step on to the sidewalk. He instantly halted, and looked down. Jake saw him stop, and a sudden chill went through his body. He took a quick step towards Kovian, and was stopped when he felt a pinch in his arm. He grabbed his left bicep with his right hand. He looked at his arm. It was covered with blood. He had been shot.

Kovian fell to his knees. He had been shot in the chest. He looked up at Jake, and said, "Tell my wife, I'm sorry." He dropped face first to the ground. The upper half of his body was on the sidewalk, and the lower half on the asphalt. A pool of blood quickly spread around his body. Charles Kovian was dead.

There was a hail of gunfire from numerous directions in the crowded parking lot. It was all aimed at the top of the mall. Jake looked up at the roof, and made eye contact with the shooter who had a rifle aimed at him. Before the shooter could pull the trigger, he was hit in the head by a bullet,

and killed instantly. He fell off the roof to the sidewalk.

Shoppers ran in every direction to find cover. Parents yelled at their children to stay together. The police directed civilians to get down on the ground.

Police helicopters hovered over the mall. Within minutes they were joined by news helicopters from: FOX, ABC, NBC, and CBS. This was the most chaos that had been seen at the mall since a pop star made a surprise appearance there a few months earlier.

The people inside the mall were clueless about what was happening outside. An announcement was made over the public announcement system that the mall would be closing immediately. Employees escorted shoppers out of their stores. This added to the frenzy.

If there were multiple shooters, they could have easily disappeared into the crowd. The FBI and the police department hadn't prepared for the pandemonium.

Agent Clarkson ran towards Jake. He was standing over Charles Kovian's dead body. The

only thing he was thinking about was Jenny. He wondered if he would ever see her again.

"Jake…Jake…are you alright?" asked Agent Clarkson.

"Yes, I'm fine. The bullet just grazed my arm. It's only a flesh wound," answered Jake. He didn't seem to care that he had been shot.

An ambulance stopped a few feet away from Jake, and an EMT rushed towards him. The EMT led him to the back of the ambulance. He tried to get him to lay down on the gurney, but Jake refused. He wanted to see what was happening around him. He was hoping to see his daughter run out of the crowd, and jump into his arms. He looked at the dead shooter, and thought if he was the man who had murdered Nadine and kidnapped Jenny.

32

Craig Nealis had been fascinated with guns ever since he was a young boy. He read gun magazines when other kids his age read comic books or watched cartoons. While kids were imagining themselves to grow up to be superheroes, athletes, firemen, and policemen, Nealis wanted to be an assassin. He convinced his father to buy a pellet gun for him for his sixth birthday. It wasn't difficult for young Nealis to convince his parents for almost anything.

At first Nealis practiced his marksmanship on

bottles and cans. He was a quick study, and developed his skill in a short period of time. Once the stationary targets became boring, he began looking for moving marks. There were plenty of kids he would envision shooting at as they walked passed his house. He refrained from doing it as that would have gotten him into trouble. He began shooting at pigeons, sparrows, and other small birds. This was a whole new ball game for aspiring killer. Hitting moving targets was more difficult than he had anticipated. He would sit by the window, or in the woods wearing camouflage for hours waiting for the perfect shot. He was patient as most predators tend to be. After several month of training, birds were no match for him.

Nealis recognized it would be impossible to convince his father to buy him a real gun. He would have wait until he could get one for himself. Until that time came, he continued to practice for an hour every day. He was turning out to be quite a sniper.

Nealis realized that he had no use for his friend, Charles Kovian. He wanted to eliminate the Armenian just in case he still hadn't given him up to the authorities. Nealis didn't want to take a chance, and trust his friend to remain quiet.

It took a while for Nealis to plan how he was going to outsmart his pursuers. He was confident that he would prevail. Though the thought of doing it himself did cross his mind, he felt it would be better to hire someone to do the job for him.

Nealis spent a significant amount of time at several different gun ranges once he was able to get a real gun. During this time he made acquaintances with a number of people who had served in the military. He found the Marines were more to his liking than any of the other members of the armed forces. They were dedicated and driven. He developed a great deal of respect for them.

One young man at the firing range, who happened to be a Marine, stood out from the rest. Nealis watched as the young Marine hit his targets with extreme accuracy.

Nealis wasn't the type to make light conversations. He rarely spoke to anyone at the firing range. As he spent an increasing amount of time at the particular range the young Marine frequented, the two gun aficionados began to acknowledge each other's skills. Most of their conversations revolved around guns; neither the Marine nor Nealis were interested in anything else. At least nothing they would openly share with each other.

The two became friends over the years, though they never spent time together outside of the range. One day the Marine confessed to Nealis that he had been discharged from service due to what he called a misunderstanding. Since the discharge, he had a difficult time finding work. Nealis didn't care to find out what the misunderstanding was. The Marine told him that he knew people who, from time to time, called upon him to use his special skills. Nealis found this intriguing. He asked his friend what those services were.

The Marine, in confidence, told him that he was working as a contractor. He would take

contracts to kill people. This bit of information brought a smile to Nealis's face. He had finally found someone he could look up to.

Over the years, the two friends lost contact. Now was the time for Nealis to call upon his old buddy. When the two spoke on the phone it was as though they had never lost touch.

Nealis explained what needed to be done. The Marine accepted the contract.

33

The forensics team gathered evidence from the rooftop of the mall. The consensus was there may have been more than one shooter given the number of rounds fired. They collected the spent bullet shells found in the vicinity where the shooter had been killed. There was a splatter of blood, a towel, and a copy of "The Catcher in the Rye," found in addition to the shells. The book appeared to have been read numerous times. Its cover was worn, and the inside pages had been annotated and underlined throughout. There were notes written meticulously

on the margins of nearly every page of the literary classic. The team also located a portable music player. The shooter was listening to a song by Depeche Mode: "Barrel of a Gun." The volume was turned up, and the haunting vocals of Dave Gahan could be heard spewing out of the headphones. The song was set on repeat. The investigators gathered evidence, and placed it in specifically marked bags.

The body of the shooter was splattered on the ground. The mall parking lot was cleared of civilians. The local media outlets gathered by the crime scene. They established their ground crews as all of the video thus far had been shot from the helicopters above. The reporters were blocked from getting close to the body of the shooter which had been covered with a black body bag. This was big news. There was rarely any major crime in the area. The reporters interviewed the few civilians who had remained, behind barricades, on the scene. Most of them were employees of various stores from the mall. They hadn't seen the actual shooting, but that didn't stop them from giving thorough accounts of

the mayhem that had ensued. They were relishing in their fifteen minutes of fame.

A FBI agent approached Agent Clarkson, and whispered in her ear. She excused herself from Jake, "I'll be right back."

The sensation in his arm started to return, and he could feel the pain. He looked at the dressing, soaked in blood, around his bicep.

A moment later Agent Clarkson approached Jake. She updated him on what she was told by the agent who had pulled her aside.

"They found a wallet in the shooter's jeans. There was cash in it along with a picture ID and an address," said Agent Clarkson.

"It doesn't make sense. Was he an amateur?" asked Jake.

"A team is headed to investigate the address on the ID. It could be a trap."

"Where's the house?"

"New Jersey," responded Agent Clarkson.

34

The FBI agents arrived at the address that was listed on the shooter's ID card. They surrounded the house with guns drawn. They approached it with extreme caution, knocked on the door, and waited for a response. One of the agents turned the knob. The door opened; it was unlocked. He looked at the other agents and nodded before pushed it open, but couldn't avoid the noise the old hinged door made.

"FBI!" yelled the agent.

There was no response. The house was minimally furnished. There was an old couch, a

coffee table, and two folding chairs in the living room. There was an old television set which had been left on. The volume was turned low. A classic episode of a Bugs Bunny rerun was playing on screen.

The agents checked the rest of the house. There was no one there. The bedrooms were empty, and looked as though they hadn't been used for some time. The walls were bare and painted off-white throughout the house. The kitchen was clean as well. The refrigerator was mostly empty except for a few cans of soda and bottles of beer. The freezer had a tray of ice and a sealed box of vanilla flavored Haagen-Dazs ice-cream.

An agent opened the door to the basement. He gave a hand signal to his partner to move. The two agents walked down the stairs to the dark basement. They pointed their flashlights on the walls to search for a light switch, and to see what was around them.

They located a switch at the bottom of the stairs. An agent flipped it up, and the lights came on. There were several rooms in the basement. The agents couldn't believe what they saw; the rooms

were the same as the ones in some of the sex videos. The agents took photographs as they searched for evidence. Each room had a picture of a young girl hanging on the wall.

One of the agents looked at a photograph and said, "This looks like the girl who was found at Jake Burke's house...the young girl that was left there, dead."

"I think we got the son-of-a-bitch," said another agent.

"It doesn't look right. Something doesn't fit. It's too perfect," said his partner.

BOOK 2

35

The thought of authorities catching up with him, had never crossed Craig Nealis's mind. He liked the way he lived his life. He had everything he could ever want. As he got older and dreamt of new luxuries, he made sure to satisfy those desires as well. No one had it better than him, he thought. He lived a life fit for a king.

He had kidnapped or rescued as he interpreted countless young girls. He played with them until he felt they were too old. He had convinced himself, they were dolls until the ripe old age of eight. After

that life was over for them.

Nealis was just about to turn eight years old when his mother stopped breastfeeding him. She told him that he was getting too old. It was awkward for her when she was at the house with friends, and he would come crying asking for her to breastfeed him. He would jump on her lap, rest his head against her breast, and pull down her top. Her friends would feel uncomfortable and leave.

Even though he still felt like a baby, his mother told him that he wasn't one any longer. Then, it was settled, eight was the age when a kid became too old. He had taken it upon himself to save the childhood of as many children as possible even if it meant he had to kill them. He thought of himself as a saint. Boys didn't interest him. He liked girls. He only wanted to play with them.

Nealis would have the girls do what he imagined his father had done to him. Over the years he had made up stories in his mind on how his father had treated him when he was a young boy. His father would take off his pants, pull out his penis, and tell young Nealis to put it in his mouth.

225

He told him that he would grow up to be big and strong if he did that. He made his son promise not to tell anyone about their secret. This was a story Nealis had convinced himself to be true. It wasn't.

Nealis forced the girls to perform unimaginable sexual acts with him. They hesitated at first, but would eventually give in. Sometimes it took small doses of cocaine to convince them. He felt justified in his own mind for doing this. They needed to learn as he had done when he was a young boy, he thought.

Nealis was quite handsome as a teenager. His mother regularly set him up on dates with her friends' daughters. He was never too interested in going out with them. When he was with them he acted like a gentleman, at least at first. He treated them with the respect he thought they deserved considering his mother knew their parents. However, they didn't excite him.

If he was even a little bit intrigued by the

young ladies, he asked them out on a second date just to please his mother. It never went beyond that. He would manage to freak them out just enough so they wouldn't want to see him again.

For the second date he invited them to come to his house. He told them it would be more fun to spend time at home rather than going out which is what everyone else did. His dates were usually intrigued by this proposal and would agree.

Young Nealis would ask his parents to leave the house while he was home entertaining the young ladies. His father would hesitate, but his mother was always able to convince him to leave their son alone. That is one of the many reasons Nealis loved his mother, she understood him.

Once his dates came to the house, he would take them to his room. There he would begin to seduce them. He told them stories about his travels abroad, all of the interesting people he had met, the books he had read, and the girls he had been with. He exaggerated his sexual escapades. He would go into details about things he had mostly imagined, but convinced himself to be true.

The girls found his stories intriguing, but eventually would start to get freaked out by them. They would start to think that Nealis was weird and strange. Without an exception, they tried to end the date early and leave.

Nealis would get upset with his dates, and accuse them of being immature. He told them they didn't know how to be with a sophisticated man such as himself. He told the girls they wouldn't become mature women unless they allowed him to show them how to behave in the company of a man. He did his best to convince them to stay. Most of the young ladies who agreed to go out on a second date with him had low self-esteem. They were easily persuaded. They wanted to become women, and know how to treat their man.

Nealis would put one hand around their shoulder, and feel their legs with the other. If they tried to push him away, he wouldn't let them. "Relax, just relax," Nealis would say. He would take off their tops, and the girls would try to cover themselves. "It's okay, trust me," he'd say.

He convinced them to close their eyes as he

took of their braziers. Some of the girls were afraid or confused, and didn't attempt to stop him. They sat on the edge of the bed with their eyes closed, and breasts exposed. They felt vulnerable. He would lean forward, put his lips over their nipples, and kiss them gently. The girls weren't sure how to react.

"Stop, that tickles," the girls would say.

Nealis would leisurely transition from kissing to suckling their breasts. This was too much to handle for the easily impressionable girls. A feeling in their gut told them what Nealis was doing wasn't normal. They would hurriedly grab their clothes, and begin to dress. Nealis would stare at them with an ominous smile; the smile of a boy who was wild and demented. The girls would rush out of his room, and out of the house as Nealis sat on the edge of the bed laughing out loud.

36

Agent Clarkson reviewed the video footage of the bedrooms the investigators had recorded at the address found in the shooter's pocket. She compared it to the footage of the bedrooms on the sex videos found in Charles Kovian's computer. She had a feeling that it was all too perfect. She sensed they were being led on a wild goose chase. There was something more. There had to be.

The fingerprints of the shooter matched those of a former Marine, but nothing in his record indicated he was a kidnapper or a murderer. He had

been arrested a few times before on minor drug charges. Regardless of how much Agent Clarkson tried to connect the dots, the whole thing just did not add up.

Jake and Agent Clarkson met at the park in front of City Hall. They found an empty bench and sat down. Jake had brought a cup of coffee for her. He knew how she liked it, light and sweet.

"This isn't right. There are too many loose ends," said Agent Clarkson as she took a sip of the hot coffee. She brought Jake up to date on what the agents had discovered at the shooter's home.

"I don't know. The dots aren't connecting," said Jake.

"Those were my thoughts exactly. The shooter can't be our guy, he can't be the one who kidnapped Jenny and…" Agent Clarkson stopped herself before she said, "…murdered Nadine."

"Whoever it is, he wanted to get rid of Charles Kovian," said Jake. "Kovian knew something that

may have taken us straight to him."

Jake and Agent Clarkson sat in the park as people passed them by. He looked at kids walking in the park holding onto their parents' hands, while other kids sat in strollers with smiles on their faces. Each kid reminded Jake of his daughter.

"There is one more thing," said Agent Clarkson, "My director is threatening to take me off the case. He's putting the blame of Kovian's death on me. I may to have to take the heat on it. There is a possibility I may be reassigned."

"So that's it?"

"Look, there is nothing I want more than to get that son-of-a-bitch. But my hands are tied. If I'm taken off the case, I'll do my best to continue to pass on as much information to you as possible."

Agent Clarkson got up off the bench. Jake followed her lead. They looked at each other for a brief moment, and then walked away in separate directions.

37

A man stood in an office at the top floor of One Liberty Plaza located in the financial district of Manhattan. He was dressed in a tailored black suit. His back was to the door. He looked out the window that stretched from floor to ceiling. The office had spectacular panoramic views of New York City. One of the office walls had five flat screen televisions mounted on it. Each television was set to a different news channel: CNN, CNBC, FOX, BBC, and Al Jazeera.

"How was your trip, Mr. Nealis?" asked a

woman as she entered the office.

"It was fine Lydia. Thanks for making the arrangements," said Nealis. He turned around to face his executive secretary.

Nealis had hired her after conducting extensive interviews. The previous twenty of his secretaries had resigned for unknown reasons. At least they hadn't indicated any particular reasons for resigning on their exit interviews that were common among Wall Street firms. In fact, Nealis had made them mandatory. He wanted to be certain that after the secretaries resigned they got everything off their chest. As everything they stated was documented, it could be used against them if they ever decided to bring charges against him or the firm.

Lydia was the first woman he had hired that was over twenty years of age. She was an African-American woman in her late fifties. She was one of the most unattractive women Nealis had ever laid eyes on. This was the main reason why he had hired her.

The board members of the firm had begun to question Nealis about the frequency at which his

previous secretaries had resigned. This became quite a nuisance for Nealis. He realized the only way to get the board off his back was to hire a secretary he wouldn't be inclined to harass.

"Sir, you have a busy day today. There are five meetings scheduled. The first meeting begins in thirty minutes. It's with the board of directors," said Lydia. She brought Nealis up to date on the other four meetings scheduled for the day.

Nealis was not paying attention. He was bored with his job. He had taken over the bank a few years after his father passed away. When his father was alive, Nealis wouldn't step a foot inside the same building he was now standing on top of.

"Craig! It's great to have you back in the office," said a man in his thirties as he entered the office.

"Hey, Fred," said Nealis begrudgingly.

"I'm better now that you are here, buddy. It was starting to get boring here without you," replied Fred. He was among the best at brown nosing and posturing, a skill that had been mastered by many at Wall Street firms.

Nealis excused Lydia, and asked her to buzz him once the board members had gathered in the conference room which was located across his office.

"Please close the door on your way out," said Nealis.

Fred waited for the door to close before speaking again, "I don't get you. You go from having some of the most beautiful girls on Wall Street work for you to hiring the ugliest woman I've ever seen."

Fred was one of the very few people Nealis could tolerate. He was the closest anyone came to being his friend at work. There was a good reason for it. Fred was a math genius. He had set up trading algorithms which allowed the bank to generate hundreds of millions in profits each year. Because of his success, he was promoted to Chief Investment Officer. The title was a big deal for Fred. It meant that he would report directly to Nealis. The man he held in high regard.

One of the reasons Nealis didn't have many friends was the fact that he didn't speak much.

People would start conversations with him, and all Nealis would do is acknowledge them by nodding his head. Fred didn't seem to be bothered by this peculiar habit of his boss.

Fred was one of those people who could talk non-stop, ask questions, and answer them at the same time. This made it easy for Nealis. He was one of the few people at work Nealis didn't fantasize about killing.

Lydia buzzed Nealis, "They're all in the conference room."

Fred stood up off the chair, and followed his boss as he walked towards the door.

"Some of the guys are going out for drinks tonight. It would be great if you would join us," offered Fred. "And if you can't that's okay too. We will do it another time."

Nealis walked out of the office without acknowledging Fred's invitation.

The boardroom was filled with men in their seventies. Nealis entered the room with a spurious smile. He shook hands with every board member. This was customary at boardroom meetings.

Nealis, without success, had tried to do away with the custom.

As Nealis took his seat he picked up a file which was placed on the conference table in front of everyone in the room. He kept his head buried in the file as the rest of the board members discussed issues at hand.

Nealis made sure to run his bank so that all i's were dotted, and t's crossed. Since he took over the job, the bank had reported consistent profits, and survived a global financial crisis. The bank refrained from taking on high risk investments. It was conservative with its clients' investments. This meant that during times of a booming stock market the bank didn't make as much money as its peers, but didn't lose money in times of an economic downturn either. This was fine with Nealis, and the bank's loyal customers.

The success had less to do with Nealis's ability to lead a multi-billion dollar investment bank, and more to do with his ability not to micromanage its employees. He couldn't do it even if he wanted to, there was always too much on his mind. He had

found the secret of success without actually caring much about it.

The staff was under the impression that Nealis was always thinking about how to make the bank more profitable. He had them all fooled. The board members were no exception; he had them just as bamboozled as the rest of the staff.

He thought about retiring. He would rather be home with his little dolls, and play with them to his heart's content. But if he became totally reclusive, he would have drawn unnecessary attention towards himself.

Nealis looked up as he heard his name being called.

"Mr. Nealis," said Ferdinand Powell.

"Yes, sir," said Nealis.

Ferdinand Powell was the only African-American member of the board. It was becoming common at big banks to have diversity amongst their boards. It was evident that he did not trust Nealis. He was suspicious of him.

"As per the policy you signed off on, it is required for all employees to be present in the firm

at least one week every calendar month. Yet, this is the fifth time in the last two years that you have been away for longer than that," accused Ferdinand Powell.

Nealis, as well as everyone else in the room, knew this was not a matter that needed to be discussed at a board meeting. However, Ferdinand Powell made a point of bringing it up, and now it had to be dealt with.

"I will make a note of that," said Nealis after a long pause.

Ferdinand Powell and everyone else present at the meeting sat quietly. They expected to hear more from Nealis. However, he did not say another word. Instead, he went back to looking at the file which he had been staring at for the length of the meeting without flipping a page.

Nealis had contemplated killing Ferdinand Powell on numerous occasions. He had even driven by his house to stalk him. Nealis would go as far as aiming his index and middle finger at him, while pretending to shoot. The only thing that had kept him from actually killing Ferdinand Powell was the

fact that his murder would've attracted too much attention towards the bank. Attention was the one thing Nealis avoided at all costs.

The board meeting lasted for the usual two hours. Nealis immediately stood up off his seat as it came to a close, and proceeded to shake everyone's hand once again. This too was customary. He did it as quickly as possible and avoided making eye contact for longer than a second with any one person. Over the years he had come to a realization that if he made eye contact with an individual for more than a second, it was likely to lead to a conversation. Nealis wanted to be left alone.

38

To Jake, it seemed as though years had passed since his ordeal began. He had taken an indefinite leave of absence from the CIA. His life had been turned upside down. He decided to move back to his house. He had considered selling it, and moving to the city. However, the thought of Jenny miraculously coming back home one day and not finding him there, kept him from pulling the trigger.

Even though home prices in the town of North Hills dropped drastically, immediately following the kidnapping and the murder, they rebounded just as

quickly. Regardless of what had happened, it was still a good place to live.

Real estate brokers sent letters to Jake with offers to sell his house. Occasionally they would come to the house with hopes of finding him there, and asking him for an exclusive listing.

The Daily News and the New York Post eventually stopped printing stories about the horrific murder and the kidnapping. Jake had saved all of articles. Perhaps there were clues in them that would help him find Jenny, Jake had thought.

He had been invited on several talk shows, and on television news programs. At first he accepted the offers. He gave interviews on television in hope that Jenny would see him, and possible call for help. He wanted her to know that he loved her, and was doing all he could to find her. He realized he was being exploited for sympathy, and for the ratings he generated for the programs every time he made an appearance. The unsolved case had become a national sensation.

Jake sat for hours at a time watching home videos of Nadine and Jenny. They kept him sane.

Seeing them together, gave him hope.

At first visits by his in-laws were frequent, but they waned as time passed. Jake couldn't manage to look at his mother-in-law as she broke down every time he saw her. She blamed him for her daughter's murder, or at least that is what it felt like to him. She never said anything which indicated she actually felt that way. It was how she looked at him, or perhaps it was all in his head. Jake blamed himself.

39

Jake had passed out on the couch in the living room. He struggled to get up when the persistent ringing in his head turned into a knocking sound. It took a while for him to realize that someone was at the front door. He hadn't seen anyone for days. The only visitors he had in the last month were delivery boys from the local pizza shop and the Chinese takeout restaurant. It was too early in the day, and he hadn't ordered food yet.

Jake unlocked the door and opened it. He was surprised to see Agent Clarkson standing there. He

ran his fingers through his hair to straighten them out. He was aware that he looked terrible.

"Hello, Jake," said Agent Clarkson, "may I come in?"

Jake, at first, seemed lost for words. He moved out of the way to let her in.

"Of course…I'm sorry. I wasn't expecting anyone."

Agent Clarkson was dressed in a black suit. Jake noticed the gun strapped under her jacket. She stepped in to the living room, and looked around before sitting down on the sofa. Jake poured a drink, and offered one to her. She accepted. He poured a second drink, and handed her the glass. She took it and set it down on the coffee table. He sat down across from her.

"What brings you to the Island?" asked Jake

"Work…how have you been holding up?"

"Look at me," said Jake as he held up his hands.

"I wish I had good news for you."

Jake looked at her as she spoke. It struck him again how beautiful she was. He had a sudden urge

to ask her: "What's an attractive woman like you doing working for the FBI?" But he managed not to make a fool out of himself. He couldn't remember if he had already asked her that question.

"I know the Bureau didn't show their appreciation for what you did for the parents of those kids...well you know how they feel," said Agent Clarkson.

After the incident with Charles Kovian, Jake had asked Agent Clarkson to alert him anytime a new lead came in regarding Jenny. It was against Bureau protocol, but Agent Clarkson had agreed. She gave Jake her word that she would keep him updated.

There were many leads that came into the Bureau about Jenny. As she had promised Jake she would, Agent Clarkson passed on every one of the leads to him. He followed up on each one. He didn't care how crazy they seemed, he investigated them. He used his resources at the CIA whenever he needed to.

Some of the leads were from outside of the country. Most of them lead to Mexico; a country

that was notorious for kidnappings. Almost all of the kidnappings in the neighbor to the south eventually lead to a monetary ransom. If the families paid, the victims were released. If the ransom wasn't paid, the victims were killed. There was no middle ground in the mostly lawless country.

Though none of the leads helped Jake find Jenny, several of them did aid in foiling ransom plots. Without them knowing, Jake helped the FBI solve numerous cases. The Bureau eventually found out what was happening as Jake was involved in helping them locate victims, and capturing the kidnappers. They warned him to stop, and threatened to prosecute him for interfering with a government agency.

Agent Clarkson's superiors were aware of the relationship which had developed between her and Jake. They cautioned her to stop passing on leads to him. As much as she wanted to continue to help him, she realized that she would be of no use if the Bureau took disciplinary action against her, and she lost her job.

Agent Clarkson got up to leave. Jake wanted her to stay. He enjoyed her company. He was aware that he was in awful shape, and she wouldn't feel comfortable staying. He stood up to walk her to the door. She took a step forward, and gave him a hug. This came as a surprise to Jake. He welcomed the gesture.

40

Jake entered the vacant house in Hoboken, NJ.

He had asked Agent Clarkson for the address many times. She told him that she would lose her job if the Bureau found out that she gave it to him. What had made her change her mind? Why had she visited him months after the incident at the mall? These were only two of the many questions that were going through Jake's mind.

He rode to New Jersey immediately after Agent Clarkson left his house. She had whispered in his ear, when she hugged him, to look inside the

mailbox after she had been gone for an hour. She told him whatever was in the mailbox didn't come from her.

Jake was standing in the house of the man who had shot Charles Kovian, and had attempted to kill him as well. He walked through the rooms which were lit by sunlight. That was the reason Jake had decided to visit the house during the day. He didn't want to use flashlights. He walked down to the basement, and entered the room which looked exactly like the one where Jenny was being held in the video.

He walked around the room without touching anything. He wanted to study every inch of it. He was wearing gloves. The house had been dusted for fingerprints. Jake made sure not to leave his. In case it was dusted again, he didn't want his fingerprints to be discovered. If he was caught, it would have been difficult to explain what he was doing at the house without jeopardizing Agent Clarkson's position.

The room was exactly the same. There must be something here that the detectives or the forensics

team had missed, thought Jake. He was excited. This was the first time in months he felt alive.

Jake looked up at the window, and noticed it was same as the one in the video. It was covered by a curtain. Jake moved it to look outside. To his surprise, he noticed someone standing outside by the window. All he could see were a pair of black boots covered in mud. He looked up to see who was standing there, but couldn't. The basement window was too small, and whoever was outside was standing too close to the house for Jake to be able to see the person's face.

Jake ran upstairs to the main floor and out the front door, but the person standing by the window was gone. He looked around in every direction. There was nobody there. He rushed to his motorcycle, and noticed both of the tires were flat. They had been slashed. He grabbed his head as he tried to think. That's when it occurred to him, the windows in the room where Jenny was being held didn't have light coming through them from the outside.

It wasn't the right house!

41

Though she didn't know it, Jenny was six years old now. There were no calendars that she could look at to see when it was her birthday. The calendar in her home had the date marked: January 10 - Jenny's Birthday. Jenny would start flipping through the calendar months before her birthday just to see the date. She loved Christmas, but her birthday was even more special. She loved having all of her friends over for her birthday party. Every year she would put on a dress that made her look and feel like a princess.

Jenny had become mature. She understood her parents didn't want to see her anymore. They had given her away to someone else. She would clasp her little hands every night, when the light went out, to pray. She asked God to let her parents know that she would be a good girl if they took her back. But if they didn't love her anymore, it was okay as she still loved them very much.

She had stopped crying. She had also stopped soiling her bed and underwear. She was a big girl now, and knew how to take care of herself.

Another little girl had moved in to the room next to Jenny's. Zoey had left without saying goodbye. Jenny missed her very much. The new girl was younger than Jenny. Her name was Emily. Her parents didn't want her either so they had sent her to this terrible place, thought Jenny.

Emily and Jenny became friends. Jenny told her to pray every night, and ask God for forgiveness. She told Emily that the girl who was there before her used to pray before going to bed, and now she was back home with her parents. God had answered her prayers.

Emily would ask, "Is Zoey with her mommy and daddy now?" To which Jenny would reply, "Yes. Where else could she be, silly?" To this, both girls would giggle. It gave their little hearts, big hope.

42

Craig Nealis sat in his car. He was waiting patiently for Jake to leave his house. He was parked around the block on a busy public road where he would not raise suspicion.

Nealis saw the black SUV as it approached the street Jake lived on. He pulled out a camera, equipped with a high powered lens, and snapped multiple photographs. He recognized the female driver. It was Agent Clarkson.

"Hello, Samantha," said Nealis.

This added a twist to his plan. Nealis's plan

was simple, as soon as Jake left his house, he would break in through the back door. He would then wait for Jake to return and kill him, piece of cake.

Nealis had watched several homes being raided in recent months. The raids were reported on the news. Abducted children were found. Watching the raids take place on television, he noticed Jake was present at each of them. If Jake was still looking for his daughter, there was a chance he would get lucky and track him down. As a precaution, Nealis thought it would be best to get rid of Jake. This time he would do the job himself.

After Agent Clarkson left Jake's house, Nealis watched as the black SUV turned the corner and headed towards him. He turned his head, and looked the other way. He was certain she hadn't seen him. He looked in the rearview mirror to make sure the SUV did not stop.

An hour and a half later Nealis watched as Jake turned the corner on his motorcycle, and rode towards him. He waited until Jake was a safe distance away before making a U-turn. He changed his plan of waiting for Jake to return to his house.

Instead, Nealis decided to follow him.

Jake merged onto the Long Island Expressway. He followed the flow of traffic.

"Where are you going," said Nealis aloud as he drove a safe distance behind Jake.

The Expressway wasn't packed with the usual bumper to bumper traffic. This made following a motorcycle easier. Nealis followed Jake through the Midtown Tunnel, down 34th Street, and across the Lincoln Tunnel.

Nealis stopped a block away from where Jake parked the motorcycle. He was familiar with the area. What was Jake doing there? Nealis thought. He watched as Jake entered the house he had remodeled to resemble the place where he kept his little dolls.

"Jake, Jake, Jake, what are you doing here?" asked Nealis in a whisper.

Nealis got out of the car after a few minutes, and walked towards the abandoned house. He pulled out a knife, and punctured both tires of the motorcycle. He was standing by a basement window, on the side of the house, when he saw the

curtain shift. He realized if he moved Jake would've seen his face. He stood still.

Nealis was gone by the time Jake came out of the house. He drove back to Long Island. He was going to follow his original plan. He arrived at Jake's house an hour after leaving Hoboken.

The neighborhood was quiet. It was early in the afternoon. Most people were at work, and their children at school.

Nealis walked to the back of the house, broke the glass of the sliding door, and entered the kitchen. The alarm warning sounded. He pulled out a piece of paper from his pocket, looked at the numbers written on it, and entered them in the central control unit to shut off the alarm. He had gotten the code from Nadine. She had given it to him after he threatened to kill her daughter. It was something he had done as a precaution, but never thought he would actually need to use it. He was proud of his foresight.

Nealis looked around the kitchen and smiled. It brought back memories of the events which had turned him into a celebrity. He had become one of

the most notorious and wanted criminals in history.

Paul had been looking out of his living room window. This was normal for him to do. When he wasn't outside his home working on the yard, he would spend hours sitting by the window surveying the neighborhood.

At first Paul thought about alerting the police when he saw a man approach Jake's house, and then walk to the backyard. He had called the police on three previous occasions since the murder of his neighbor's wife. The first time the police found a mail man who was leaving a package at the back door. The second was a man from the electric company. The previous time Paul had called the cops, they did not find anyone.

Paul put on flip flops, and left his house. As he walked out he saw his neighbor from across the street. Paul waved and said, "How are you Mrs. Fielding?" She waved back, and mumbled something he couldn't hear. Mrs. Fielding wasn't

the friendliest person he had ever met.

On the way back to her home, Mrs. Fielding turned around and saw Paul walk up to Jake's house. She watched him peep inside through the living room window. She shook her head, and rolled up her eyes. Once inside the house, she looked out the kitchen window which faced the street. Paul turned around, and saw her looking at him. She shook her head once again before stepping away from the window.

Paul walked to the back of Jake's house. He knew someone was there as he had witnessed it through his window. When he approached the patio, he saw the shattered door. He immediately turned around, and pulled out a phone from his pocket to call the police. He had done it. He had caught an intruder in the act. The phone slid out of his hand as he pressed "9." He fell to his knees, and grabbed his neck. He opened his mouth and gasped for air. He didn't have enough time to look at his blood filled hand. His throat had been sliced with a knife. He fell, face first on to the floor. Paul was dead.

43

Detectives Jones and O'Brian arrived at Jake's house. They stood over Paul's body as it lay in a pool of blood.

"Remind me not to buy this house when it's listed for sale," said O'Brian. "Real estate prices around here are dropping faster than the Dow Jones during the market crash. This time they are not getting back up, just like him," continued O'Brian as he pointed to Paul's body with a Mont Blanc pen that he was taking notes with.

As Jake rode up the street, towards his house, he noticed the police activity. He kicked down the stand, took off the helmet, and leaned the motorcycle next to a marked police car. He looked towards Paul's house. He found it odd when he didn't see him standing there. He shrugged it off, and walked to the back of his house.

"Jesus Christ!" said Jake as he walked up to Jones and saw the covered body.

"It's your neighbor, Paul," said Jones.

"What the fuck is going on here?" asked Jake.

"We were hoping you would have some information. I've been trying to get through to you for over an hour."

Jake hadn't felt the phone vibrate when he was riding the motorcycle. He took the phone out from his coat pocket, looked at the screen, and saw ten missed calls from Jones.

"I was riding," said Jake.

"How long have you been out of the house? Where were you?" asked Jones.

Jake looked at Jones quizzically. "I went out for a ride. I've been cooped up inside the house," replied Jake as he looked down on the ground at Paul's dead body.

He couldn't tell the detective where he actually was, as it didn't have anything to do with Paul's murder. Or did it? Thought Jake as the image of the person's boots he had seen standing by the basement window flashed through his mind.

"Did you get the fucker who did this?" asked Jake.

Jones shook his head. "We got here as soon as we could after we received the call from your neighbor across the street."

"Who?"

"Mrs. Fielding," replied Jones.

"How did she find out? Did she see who did this?" asked Jake.

"Apparently, Paul's wife was inside the house when her dog began barking hysterically. She began shouting for Paul to take it out for a walk. The dog wouldn't stop barking as she kept yelling. When she opened the front door to look for him, the

dog ran out. He ran here, found Paul on the floor, and started licking him," said Jones as he looked at the body. "The dog ran back to his house. Paul's wife was horrified when she saw his mouth covered with blood. The dog barked a few times before running back out of the house, and she followed him. She screamed when she saw her husband lying on the ground in a pool of blood. That's when your neighbor, Mrs. Fielding, called the police."

"Where is Tulip now?" asked Jake.

Jake had never cared for his nosey neighbor's wife. She was always shouting at Paul. She was rude to all of the neighbors. Nadine had made several attempts to get to know her, but Tulip wasn't interested in getting to know anyone. Tulip always looked miserable. She seemed to have a chip on her shoulder. She always gave the impression that she was upset at something, but only she was aware of what it was.

"She had to be taken to the hospital after she fainted on the street. She's lucky not to have hit her head on the pavement," said Jones.

"Has Mrs. Fielding been questioned?" asked

Jake.

"Agent Clarkson is with her now," answered O'Brian. "She got here a few minutes before you did."

Mrs. Fielding was sitting across from Agent Clarkson in the living room when the bell rang.

"Excuse me dear," said Mrs. Fielding. She stood up, and walked to the front door to see who it was. She managed a smile when she saw Jake standing there.

"Come in dear," said Mrs. Fielding.

Jake followed her to the living room. As he walked in, Agent Clarkson stood up to greet him.

"Are you okay, Mrs. Fielding?" asked Jake.

Everyone in the neighborhood called her Mrs. Fielding. That is how she had been introduced to Jake and Nadine when they moved to their house across the street. She had taken an immediate liking to Nadine. The two had developed a friendship. Often, when Jake was away, they would spend time

together. Mrs. Fielding loved to invite Nadine to her house for tea. She looked forward to her company. The feeling was mutual.

Mrs. Fielding was a strong woman. She lost her husband in the Vietnam War, three years into their marriage. From the way she spoke about her late husband, Jake and Nadine could tell she loved him very much. She had never quite gotten over his death, and hadn't remarried. Jake had seen her pictures from when she was younger. She appeared to be much happier back then.

From time to time, Jake and Nadine would talk about Mrs. Fielding when they were alone. They both felt she looked beautiful when she was younger. They spoke about how happy she seemed as well. They couldn't help, but sorry for her. The conversation usually led Jake to ask Nadine how she would cope if something bad happened to him. She always gave him playful slaps on the back or a nudged his arm, whenever he'd ask that question. "Don't say such terrible things," Nadine would say. "Would you remarry?" Jake would ask. Her response was always the same: "I wouldn't. There

isn't anyone in the world that can keep me as happy as you. I'd rather die."

"Mrs. Fielding saw Paul walk up to your house, and look inside through the front window. Then she saw him walk to the back yard," said Agent Clarkson.

"After he walked to the back of the house, I went to the basement. I was doing laundry, and went down to put the clothes in the dryer. When I came back up, that's when I heard Tulip screaming and crying. I asked her what happened, but she couldn't get the words out of her mouth. The poor girl was absolutely helpless. She kept repeating his name over and over again, 'Paul…Paul…Paul,' the poor thing. I didn't know what to do…I just called the police."

Mrs. Fielding told them she hadn't seen anyone enter or leave Jake's house. She said that Paul must've seen something or someone that made him suspicious. She had dismissed it, because everyone in the neighborhood knew Paul was nosey.

It was obvious to Jake that whoever had murdered Paul was there to kill him instead. Paul

must have caught the killer off guard and spooked him, thought Jake. Jones had mentioned the way Paul's body was positioned on the ground it appeared that he was facing away from the killer. The killer grabbed him from behind, or perhaps didn't grab him at all when he slit his throat. The cut was similar to the one on Nadine's neck. It was the same killer. It had to be.

Jake entered his house. He was accompanied by Agent Clarkson. They found Detectives Jones and O'Brian sitting on the couch in the living room. Jones had a tablet on the coffee table in front of him. He was watching a video.

There were numerous traffic cameras, both still and video, on major intersections across Long Island. The main use of the cameras was to cut down on the number of accidents caused by drivers breaking traffic signals. At first there was uproar from the public about the devices. They felt it was an invasion of privacy. They also complained it

was unfair to receive a summons unless they were caught in the act by a police officer. Overtime, the complaints subsided, and the public learned to live with them.

The traffic cameras had turned into an unexpected revenue stream. Due to the ongoing budget cuts and deficits, the city needed to cut down on the number of police officers to solely monitor drivers who ran red lights.

The cameras also caught what the human eye couldn't. The drivers couldn't argue their way out of the tickets as the proof was in the pictures snapped by the motion sensitive cameras.

The video cameras were mostly installed in neighborhoods with high rates of crime. The camera which had caught the footage the two detectives were watching on the tablet had been installed soon after Zoey's body was discovered at Jake's house.

"Do you recognize this car?" asked Jones as he pointed to a car parked on the street.

"No," replied Jake after looking at the video closely.

"I've been going through the video of the time you said you left your house, and the time when you came back. As you rode off, the driver of that car followed you. Look," said Jones as he pointed at the screen. "The second time, which is about the time of Paul's murder, that same car came back. The driver didn't stop and park the car at the previous spot. Instead, he or she turned the corner and drove up your street. And there's the car," said Jones as he pointed at the screen again. "The tech guys at the station are working on getting zoom shots of the driver. The car's windows are tinted, and it may be difficult to get a clear shot of the driver's face."

"That has to be the killer," said Jake.

Jake was thinking about Jenny. He prayed she was alive.

"Have you run the license plate?" asked Agent Clarkson.

Detective Jones's phone rang, and he quickly answered it. It was a short call. "That was the station. They ran the license plate, and confirmed the car is registered to a bank in Manhattan."

44

It was Friday and Craig Nealis made plans for the weekend. It had been a while since he had a chance to play with his little dolls. Work, though he didn't do much, had kept him busy. The bank was about to post yet another record quarter of profits. With the earnings release, he would have to make another speech. He dreaded making the quarterly speech in front of analysts and financial reporters.

The speech was prepared for him by someone he didn't know. He would stand in front of the mirror in his office, and practice delivering the

speech while also recording it. He couldn't tolerate looking at his own reflection. He was getting older. Regardless of the beauty products he used, his skin showed his age. He would look in the mirror, and pull at the sides of his eyes to make the crows feet disappear. He would put his fingertips over the top of his forehead, and pull the skin up to hide the stress lines.

When he played back the speech, and listened to his voice, he would feel like cutting his own throat. He despised the sound of it. He sounded old, he thought. He felt disgusted.

Nealis turned as he heard the speaker phone ring followed by his secretary's voice. "Sir, you are wanted in the boardroom."

"What's it about? I checked this morning, I didn't see any meetings scheduled on the calendar," said Nealis in an irritated voice. He tried to keep meetings at a minimum. "Is it important that I be there?" Nealis sounded like a child about to throw a tantrum. His secretary found this to be quite amusing.

"Come on Mr. Nealis. You know you have to

go. It will be over before you know it," said the secretary as though she was speaking to a kid.

Nealis walked in to the boardroom. "Surprise!" everyone yelled at once. The room was packed with senior members of the firm. They had gathered every year since he joined the bank to throw him a surprise birthday party.

People, most of whom he did not recognize, came up to Nealis to shake hands or hug him. They wished him a happy birthday. Nealis didn't know what there was to celebrate. It wasn't as though he was getting younger. Moments earlier he had been standing in his office, looking at his reflection, and thinking about how old he looked. Why can't these people understand that I don't like parties, thought Nealis as he smiled, shook yet another stranger's hand, and said, "Thank you."

Nealis was beginning to feel disgusted. He hated being around people. It made him feel claustrophobic. He looked around the room; everyone appeared to be having a wonderful time at his expense. He detested them all.

Nealis had never kidnapped a child of an

employee of the bank. As he looked around the room, he noticed there were several attractive women. He pondered if any of them had young children, daughters to be specific. This thought seemed to give him some pleasure. He even managed a genuine smile.

Everyone in the room began cheering him on to cut the birthday cake. This gave Nealis some joy as it made him feel young again. He picked up a knife, looked at the shiny blade, and contemplated the amount of time it would take to slice someone's throat with it. The knives he used at home, and the two he always carried on him, were razor sharp. The knife he was holding seemed dull.

As he cut the cake, everyone in the room sang, "*Happy Birthday to you, Happy Birthday to you, Happy Birthday dear Mr. Nealis, Happy Birthday to you.*" Nealis knew that he would totally lose it if they sang the last part of the song, "*How old are you? How old are you? How old, how old, how old are you?*" He thought how fortunate for them to not sing those dreaded lyrics. He would have stabbed each and every one of them with the dull

knife just to make them feel as much pain as he felt at that very moment. His secretary took the knife from him. She felt it was odd as she had to force it out of his hand. She proceeded to cut the cake into small slices. It was another person's responsibility to place the pieces on the disposable plates before passing them around the room.

It would only be a few more minutes; Nealis comforted himself with the thought. He wanted to go home immediately to be with his little dolls. He needed to be with them now more than ever.

45

The two police detectives, the FBI agent, and Jake entered the skyscraper located in downtown Manhattan. The address outside read, in large block letters: ONE LIBERTY PLAZA. They stopped at the security desk, and displayed their identifications.

"Who is in charge of the corporate car fleet?" asked Jones.

The receptionist directed them to the fifteenth floor. She called a security guard on a two way radio, and asked him to escort the four visitors.

The elevator stopped at the lobby. They received curious looks from people exiting the elevator who were staring at the badges hanging from their necks. It wasn't every day the bank employees saw the police and the FBI in their building. They whispered amongst each other about what was going on, and why the authorities were in the building. They couldn't wait to get back to their offices and cubicles to tell their colleagues about what they had seen.

As the elevator stopped on the fifteenth floor, the security guard led the four visitors to a conference room. He asked them to be seated. The guard closed the door behind him as he walked out of the room. A few minutes later a young lady came in to the room. She introduced herself as Audrey. She offered refreshments to the guests. It was tough for the two detectives to pass up on coffee. They had hoped she would have also offered donuts.

"I'll be right back," said Audrey. She left the room.

A few minutes after the young lady left the

conference room, an older woman entered. She appeared nervous as she looked at the four guests. She was the manager of the corporate vehicle fleet. The first thought that went through her mind was: I hope I don't lose my job. I'm almost sixty-five years old, and this is the last thing I need.

"Hello, my name is Margaret Sama. How can I help you?" She proceeded to shake hands with everyone in the room.

"We would like to see your log of corporate vehicles," requested Jones.

"May I ask what this is about?" asked Margaret Sama.

"It's a routine investigation. We are searching for a specific car," answered Jones.

Even though Margaret Sama was not satisfied with the answer, she thought it would be best not to ask for a more specific reason. She didn't think to ask if they had a warrant. They hadn't produced one.

Audrey walked back in to the conference room with a tray. Jones and O'Brian were relieved to see some pastries on it. She set the tray down on the

table.

"Sweetheart, please bring in the laptop that's on my desk," instructed Margaret Sama.

Audrey immediately left the room to do as she was told.

"What kind of investigation are you doing?" asked Margaret Sama. The curiosity had gotten the better of her. "I hope you don't mind my asking. I'm not sure of the proper protocol regarding this sort of thing."

"It's a criminal case," said Jones.

"Oh, my!" said the startled elderly woman. She covered her mouth which was wide open with shock. "What a terrible thing."

Audrey walked back in to the conference room with the laptop. She placed it in front of Margaret Sama.

"Thank you sweetheart…that will be all."

The two detectives thanked Audrey for her hospitality as they each picked up a cheese tartlet.

Margaret Sama turned on the laptop. She adjusted the glasses to the tip of her nose as she focused on the screen. "May I have the license

plate number?"

"JNZU 57489," said O'Brian.

Margaret Sama entered the license plate number, and waited for the computer to search all records. "Ah, yes. Here we are." She looked up at the four faces that were eagerly waiting to hear who had use of that particular car within the last twenty-four hours.

Agent Clarkson looked at Jake. They were both thinking the same thing. This was it. They were going to get their man. They were going to catch the animal that had killed and kidnapped an unknown number of people.

"I'm sorry but that car hasn't been used in over a month. The record here indicates that it's had engine problems."

"Where is the car now?" asked Jake.

"It should be in the garage with the rest of the company cars," said Margaret Sama who seemed relaxed, and wasn't worried about losing her job any more. "Would you like to see it?"

"Yes," said Agent Clarkson.

"Please follow me," said Margaret Sama as she

shut the laptop.

They took the elevator down to the garage level.

"Well, it should be right here," said Margaret Sama

The car wasn't parked where it was supposed to be according to the records on the computer. Everyone looked around to check the license plates of other cars in the garage. They didn't find the car they were searching for.

"It should be right here," repeated Margaret Sama anxiously.

"Is there a security desk in the garage?" asked Jones.

"No, it's only used by our employees, and each person has a remote for the garage door."

"Are there security cameras down here?" asked Jones. He looked around the garage, but didn't see any cameras.

"I'm afraid not. It was never deemed necessary to have them installed. The bank's been a tenant in this building for over fifty years. We've never had anything missing or stolen, let alone a car," replied

Margaret Sama to reassure the detective of the safety and security of the building.

"You said the car hadn't been used in a month, who was the last person to use it?" asked Jones.

Margaret Sama flipped through the papers in her hand, and searched for the name of the employee who had used the car last.

"It was Vincent Brooks," said Margaret Sama with a saddened look.

"Where can we find Mr. Brooks?"

"I'm sorry, but he passed away. In fact he died in his office, right here in the building, two weeks ago.

"What was the cause of death?" asked Agent Clarkson.

"He had a massive heart attack, the poor man."

Detective Jones asked Margaret Sama to immediately file a stolen car report with the local police department. She said that she would as soon as she got back to her office.

46

Craig Nealis walked to the security desk in the main lobby. He had remained calm when he saw the four familiar faces waiting to enter the elevator as he stepped out.

"Where are they headed?" asked Nealis.

"Sir, they asked for the person in charge of the bank's vehicle fleet," replied the receptionist.

"Did they say why?"

"No sir," replied the receptionist nervously. This was the first time the receptionist had spoken to the CEO of the bank.

Nealis turned around and stepped away from the security desk. He walked out of the building, stopped a yellow cab, and instructed the driver to take him to Alpine, New Jersey.

He realized what the detectives were after as soon as the receptionist at the security desk told him they were looking for the person in charge of the bank's vehicle fleet. It occurred to him that they must have seen the car in one of the traffic cameras.

"How could I be so stupid," said Nealis loud enough for the taxi driver to hear.

"Excuse me sir?" asked the driver.

"Nothing…nothing…it was nothing," said Nealis.

He looked up at the driver who was looking back at him through the rearview mirror. It took thirty-five minutes for Nealis to get home. The same drive during rush hour could take well over an hour.

The company car was parked in the driveway. Nealis got in the driver seat and pushed the start button, but the car did not start. He tried again, but the result was the same. He remained calm. He

stepped out of the car, and walked towards the side of the garage. There was an electronic keypad located on the wall. He entered a four digit code, and within seconds the garage door opened.

Nealis walked back to the car. He pushed the gear in neutral, and stepped out. The driveway was on a slight down slope. He pushed the car with his right hand on the steering wheel and the left on top of the door. It didn't take much of an effort to move the car. It picked up momentum as it started to roll. He jumped inside to steer, and parked it next to a pickup truck.

Nealis recognized the fact that the authorities were gaining on him. He would have to be more careful in the future.

47

Margaret Sama entered her office, and closed the door. She sat down on a chair behind the desk, and flipped open the laptop. She looked at the log of employees who had use of the company vehicles once again to confirm she hadn't made a mistake. She read the name of the bank's CEO.

Craig Nealis was the last person to use the car the detectives had inquired about. She didn't want to tell them Nealis had possession of the car. She had lied to them. She wasn't sure why she hadn't just told them the truth. At the moment she felt in

her gut that she couldn't give them his name. She was concerned about losing her job. The fact that she was close to retirement, she was afraid getting fired.

Margaret Sama felt certain there was no way the bank's CEO was involved in a criminal case being investigated by the police and the FBI. He was rich. That was her logic for the way she felt. Just because he was rich, he wasn't capable of doing anything criminal.

She entered Craig Nealis's name on the company directory, picked up the phone on her desk, and dialed his cell number. She wanted to tell him about the two detectives and an FBI agent who had questioned her about a company car he was using. She thought she may even receive a bonus for not giving them his name. She had acted on her feet in a difficult situation, and would be rewarded for it. Everything would be alright. She smiled as she listened to the phone ring.

To her disappointment, there was no response. She left a message: "Mr. Nealis, this is Margaret Sama. I wanted to tell you that two police detectives

and a FBI agent came into my office today to question me about a company car. You were the last person to use the car they inquired about. Please call me at the office when you have a moment. Thank you." She hung up the phone and started feeling sick. She picked up a bottle, loosened its cap, and drank some water. "Why am I so nervous?" she said aloud. She looked at her hands and noticed they were shaking.

A few minutes later Margaret Sama nearly jumped out of the seat when her phone rang. She had never noticed how loud the ringer was until that moment. She picked up the receiver, "This is Margaret Sama."

"Hello Margaret, this is Craig Nealis."

Margaret Sama was surprised how quickly Nealis had returned her call. No wonder the bank was doing well financially, with such a diligent CEO at the helm, how could it not?

"Thank you for calling me back so soon Mr. Nealis," said Margaret Sama excitedly.

She felt like a young lady going out on her first date. She was nervous. Her palms were sweating.

"So, what is this matter you mentioned about the police and the FBI?" asked Nealis in a calm, almost playful voice.

"I'm sure it's nothing to be worried about"

"Let me be the judge of that," snapped Nealis with a sudden change in the tone of his voice.

Margaret Sama was taken aback by the outburst. "I'm sorry Mr. Nealis. I just…"

"I apologize, I shouldn't have snapped like that. Please tell me what happened."

Margaret Sama composed herself. She was in shock. "The detectives wanted to know who had used a particular car. When I looked it up, I saw your name on the log. I didn't think it wise to tell them that it was you. I told them the car hadn't been used in a month, and that it had engine problems."

"Does anybody else know about this?" asked Nealis guardedly.

"Well, no sir. I just got back to my office, and called you immediately. The detectives asked me to file a stolen car report. I'm not sure what to do."

"I want you to keep quiet about this matter.

Don't mention anything to anybody at the bank, or to anyone in your family. If the press finds out that the FBI is snooping around the bank, the stock price of our company is going crash. And you know that no one wants that, right?"

"Yes, sir" said Margaret Sama.

She had substantial amount of equity in the bank in the form of common shares and options. She was banking on them to live the rest of her life comfortably in a state where taxes were low, and the cost of living was manageable. She had even contemplated moving to another country.

"Is there a way to remove my name from the log?" asked Nealis.

"I think that can be done. I'll get one of the tech guys to do it."

"No…no…no…listen to me…do it yourself. I will hold while you do it."

Margaret Sama began typing as she tried to find a way to delete Nealis's name from the register. She wasn't computer savvy, but knew how to navigate the company software. "I think I got it."

"Can you make sure?" asked Nealis.

"It's done. I'm certain of it," replied Margaret Sama excitedly.

"That's great. You did well. I am going to make sure you are rewarded for it. Remember do not mention this to anyone. I mean no one in your family, and especially no one at work."

"Yes, sir, I won't tell anyone."

"Great. You are an asset to the bank. I will see you tomorrow," said Nealis.

Before Margaret Sama could say anything, Nealis ended the call.

48

It had been a long day for Margaret Sama. She was exhausted, and couldn't wait to get home to take a long warm bath. It was the first time in years she felt as though she had really done something important. However, at the same time she felt sick to her stomach. The thought that Nealis was a criminal kept circling in her mind. Regardless of how hard she tried to stay positive, she couldn't get the thought out of her head.

She got off the Q28 bus in Bayside, Queens. She lived alone in a ranch style house. It was one in

a row of many that had been built in the 1950's. She had two cats to keep her company. She would frequently talk to them as though they were her children. She loved them dearly.

She unlocked the front door of the house, and stepped inside. It was dark. She turned on the living room lights. As she had done for years, she picked up the remote off the coffee table, and pressed the power button. The television screen lit up instantly.

With her two feline friends following closely, she walked to the kitchen, and took out two cans of cat food from the cabinet below the sink. She poured the cat food in two separate dishes. The cats began to chomp on their nightly ration immediately. Margaret Sama bent down to pet them as they ate.

"How are you two doing? You sure are hungry today. Yes, yes you sure are," said Margret Sama as though she was speaking to a couple of babies.

She picked up her purse, and walked upstairs to the second floor. She stepped in to the bedroom, took off her scarf, and placed it on the bed next to the purse. She walked to the bathroom to turn on

the faucet. This had been her routine for years.

She walked back in to the bedroom to undress. Her body had held up well for a woman her age. She picked up a bottle of body cream, and squeezed it on the palm of her left hand. She rubbed the cream on her body. She liked to put it on before and after taking a bath. It was her secret to keeping her skin looking young. She opened the closet door to take out a robe.

Margaret Sama's eyes popped open as though she had seen a ghost. The knife wound was deep. How long had he been standing there in the closet watching her? Why didn't she just tell the detectives the truth? Was God punishing her for lying? These and many other thoughts flashed through Margaret Sama's mind.

The blood oozed down her oily skin from the neck to her bare breasts, and continued on to her stomach. It paused for a moment as the pubic hair between her legs soaked it in before continuing down her legs. She fell backwards on to the carpet. Her eyes were open as she stared up at the ceiling. She gasped for air. This is how they would find

her.

The cats heard the commotion, and came running to the bedroom to investigate. They sensed something was wrong. They pressed their furry bodies along Margaret Sama's head. They wanted her to get up, and play with them.

Craig Nealis had his boots covered with plastic bags. He was wearing gloves like a surgeon. His head was covered with a shower cap. He was an experienced killer. He stepped over Margaret Sama's dead body making sure not to step on the blood. He stopped in front of the dresser, looked in the mirror, and smiled.

49

Detective Jones arrived at the house in Bayside, Queens.

Before it was developed in the 1950's, Bayside was considered the Hamptons of New York City. The beach along Little Neck Bay was converted to a highway, Cross Island Parkway. The area had become congested with commercial and residential buildings, multi-unit houses, and mini-mansions. The roads which were manageable just a decade ago were now packed bumper-to-bumper with traffic. There was no shortage of wealth. Mercedes-Benz,

Lexus and BMW were the automobiles of choice.

As the area began to develop, it was mostly occupied by Italian, Greek, and Irish families. In the eighties there was a heavy influx of Asian immigrants. Within twenty years the neighborhood transformed completely. The Italians and the Irish began to sell their properties to Asians who kept bidding them up. Real Estate prices more than quadrupled in a relatively short period of time. It was a housing market like none other in the country. Even the collapse of the housing market, which crippled the rest of the nation, did not make a dent in the real estate prices in Bayside. It was a city within a city, a country within a country, a world within a world.

Margaret Sama was one of the few old timers who had remained. Her entire family had either moved out east to Long Island, or relocated to Florida and Arizona. She had stayed because she loved how the neighborhood had evolved during her time there. She loved the cultural diversity it offered.

Her fate, even if she had moved out of Bayside,

may not have been different. Whoever killed her had targeted her. This was not a robbery. Nothing had been stolen from the home. All of the windows and locks on the doors had been checked. There were no signs of forced entry. Police officers interviewed Margaret Sama's neighbors about what, if anything, they had seen. The neighbors, who were mostly immigrants, did not like to talk to the police. They tried to end the interviews as quickly as possible. Interpreters had to be called in as there were some residents who couldn't speak English.

Evelyn Sama had called the police after her Aunt Margaret didn't return her calls. For years she had called her every morning to wish her well. She loved her aunt. She thought of her as her mother. She had lost her biological mother to cancer when she was eight years old. Margaret Sama had been there for her niece ever since.

Detective O'Brian was listening to the news on the radio when he learned of the murder in Bayside. He was driving to the precinct when he heard the reporter say the name of the victim, Margaret Sama. He called Jones immediately.

"Are you listening to the news?" asked O'Brian

"No," replied Jones, "…what's up?"

"They just said the woman by the name of Margaret Sama was found dead in her house in Bayside this morning."

"Jesus! I'm on my way there," said Jones. As soon as he was off the phone, he called Agent Clarkson, and advised her of the murder.

Agent Clarkson arrived at Margaret Sama's house. She was greeted by Jones and O'Brian.

"It's the same killer. The cut on her neck is identical to the others," said Jones.

"Why her?" asked Agent Clarkson.

"It must have to do with us questioning her about the company car. The killer found out about it, and wanted to tie up a loose end," said Jones.

"Whoever the killer is, he must work at the bank, or is affiliated with it somehow. Maybe he saw us there, or perhaps she knew who he was," added Agent Clarkson. "I'm going to her office to

have a look around before someone else has a chance to go through it, and destroy potential evidence."

Agent Clarkson left the two detectives at the house. She told them that she would touch base later in the day. As soon as she left, she called Jake and brought him up to date. He hadn't heard about the murder.

"Meet me at the bank," said Agent Clarkson before ending the call.

50

Jake pulled up in front of the bank on his motorcycle. Agent Clarkson was waiting for him in the lobby. She flashed her ID at the security desk, and proceeded to the elevators. A security guard escorted them up.

As the elevator doors opened on the fifteenth floor, there was silence. Every employee of the bank had heard about Margaret Sama's murder. They looked terrified.

Agent Clarkson walked up to the young lady, Audrey, who she had met the previous day. Audrey

was in shock. From the look on her face she appeared as though she had been crying.

"I'm very sorry," said Agent Clarkson.

"Me too," said Audrey.

"Please take us to Margaret Sama's office."

"Of course," said Audrey. "Please follow me."

Agent Clarkson and Jake followed her down the hall, made a right, and stopped in front of an office. Audrey unlocked the door. The office was a mess.

"Someone's been here. Margaret was organized. She would never have left the office like this," said Audrey. "She was anal about organization." Audrey looked at the two agents. She was scared.

"Listen, everything is going to be fine. Who was the first person on this floor today?" asked Jake.

"It was me. Usually, it was Margaret, but when I came in this morning there was nobody here. It was unusual because she never took any days off work without letting everyone know. She never called in sick. She was a hard worker." Audrey

was rambling. She was trying to maintain her composure. She was too young for this sort of thing.

"We are going to have a look around the office," said Agent Clarkson. "Is there any way to find out who was the last person on this floor? When I walked in, I noticed an electronic key is required to enter the floor. Is there a record kept of who comes and goes every time a key is used?

"I will check with security," said Audrey, and walked out of the office.

Jake went behind Margaret Sama's desk, and sat down on the well used office chair. He pressed a button to turn on the computer, but it didn't power on. He turned the computer on its side. It appeared to have been opened.

"Son-of-a-bitch," said Jake, as he pounded his fist on the table, "the hard drive is gone."

Agent Clarkson went through the papers on the desk, and inside the file cabinets to look for anything that may have looked suspicious, but didn't find anything.

"The phone...maybe she called someone before

she left the office last night," said Agent Clarkson.

Jake immediately picked up the receiver, and pressed the redial button on its base. He waited for the bell to ring. As it rang, Jake's phone began to vibrate. He took the phone out of his pocket, and looked at the caller ID. The last number dialed from the office phone had been his. Whoever called him had hung up before the bell rang. He searched the call history on Margaret Sama's phone. There was nothing there. It had been deleted.

"Fuck!" yelled Jake, "Who the hell is this guy?"

Audrey walked in to the office. "I checked with security. They said the last person to enter this floor was someone with a master key. That means it's not registered to any particular person. It could've been anyone."

"Who's authorized to have a master key?" asked Jake.

"Security, the cleaning people, the officers of the bank," replied Audrey. "It could be any one of them really."

"Are there security cameras on this floor?"

asked Agent Clarkson.

"I'm afraid not. It's against company policy. When I joined the bank they had security cameras on every floor. A few months ago they got rid of them. It had something to do with employee privacy…at least that's what the memo said. I can show it to you if you like."

"No, that won't be necessary," said Agent Clarkson.

Jake's cell phone vibrated again. He looked at the caller ID. The number was blocked. He pressed the end button. The phone vibrated again. This time he answered it. He pressed the speakerphone button, and said, "This is Jake."

"If you want Jenny to live, stop looking for me. Stop trying to find me. Do you want Audrey to die as well? Her murder will be on your hands just like Margaret Sama's," said the caller.

"Listen asshole, I'm going to find you, and make you suffer. Are you listening to me, motherfucker?"

"Now, now, there's no need to get worked up. I want you to know I'm having a lot of fun playing

with your daughter. She is sweet, just like her mother. Hahaha." The caller began to laugh before he ended the call.

Jake looked up at Agent Clarkson and Audrey. They had heard the phone call. Audrey began to cry. She was shaking out of fear.

"I promise, you'll be safe," said Agent Clarkson. "We're going to find him before he can hurt anyone else."

"You don't understand. I know that voice," said Audrey.

"What! Who is it? Is it someone who works here?" said Jake. He knew immediately this was the break they had been looking for.

"He sounded like Mr. Nealis. Could it be him?"

"You mean Craig Nealis. The bank's CEO?" snapped Jake.

"Yes…yes…I'm certain. I never forget a person's voice. Some people have a knack for remembering faces; I am good with remembering voices. I heard his speech when last quarter's earnings were released. He rarely speaks

publically, but I swear the person on the phone was Craig Nealis."

It was a far cry, but a lead worth following up on.

"Where is his office?" asked Jake.

"He's on the top floor of the building," replied Audrey.

Agent Clarkson and Jake left Margaret Sama's office. They rushed to the elevator. They had to get to the top floor as quickly as possible. The elevator seemed to take forever as Jake pressed the button repeatedly. They stepped inside the elevator, and he pressed "50."

The elevator stopped on the 50th floor. They approached the receptionist. Agent Clarkson flashed her ID. "Where's Craig Nealis? Is he in his office?"

"Let me check. Please have a seat," said the receptionist calmly.

"Where is his office?" yelled Jake.

"Follow me," said the receptionist. She led Agent Clarkson and Jake to an office on the far end of the floor. She knocked on the door, but there

was no response. "Looks like he's not in the office, would you mind coming back another time? Please leave your business card with me, and I'll pass it along to him. I'm sure he'll get in touch with you when he returns."

Jake couldn't believe the receptionist didn't comprehend they weren't there to leave business cards. How could she not sense the urgency?

"When did you see him last?" asked Agent Clarkson.

"About thirty minutes ago," replied the receptionist.

"How could you be sure?"

"Because I passed a call to him about half an hour ago, and he took it. He was in his office then," said the receptionist sarcastically.

Jake had never hit a woman, but he was on the verge of knocking out the receptionist.

"Who was the call from?" asked Jake.

"It was the security desk from the lobby downstairs."

"Is there a number Craig Nealis can be reached?" asked Agent Clarkson.

"Yes, hold please," replied the receptionist as she looked up the number in the directory. She wrote it down on a piece of paper and handed it to her, "Here you go."

Agent Clarkson pulled out her phone, and dialed the number. There was no response. She looked at Jake, and shook her head. She handed her business card to the receptionist, and advised her to call the number as soon as she saw Craig Nealis.

"What is his home address?" asked Agent Clarkson.

"I'll write it down for you," replied the receptionist. She wrote the address on a piece of paper and handed it to the FBI agent.

Jake and Agent Clarkson took the elevator down to the main floor. They walked up to the security desk. Agent Clarkson flashed her ID again. "Who called Craig Nealis half an hour ago?"

"I did," said a receptionist who was sitting behind the desk.

"What was it about?" asked Agent Clarkson

"We have direct orders from Mr. Nealis to notify him if anyone from the police, the FBI, or the

press comes in to the building," replied the receptionist.

"Did you happen to see him leave the building?" asked Jake

"Yes, in fact, he left soon after I called him. He even stopped by the desk, and thanked me personally," replied the receptionist proudly.

Jake and Agent Clarkson stepped away from the security desk.

"We need to search his office," said Jake.

Though they had a warrant to check Margaret Sama's, they didn't have one to check Nealis' office.

"We'll have to get a warrant."

51

The streets were blocked to traffic on 65th Street between Madison Avenue and 5th Avenue. This wasn't unusual in Manhattan. It was especially true for the area between 57th Street and 65th Street, between Lexington Avenue and 5th Avenue. This is where most foreign diplomats resided, and the President stayed while in New York.

Agent Clarkson had called Detective Jones from the main lobby of the bank after talking to her superiors at the Bureau. FBI agents and police officers were dispatched immediately after the call

as per her instructions.

Agent Clarkson told Jones that Audrey's life was in danger. She requested uniformed officers be sent to the bank for the young lady's protection.

Detectives Jones and O'Brian had just crossed the Ed Koch Queensboro Bridge in to Manhattan when Jones received Agent Clarkson's call. They drove directly to the brownstone, and waited for the unit to assemble. They wanted to get this done before the press arrived. It would be any minute before they were all over the news. As much as the media helped in solving crimes, it did no less in helping criminals get away. It was their best warning system.

The FBI broke down the front door of the brownstone, and entered with guns drawn. From the outside the building looked like an unassuming structure. However, from the inside, it was anything but simple. It was decorated with antique furniture. A chandelier, which looked to be a hundred years old, hung from the high ceiling. It appeared as though no one had lived at the glorious brownstone for some time. The cops and the FBI

agents searched each room without concern for anything fragile. It almost seemed deliberate the way they knocked things down.

The officers and agents entered the basement. It was vacant as well. The investigators searched each room in the basement for anything that would lead them to Craig Nealis.

"There's nothing here. He knew we would catch up to him, and from the looks of it he cleaned out the place some time ago," said Jones.

Agent Clarkson and Jake received the warrant to search Nealis' office. The receptionist on the 50th floor, who had resisted at first, opened the door to his office to let them in. The room appeared to be in order. It had windows which displayed a spectacular view of Manhattan, including the Statue of Liberty.

Jake turned on the computer. Just as he had found in Margaret Sama's office, the CPU had been opened, and the hard drive removed. They went

through file cabinets to look for evidence. After several hours of searching the office they came up empty handed. Everything they found was related to the bank. There were no personal items in the office.

Agent Clarkson's phone vibrated. She took it out from the belt clip, and said, "Hello."

"There's nothing here. From the way it looks, no one has lived here for months. The investigators are going through the home in detail, but I have a strong feeling we are not going to find anything," said Jones.

"The story's the same here. We've searched Craig Nealis' office. There's nothing here we can use to get to him," said Agent Clarkson.

52

The photograph of Craig Nealis was plastered on every television screen across the country. Several European countries had picked up on the story also as it related to a major international bank. The stock price began plummeting as soon as the story broke. Trading on the stock had to be halted as shareholders began liquidating their holdings as fast as they could. Clients who had investments in the bank filed for immediate redemptions. The firm, which just a day prior had been considered a premier global banking institution, was quickly

becoming insolvent.

Craig Nealis had sold shares short of the bank in numerous numbered accounts he held across the globe. To ensure the stock trades would not be associated with him, or raise red flags which would lead to his assets being frozen, Nealis shorted the stock through derivative positions. He was betting on the share price of the bank to drop. The more it dropped, the higher his profits would rise. This was a major violation of rules set forth by the Securities and Exchange Commission to protect the public from insider trading.

Once the banks' shares resumed trading, the projection was the stock price would be seventy to eighty percent below previous day's market close. This translated to more than five hundred million dollars in profit for Nealis.

It was quite amazing for a person as insane and demented as Nealis to make astute trading decisions while he was being hunted by federal and local authorities.

This was a calculated decision by Nealis. Domestic and foreign bank and brokerage accounts

that were registered under his name had already been frozen by the FBI. He had several million dollars in cash locked in a safe at his home in Alpine. He also had money stashed in public lockers at bus and train terminals in New York, New Jersey, Georgia, and Florida. Nealis calculated if he had to flee to a country which did not have an extradition treaty with the United States, he'd need sufficient funds to ensure the host country's officials could be bribed. This would keep them from harassing him while he lived out his sadistic and masochist, fetishes and fantasies, in peace. He had narrowed down the list to Indonesia, Morocco, and the United Arab Emirates.

Craig Nealis was in the driver's seat.

53

The restaurant, Campagnola, on 1st Avenue was among the best Italian eateries in Manhattan. Jake and Nadine went there frequently. They never needed to make a reservation as they had gotten to know the staff well. It was where Jake had taken Nadine on their first date. It was also where he had proposed to her. They were treated like family every time they went there.

Campagnola was a favorite of Hollywood types, athletes, and businessmen. While celebrities impressed their dates with witty conversation,

businessmen did their best to impress their clients with pitches about their products and services. Athletes congregated at the restaurant to celebrate their victories.

Jake missed Nadine. Over a year had passed since her murder. They often spoke about what either of them would do if they lost each other. At the time Nadine would playfully say that she would die before he did. She told him it would be unbearable for her to live without him. Jake couldn't remember what he had said to her. The thought had become blurred in his mind. The reality of losing her was too painful.

At first Jake thought about taking Agent Clarkson to another restaurant. In many ways she had been exactly who he needed to keep him sane after Nadine's murder and Jenny's kidnapping. He felt lucky to have met her at the most terrible and painful time of his life. She was beautiful. She was smart, and had a great sense of humor. She cared about people. To him she was almost everything Nadine had been. Deep down, he knew she would never replace Nadine. No one could.

"Hello Jake. It's been too long my friend," said the maitre d' as he hugged Jake. He learned of Nadine's murder on the news when it happened. He had reached out to Jake at the time to extend his condolences.

"It's great to see you too my friend," said Jake.

"And who is this lovely lady with you this evening?" asked the maitre d' as he stepped closer to Agent Clarkson.

Jake introduced her to the maitre d'. He took her right hand in his, and kissed it on the back.

"It's a pleasure to meet you," said Agent Clarkson.

The maitre d' smiled. He kissed her on both cheeks. "The pleasure is all mine," he said, and led her and Jake to their table.

"Enjoy," said the maitre d'. He excused himself.

"Wow, this place is nice," said Agent Clarkson. She looked around the restaurant which was filled with celebrities. Although, she was not a person who was easily impressed, she couldn't help but be a little star struck.

Jake ordered the food and drinks without looking at a menu. He had been there enough to know exactly what to order. All of the waiters in the restaurant knew him. They stopped by the table to ask how he was doing.

"You seem to be the mayor of the place," said Agent Clarkson.

"They really make you feel like it in this place. I've been coming here for years. This is actually where Nadine and…" Jake stopped midsentence.

"What?"

"Nothing, it's nothing," said Jake.

Agent Clarkson smiled. She had an idea of what Jake was about to say. She did not want to make the dinner uncomfortable. She liked Jake, and enjoyed his company. She hadn't been out on a date for well over a year. Was this actually a date, she thought, or was it just two lonely people in the big city giving each other company? Either way, she was happy to be with him.

The two enjoyed the food and drinks. They told each other stories about their childhoods, and their college years. They talked about their

families. They talked about music they listened to, books they read, and movies they had seen. At the end, they had more in common than either of them expected. At times they laughed, and others they looked at one another quietly. Each wanted to know more about the other.

It was late. The restaurant had emptied out. Only a couple of other tables were occupied, beside theirs. Time had passed quickly. Jake asked for the check. The maitre d' walked over to their table, and told Jake dinner was on him.

"It has been too long, and I hope to see you again soon," said the maitre d'.

"Thank you my friend. Thank you for everything." Jake stood up, and hugged the maitre d'. Jake was referring not only to the dinner, but also his kindness.

The maitre d' kissed Agent Clarkson on both cheeks once again.

"It was a pleasure to meet you. I hope to see you again very soon," said the maitre d'.

She smiled, and said, "It was a pleasure to meet you as well, and the food was delicious. I can

hardly wait to come back."

Jake's motorcycle was parked on the street in front of the restaurant. Agent Clarkson said yes when he offered to give her a ride to her apartment. It was a clear and warm night in New York.

She put her arms around his waist as she sat on the back seat. She held onto him tight. She felt safe. Jake started the engine, and the Harley Davidson roared. As they began to move, she closed her eyes, and felt the breeze hit her face.

Jake rode up to the front of Agent Clarkson's building. He shut off the engine, and leaned the bike on its stand. She took off the helmet, and ran her fingers through her hair. Jake looked at her. He thought she looked beautiful.

A man who was walking out of the building held the door open for Agent Clarkson. "It's okay Charlie," she said. He smiled, and closed the door.

Jake grabbed her arm, and drew her close. He paused for a moment, and then kissed her. She didn't resist. She wanted him more than he would ever know. She had hoped for this.

They parted their lips, looked into each other's

eyes, and kissed again. She had dreamt about this day. She thought it would never come. This was the first time in her life she felt truly alive.

She invited Jake up to her apartment. They kissed in the elevator. She wondered how long the ride would be before it reached her floor.

Once they entered the apartment, she took Jake by his hand, and led him to the bedroom. They kissed as they undressed. She ran her fingers through every muscle on his body as he felt every curve on hers. They made love. How many times had each of them thought about this night, and now it was happening. It was perfect.

54

Craig Nealis was driving to Southern New Jersey, not far from the shore, to a house he purchased five years earlier. He had paid cash for it. He made certain there was no link between him and the house. It was titled under a foreign corporation, and listed as a corporate housing property.

Nealis was going to the house to ensure it was in order, but more specifically to observe if there were any cops snooping around the neighborhood. There was low probability of that, but he wanted to be positive nonetheless. He hadn't been there for

six months. The last time he had used the property was when he was driving back from Pennsylvania. He had kidnapped a six year old girl right from under her parents' nose.

The girl was at a playground with a group of other children. Her mother was talking to one of the other parent's while her father had gone to the ice cream truck. Nealis had been sitting nonchalantly on a bench paying close attention to the children. He wanted to get the prettiest doll for his collection. After he picked out the perfect little girl he waited for the right opportunity to collect her.

The opportunity presented itself when the little girl went to hide behind a bush. She was playing a game with her friends. Nealis got up off the bench, and leisurely walked to the bush. He was careful not to raise suspicion.

"Come out, come out, wherever you are," whispered Nealis.

"No," said the little girl. She thought it was her friend's father who had come looking for her. She was having fun, and didn't want to come out so

soon. "There is no one here," continued the little girl as she looked through the bushes to see who was calling out to her. When she saw the man's face, she did not recognize him.

Nealis pulled out a toy doll, and held it in front of him. "I have a little doll for you to play with. Do you want it?"

The little girl giggled, and said, "Yeah."

As she went to grab the doll from the stranger's hand, he put a white cloth over her nose. She passed out before she could scream.

Nealis picked up the little girl, and put her in a hand bag. He walked past the little girl's mother to his car. The mother was still talking to her friend, while her husband was in line waiting to buy an ice-cream cone for their daughter. By the time they noticed their daughter was missing, it was too late. They had lost her.

Nealis spent the night with the new addition to his doll collection at the house by the Jersey Shore. The next morning he had driven north with her passed out on the backseat under a blanket.

Now he was going back to make sure it was

safe for him and his dolls in case he needed to escape from the house in Alpine. He was aware the brownstone in Manhattan had been raided. He had made sure not to leave any clues which could've led the authorities to him. According to his calculations it was just a matter of time before they found him. He had prepared well.

As he drove south on the New Jersey Turnpike he noticed a state trooper driving up behind him. Nealis looked down at the speedometer to make sure he was driving within the speed limit. He was cruising at sixty-two miles per hour, three below the posted limit. He maintained the speed.

The state trooper gained on him, and changed lanes. As he drove up next to Nealis, the trooper sitting on the passenger seat looked over his shoulder. Nealis stared directly at the trooper. As their eyes met, the trooper squinted. The trooper driving the car pressed the accelerator, and drove ahead of Nealis.

Nealis felt relieved as he was prepared to kill the troopers had they pulled him over. He had a 9mm gun tucked under his jacket. The fact that the

trooper had squinted gave Nealis the feeling that he may have recognized him. He slowed down. He decreased his speed from sixty-two miles per hour to fifty-five miles per hour. He wanted the troopers to drive as far ahead of him as possible giving him enough space to take the next exit without being noticed.

As Nealis approached the exit he saw the state troopers taking it. Though he couldn't be certain they were the same troopers, he changed his plan, and decided to stay on the turnpike. He drove past the exit, and increased the speed back to sixty-two miles per hour.

A few minutes later, Nealis looked in the rearview mirror, and saw a car driving up behind him at high speed. As it gained on him he could see it was the same troopers. He turned on the right indicator to take the next exit which was only half a mile ahead. The troopers kept on his tail.

The road off the exit was clear. There were tall trees and shrubbery on both sides. Nealis saw a dirt road, and turned on to it. The troopers turned on the beacons. They signaled for him to stop. Nealis

drove up far enough so the car could not be seen from the main road.

"Turn off the engine," said one of the troopers over the loudspeaker.

After they heard the engine shut off, the troopers got out of their car with hands on their guns. They approached the car with caution. One of the troopers stood by the passenger door of Nealis' car, while the other walked up to the driver's side.

"What seems to be the problem, officer?" asked Nealis.

"License and registration," ordered the officer.

Nealis reached in his back pocket to take out the wallet. He pulled out his license and registration. As he put his hand out of the window to hand them to the officer, he dropped both IDs on the ground.

"I'm sorry about that," said Nealis. He was about to get out of the car, when the trooper stopped him.

"Hand's where I can see them…keep them on the steering wheel," ordered the officer. He bent

down to pick up the documents off the ground.

As the trooper bowed down, Nealis swiftly placed his left hand under his jacket and fired two shots through the passenger window. The trooper, standing by the passenger door, died instantly.

"Nice and easy," said Nealis as he pointed the gun at the trooper holding his license and registration. "Nice and easy," repeated Nealis. "Keep your hands where I can see them, and slowly step back."

Nealis got out of the car, and walked up to the trooper. He grabbed the gun from the holster, and threw it in his car. He also took his license and registration from the trooper.

"Just in case I get pulled over again," said Nealis as he placed the IDs in his pocket.

The trooper did not find it amusing.

"Alright, do exactly as I say, and you won't end up like your partner. Dead."

The young trooper was terrified. He waited for Nealis's instructions. He was thinking about his pregnant wife. When he left the house that morning, just like any other day, she had given him

a kiss and said that she loved him. He wondered if he would ever see her again.

"I want you to call back your headquarters, and tell them everything checked out fine. I'm sure you called in my plates before you pulled me over," said Nealis with authority. He was calling the shots.

The trooper walked towards his car.

"And shut those damn lights off," ordered Nealis.

The trooper turned off the flashing lights before picking up the microphone. He told the dispatcher that everything checked out, and there was no need for concern.

Nealis grabbed the microphone from the trooper's hand, and threw it on the seat of the car. "Why did you say there was no need for concern? Is that a code for backup? That was a mistake on your part. Turn around, and keep your hands behind your head."

The trooper turned around as he prayed. This couldn't be it he thought. He had dinner plans with his wife. They were going to Olive Garden. He loved their breadsticks.

The blade sliced the trooper's throat. He didn't see it coming. He grabbed his neck as the blood gushed out on to the dry grass in front of him. He tried to speak. He wanted to say that he loved his wife. The words didn't come out. He hit the ground, face first, and bled to death.

Nealis got inside the troopers' car, and drove it in to the bushes leaving enough space for him to back out. He walked back to the trooper, whose throat he had cut, and searched his pockets. He pulled out a set of keys and a wallet. He took out the driver's license, and wrote down his home address. He placed the wallet back in the trooper's pocket.

Nealis got back in to his car, and reversed on to the main road. Within minutes he was back on the New Jersey Turnpike heading south. It was as though nothing had happened. He was calm.

55

Jenny took comfort in the fact Emily hadn't left without saying goodbye. She still thought about Zoey. She wondered what happened to her friend. She made up fairytales about her being rescued by a prince. She fantasized the same prince who had rescued Zoey, would save her as well, and bring her back to her mommy and daddy.

"Tell me about the prince again, Jenny. Please tell me the story about how the prince saved Zoey, and brought her back home to her mommy and daddy," pleaded Emily. "Pleeeeease, Jenny, tell me

how the prince saved Zoey."

Jenny felt good about having someone to talk to. Even though they were in separate rooms, they could talk to each other through the thin walls. She enjoyed telling Emily stories. Jenny's imagination had grown substantially having been locked up in a room for days at a time without getting a visit from the mean man who touched her in ways she didn't like, and made her do things to him she was disgusted by.

"There was a prince," said Jenny, "who had a white horse. He lived in a castle far, far away."

"How far, Jenny, how far away did he live," asked Emily. She was eager to find out how long it would take for the prince find her.

"Very far," replied Jenny. The story remained the same except for minor changes each time. "The prince heard Zoey singing one day as he rode in the forest. He stopped his horse and looked for her."

"Did the horse also talk?" asked Emily

"Yes, he did," replied Jenny.

Knowing the horse could talk made Emily happy. She really wanted him to be able to speak.

"Then what happened?" asked Emily. She was fascinated by the story. She imagined it like a motion picture in her mind. "Did he find her?"

"Not that day."

"Tell me, when did he find her?"

"One day when the prince was riding in the forest, the horse stopped. He heard Zoey's voice. The prince asked him 'why did you stop?' The horse told him to listen closely. The prince listened as the forest around him became quiet. He heard her voice, and rode in the direction where it was coming from."

"Did he find her?" asked Emily.

"Yes, he rode up to Zoey's window. He didn't know her name so he threw a stone at the window to get her attention."

Emily giggled. She imagined herself looking out of the window, and seeing the prince atop his horse.

"Zoey looked out of the window and saw the prince. She tried to open it, but the window was stuck. She put her hands on the glass and screamed for help." Jenny paused to hear if Emily was still

awake.

"Don't stop Jenny. Pleeeeease tell me what happened then," pleaded Emily.

Jenny smiled and continued, "The prince went to the front of the house. He knocked on the door. When no one answered, the horse kicked up his front legs and knocked the door down. The prince went inside the house. It was dark all around. The horse stood outside to keep guard. As the prince went up the stairs to the second floor, he saw two red eyes glaring down at him."

"Who…who was it Jenny?" asked Emily. She sounded scared.

"It was a big mean giant man who had stolen Zoey from her family," continued Jenny.

"Why did the big mean giant man do that? Is it because Zoey had been a bad girl, and didn't listen to her mommy and daddy?"

"He stole her because he was a big mean giant man with giant red eyes," Jenny could never think of anything else to say each time Emily asked her why he had stolen Zoey. She wanted to know the answer to that question just as much as her little

friend. Not even in her wildest imagination could she come up with the reason as to why he had done that. "He wanted her all to himself. The big mean giant man opened his big mouth and blew fire at the prince. The prince moved out of the way. The big mean giant man rushed to capture the prince…"

"Can I finish the story, Jenny? Pleeeeease," asked Emily.

"Sure you can," replied Jenny.

"The prince pulled out his sword and fought off the big mean giant man and broke into Zoey's room and then he broke the window and picked her up and jumped out of the window and landed on his horse who could talk and rode far, far, away," said Emily. She finished the story in one breath. "Is that what happened Jenny?"

"Yes, Emily, that's what happened," replied Jenny as she fought back tears. Every time she cried, Emily would cry as well. And Jenny didn't want to make her little friend cry, not now, not ever.

"I love you Jenny."

"I love you too Emily."

56

"Turn on the news," said Agent Clarkson. She called Jake when she learned two state troopers had been killed in New Jersey. It was reported at least one of the troopers was killed with a knife. "I'll call you back in a few minutes."

It was a developing story. A field reporter at the scene of the murders reported the two dead troopers were following a suspicious car they had seen on the New Jersey Turnpike. One of the troopers had recognized the driver of the suspicious car.

The operator at the station stated the trooper believed the driver was Craig Nealis. He told the operator they were going to follow the suspicious car, and would call for back up if it was necessary. The operator said the next time she heard from the trooper was when he called in to report, "everything checked out." The operator added that she sensed something was wrong when the trooper told her, "there was no need for concern." She said the last statement sounded as though the trooper was trying to tell her something was wrong. She said she attempted to get in touch with the troopers again after a little over an hour. She dispatched back-up when neither trooper responded to her call.

There was an APB out on the car the dead troopers had called in about. The authorities began a massive search in southern New Jersey to locate the suspicious car and its driver.

Agent Clarkson called Jake. There was no response. She called again, but as before he didn't answer the phone. As she hit the end button the second time, her phone rang. She looked at the caller ID and answered, "Detective Jones, I assume

you are calling about what happened down in Jersey."

"Yes, O'Brian and I are on our way down there now," said Jones.

"I'll meet you there," said Agent Clarkson before ending the call.

There was a knock on her door.

"It's Jake."

Agent Clarkson opened the door to let him in. He was holding a helmet in one hand and a backpack in the other.

"I got here as quickly as I could." Jake was staring at Agent Clarkson. She was wearing a black t-shirt and khaki shorts. She looked stunning.

"Give me two minutes to get ready," said Agent Clarkson. She walked in to the bedroom.

Jake stood in the living room. He could see inside the bedroom. She had left the door open intentionally.

"I'm almost done," said Agent Clarkson while she undressed.

Jake looked at her through the open door, and admired her body. She put on a pair of black

panties, jeans, and a t-shirt with a jacket over it. She picked up a handgun off the table, and placed it in the holster under the jacket.

Agent Clarkson looked at Jake when she walked out of the bedroom. He gave her a smile. She smiled back at him, and shook her head. They were both thinking about the night they had spent together.

They left the apartment, and went out to the street to hail down a cab. They were headed to the pier. A helicopter was waiting to take them to the location where the two state troopers had been killed in New Jersey.

57

The helicopter touched down on an open field. The flight took thirty minutes to get from Manhattan to the crime scene in New Jersey.

They were greeted by Detectives Jones and O'Brian. Jones brought them up to date on the details he and O'Brian had been able to gather about the murdered troopers.

A state trooper, who introduced himself as Blake Jordan, approached them, and said, "There is a video you need to see."

"What is it?" asked Agent Clarkson.

"Each one of the state police vehicles is equipped with a video camera. We played the video when we arrived at the scene. It would be best if you saw it for yourself," suggested Officer Jordan.

Agent Clarkson and Jake followed the trooper, and stepped inside the back of a van. Officer Jordan pressed play on the digital video player. The video was of a car being pulled over by the two dead state troopers. Agent Clarkson gasped when she saw the trooper drop to the ground after being shot by the person inside the car.

Jake and Agent Clarkson watched as the person who had shot the trooper, stepped out of the car. They recognized him. It was Craig Nealis.

Nealis stared into the camera as though he wanted to be videotaped for what he was about to do next. He stood behind the trooper who was on his knees. Nealis smiled before he slid the knife across the trooper's neck.

"He's insane," said Agent Clarkson "He's starting to believe he's invincible. He'll soon begin to think he's God."

"An animal like him doesn't believe in God,"

said Jake.

Jake and Agent Clarkson left the crime scene. They went to the nearest town which was Jackson. They checked into separate rooms at the hotel. They would think about their relationship after Jenny was found, and Craig Nealis was captured. They both knew they would be together; it was only a matter of time.

58

Craig Nealis was back to cruising at sixty-two miles per hour on the New Jersey Turnpike. He figured it would be several hours before the bodies of the two troopers were found. By the time they were discovered he would be at his house by the Jersey shore.

Initially he had intended on driving back to Alpine the same day, but after the events on the turnpike he changed his plans. He would head back the next day. He had a motorcycle in the garage which he would switch with the car. Every police

officer and trooper in the state was searching for him. It would be much easier for Nealis to get away as the police rarely pulled over motorcyclists. They mostly searched cars, vans, and trucks.

Nealis pulled out the photograph of the trooper's wife and young daughter from his pocket. He had taken it from the trooper's wallet after he killed him. He looked at the picture and said, "Maybe another time sweetheart…maybe another time."

Nealis turned on the television, and saw his face plastered on every news channel. The stations that weren't broadcasting live had "Breaking News" alerts interrupting regularly scheduled programming to report on the murders of the two troopers. Nealis saw Jake and Agent Clarkson as the news cameramen panned the crime scene.

59

Agent Clarkson entered her apartment building. She pressed the elevator button. While waiting for it to come down to the lobby, she decided to the check the mail. She unlocked the mailbox, took out the mail, and locked it again. As she turned around she saw a man standing in a corner staring at her. She thought he looked familiar, but couldn't place him. He was wearing a uniform of a utility company. He smiled at her.

"I'm sorry if I startled you. There is some trouble with the electricity in the building. I'm just

taking a look," said the man.

Agent Clarkson nodded, but didn't say anything. She entered the elevator, and went up to her apartment.

She went through the mail, most of which was junk, and tossed it on the dining table. She went into the bedroom and undressed. She powered on the stereo and turned up its volume.

She walked into the shower. Out of habit she left the bathroom door open. She enjoyed listening to music while she showered.

Suddenly the lights went out. "Damn it," she said. She searched for the towel. She found it and wrapped it around her wet body. With her hair dripping, she walked out of the shower, and in to the living room. She flipped the light switch to see if the light would come on again. It didn't. She walked to the door that led into the lobby to see if anyone else on the floor was having the same issue. As she opened the door, she was pushed to the ground. There was someone on top of her. She tried to fight her way out, but the man on top of her was too strong even for her. She had been trained

to fight out of situations like the one she was in.

Her towel came off leaving her exposed. She felt vulnerable. The man pulled out a knife, and held it to her throat.

"Don't make a sound," said the man.

She sensed instantly the man on top of her had to be Craig Nealis. She had to think. She had to stay alive.

"Alright, alright, just calm down," said Agent Clarkson.

"That's a good girl. Now get up slowly and turn around."

He got off her and stood up. He flipped a switch on the wall. The lights came back on. He looked at her from head to toe as she stood naked. Her body was still wet. He ran the edge of the knife down the length her spine. She saw his reflection on a mirror on the wall. It was Craig Nealis.

"You are real pretty, real pretty," said Nealis.

"What do you want?" demanded Agent Clarkson. She tried to stay composed. She was scared for her life. She knew the odds were against her. She could sense the knife cutting across her

throat. It was only a matter of time before he did it. It was a terrible feeling to know you are going to die. She felt cold.

Nealis took a step closer to her. He ran his hand along the side of her body. He pulled her close. He ran his hand between her legs, up the stomach, to her breasts, and grabbed her neck.

"You know who I am?" whispered Nealis. His mouth was next to her ear. "Come on, you must have an idea. Take a guess."

"I don't know who you are," replied Agent Clarkson. She wanted to buy as much time as possible. She was trying to think of a way out of the situation she was in. He held her in a way that she couldn't break loose of his grip without giving him an opportunity to stab her.

"I'm Craig Nealis. I'm the man you and your boyfriend have been looking for. Don't worry, he's still alive. I'm going to use you to get him to come out and play," said Nealis as he ran his fingers down the lower part of her back. "You feel real nice, real nice." He paused for a few seconds, "Let's get you in to the bedroom, and get you

dressed. Move real slow or this knife will end up going deep inside your body, real deep." He pressed the point of the knife in her back.

Agent Clarkson started walking slowly towards the bedroom as Nealis followed her closely.

"Now, pick out something sexy and put it on," said Nealis in a low voice sounding as though he was trying to seduce her.

Agent Clarkson pulled out a pair of jeans and a t-shirt. "No, no, no, I said something sexy. I want to get you dolled up. Here let me help," said Nealis as he grabbed her hair and swung her down on the bed. She lay flat on her stomach with her bare back facing the ceiling.

Nealis quickly went through the closet, pulled out a mini-dress, and tossed it to her.

"Here, put this on," ordered Nealis. "You are a pretty girl. You should learn to dress like a doll, and not like a man."

Agent Clarkson got up off the bed. She was standing face to face with Nealis. He looked at her, and rubbed his crotch. She was about to put on panties, but Nealis stopped her.

"There's no need for those. Just put on the dress."

She picked up the dress and slid it on.

"Now, put on some make up…don't disappoint me. Otherwise, I'm going to have to doll you up myself. I know you would like that, wouldn't you…you little slut."

Agent Clarkson tried to hold back the tears. She was terrified. She didn't want to show him that she was weak. She realized he wasn't going to kill her there in the apartment. If he was going to do that, he would've done it already. He had other plans. She wanted to know what they were.

"Now, that's more like it. Now you are behaving like a nice little girl. You are going to be fine, just fine," said Nealis. "Now put on those shoes," he said as he pointed to a pair of red pumps with three and a half inch heels. "Now we're going to take a walk. Don't be foolish and make any sudden moves. You've already seen my work, and know that I won't hesitate to slice your pretty little throat. Let's go."

Agent Clarkson began walking as Nealis

followed her closely behind. She hoped that one of her neighbors had heard the scuffle in her apartment and called the police. Most of the residents in the building were college students. They partied louder than the noise produced by the brawl in her apartment.

As they stepped out into the lobby she looked around, the hallway was empty. Her dress lifted from behind with each step, exposing her buttocks. Nealis looked at her and smiled. He walked up close behind her and cupped her left butt cheek with his right hand.

"That feels nice," said Nealis.

Within minutes they were out of the building and walking down the sidewalk. The way Agent Clarkson was dressed was nothing out of the ordinary in Manhattan, especially at night.

Where were the cops? She thought. She would have attempted to take down Nealis if she saw them. It wasn't worth the chance if she didn't succeed, and there was no one around to help her.

Nealis stopped next to a car and opened the passenger door. "Get in," he ordered as he pushed

her down into the seat. He walked around the car, and got in to the driver's seat. He pulled out a syringe from his coat pocket.

"This will make you relax," said Nealis as he pushed the needle into her arm.

Agent Clarkson felt a sudden rush go through her body. It was gone just as quickly. She felt weak. She wondered what he had injected her with. She felt paralyzed.

They drove uptown. Nealis put his right hand under her dress. She looked out of the window with tears running down her cheeks. He was hurting her. Though she couldn't move, she could feel the pain between her legs.

She looked up at the tall buildings with their lights shining bright. She watched couples walking down sidewalks holding hands. She saw people standing outside of bars smoking cigarettes, conversing, and laughing. She saw the yellow taxis drive past her. She watched the homeless people sleeping under scaffoldings on the sidewalks, while others begged for change. She wondered if she would ever see the beautiful city again.

60

Jake called Agent Clarkson for the third time. He had called twice on her cell phone, and left a message at her home phone. It wasn't like her to not answer his calls. Perhaps he was being too aggressive, he thought. He wasn't calling her to go out on a date. He wanted to talk about what they would do next. He wanted to plan their next move to hunt down Craig Nealis. He wanted to get his daughter back. He prayed Jenny was alive. She had to be. Any thought of her being dead was insane.

Jake's cell phone rang. It was Agent Clarkson. "Hi, I thought you were starting to ignore my calls," said Jake.

"Now, I wouldn't do that, would I?" said Nealis.

Jake was caught off guard. He didn't expect to hear a man's voice. He thought it was a joke. Perhaps it was her boyfriend, brother, or father. Several thoughts went through his mind as to who it could've been.

"Who is this?" asked Jake.

"Why don't you take a guess? Perhaps I should put your girlfriend on the line, and she can tell you herself," said Nealis. "Let me make it easy for you, I'm her lover."

Jake knew something was wrong. Had Craig Nealis gotten to Agent Clarkson? This was insane. "Put her on the phone," demanded Jake.

"Or what...what are you going to do?" said Nealis in a low deep voice.

"This is not a game," warned Jake.

"Oh, but it is. Don't you see? This is a game. This has been a game all along. It's my game, one

that I've created. You are just a character. You and the rest of the cast do exactly what I want you to do. I am the one in control. I am the one in charge," said Nealis angrily.

Jake's mind was racing. He had to think. He had to keep him on the phone. The man still hadn't said who he was. Jake had to make him think that he wanted to play. Whatever the sick game was, he felt that he had no choice but to play along.

"Ok, what are we playing? Tell me where you are, and I'll come out to play," said Jake.

"Oh, not so quick, you have to buy a ticket first if you want to get on this ride," said Nealis as he let out a laugh, "hahahaha."

"Where is she?"

"Who, your daughter or your girlfriend?" asked Nealis as he laughed again. "They are both with me. I'm keeping them happy. I want you to know, your daughter is growing up to be a fine young lady. She is looking more and more like her late mother. She is growing up to be just as sweet as her too," said Nealis as he made a licking sound with his mouth.

Jake was relieved to hear they were both alive. He had ignored everything else Nealis had said about his daughter.

"What do you want? Tell me what it is you want. I'll make sure you get it," said Jake.

"Don't you see? I already have everything I want. It is you who needs what I have. The question is: are you going to come and get it?"

Jake was losing his mind. He wanted to kill the man on the other side of the phone. He knew he had to remain calm.

"Let me talk to them," demanded Jake.

"I'll do better than that, check your e-mail. You can see for yourself they are both fine…just terrific. I'm taking real good care of them. And Jake, I'm ashamed of you, how could you forget your wife so soon? You are no better than me. Samantha is beautiful, but she is no match for your lovely wife who I had the pleasure of making love to just before I sliced her throat."

"I am going to kill you," said Jake as he bit his teeth.

"I bet you are. By now you should realize that

you would've been dead long ago if I didn't want you around. I'm not afraid of death. I welcome it."

"What's this sick game you are playing?"

"It's time for me to go Jake," said Nealis as he hung up the phone.

Jake signed onto his e-mail account. He noticed an e-mail that was unread with a video attachment. He opened it immediately. He was shocked by what he saw. Agent Clarkson was being held in a room similar to the one Jake had seen on the sex videos with the young girls. She was naked. Her body looked pale. She was sitting on a chair with her wrists and ankles strapped to it. Her pupils were dilated.

Jake watched as a naked man, with his back to the camera, walked towards her. The man was holding a syringe in his right hand. He sat down next to Agent Clarkson, and turned around to look directly into the camera. It was Craig Nealis.

"Hello Jake. Let me properly introduce myself, I'm Craig Nealis. I'm sure you are going to enjoy watching this video. Feel free to masturbate. I promise, I won't tell anyone."

Nealis took the syringe and punctured a vein in Agent Clarkson's right arm. As the drug went into her blood stream, her entire body shook, and then she smiled. A moment later, her body became relaxed.

"Don't stop watching now; the fun is just about to begin. Take a guess at what I'm going to do next," said Nealis as he took quick steps towards the camera. He put his mouth up against the lens.

Jake grabbed his head and pulled at his hair. He felt helpless. He wanted to reach across the computer screen and kill Nealis. He kept watching.

Nealis loosened the restraints on Agent Clarkson's wrists and ankles. Her body was limp. He put her arms around his shoulders to lift her up. He was holding her naked body against his. He began dancing with her.

Nealis was humming a song. The more he hummed, the crazier it made Jake. He kissed her on the lips as he held out her arm, and moved around the room in front of the camera. He continued to hum.

He took her to the bed in the back of the room

and laid her down. He looked at the camera and said, "It's only going to get better from here. I bet you're jerking off. Don't worry, I won't tell anyone. It'll be our secret."

Jake became crazed. "MOTHERFUCKER! MOTHERFUCKER!" he yelled.

Jake watched as Nealis spread open Agent Clarkson's legs and put his penis inside her. Nealis moved back and forth on top of her as he looked into the camera. He stuck out his tongue, and licked her face down to her breasts. He suckled her nipples as though he was trying to draw milk. With her left nipple in his mouth, he tilted his head to look at the camera.

Nealis suddenly stopped moving. He grunted as he ejaculated inside her. Agent Clarkson's face was expressionless. The video camera kept recording as he lay on top of her.

"I must say, I enjoyed fucking your wife more, but this sweet little thing isn't too bad either. You know how to pick 'em," said Nealis. He began to laugh uncontrollably.

Out of nowhere, a new face appeared in front

of the camera. It was a face Jake recognized. It was Jenny. She had grown up so much.

"Do you still love me daddy?" asked Jenny.

Jake couldn't hold back his tears. "Baby," said Jake. "I'm so sorry…I'm so sorry."

Nealis rushed towards the camera. He pushed Jenny aside. He looked directly in the camera, and said, "You see Jake. This is my game. I'm in control." He shut the camera off.

With tears running down his face, Jake stared at the blank screen.

61

Jake and Detective Jones met at Agent Clarkson's apartment. Jake had called Jones after watching the video he received from Craig Nealis. Jake couldn't find the words to describe what he had seen to the detective. Even though he hadn't deleted the e-mail, he couldn't get himself to show it to anyone. He had seen it several times for clues. He was looking for anything that would've led to finding out where it had been made.

"Jake, the forensics team has gathered fingerprints from the apartment. They are going

through the database to find matches. Even though you said you were contacted by Craig Nealis, we need to find evidence that confirms he was here."

Jake couldn't focus on what Jones was telling him. His mind kept going back to the image of Craig Nealis raping Agent Clarkson, and then seeing Jenny appear in front of the camera.

"We have questioned tenants in the building to find out if they saw anything unusual last night, or if they had seen her with anyone they either did or didn't recognize. No one saw anything," said Jones. "Jake, are you feeling okay?"

"Yeah, yes, I'm fine. We have to find them."

"Let's get a cup of coffee and some fresh air," said Jones. He sensed Jake was about to pass out. "Between the FBI forensics team and the NYPD detectives any evidence that can help us capture Craig Nealis will be found."

Jones and Jake left the apartment. They walked down the stairs, instead of taking the elevator. They stepped out of the building, and went to a diner located across the street. They ordered medium black coffees.

"Let's grab that one over there," said Jones as he pointed to an unoccupied table.

"Where's your partner?" asked Jake.

"He'll join us in a few minutes. He's following up on a lead," replied Jones as he took a sip from the cup. "I needed that."

"Look, Detective, I am not sure what we are doing here. Why aren't we out there looking for that motherfucker, Nealis?" asked Jake.

"We are doing the best we can," replied Jones. "The FBI is working with us as well. That in itself is rare, as the Bureau doesn't like us much, and we don't like them. Now one of their own has disappeared, so they are willing to do whatever it takes to find her." Jones took another sip of coffee before continuing, "This guy is smarter than most criminals we've ever dealt with. Even though his assets were frozen, which were substantial, it is likely he still has money stashed away. He's going to use it to get away."

Jake gazed out the window of the diner, and watched cars drive by. He looked at the pedestrians as they walked past the diner. There were millions

of people in the city, each with their own war stories.

The front door opened, and O'Brian entered the diner. Before he joined Jake and Jones, he asked the woman behind the counter for a cup of coffee.

"All the leads were dead ends. Nobody in the building saw anything, and none of the street vendors that were open late last night noticed anything unusual either."

A woman, from behind the counter, walked to the table holding a cup of coffee. She placed the cup in front of O'Brian.

The two detectives and Jake sat at the diner looking out the window trying to find answers none of them had.

62

The newspapers continued printing articles about Craig Nealis. The stories were covered in both, the front pages of the main section, and the business section.

The share price of the bank had taken another dive after the abduction of Agent Clarkson. There were rumors the bank was going under. If that happened, Craig Nealis would have been successful not only in taking human life, but also for destroying the financial well being of the firms' employees as well as thousands of shareholders and

investors. Multiple lawsuits had been filed against the bank. Federal agencies had stepped in to calm the unrest.

Public interest in the case was at an all time high. Unauthorized biographies about Nealis were in the works. Each one promised to reveal the factual account of the real man. Each one promised the genuine story.

Every television network was preparing to go all out, and spend as much money as possible on getting the first interview with Nealis if he was captured alive. It was projected to be the highest rated news program in history.

At first, the late night talk shows had stayed away from making jokes about Nealis, but now it was what everyone in the country was talking about. Letterman, Leno, Kimmel, and Fallon took regular shots at the notorious criminal.

Howard Stern was negotiating with his sponsors to do "The Girls of Craig Nealis Beauty Pageant" with the women who claimed to have dated the notorious criminal when he was younger. The winner would get a cash prize. This was an

outrage; an outrage that everyone was going to listen to and comment about for a long time to come.

The New York Times printed an in depth account of Craig Nealis' life. It reported on the early years of the troubled CEO, to the death of his parents. They raised questions which hinted the deaths could actually have been murders committed by Craig Nealis. They interviewed his high school teachers and college professors. Nearly every student who went to school with Nealis claimed to have known him. A few even had pictures with him. Of the women who claimed to have dated Nealis, some talked about how charismatic and loving he was, while others said they were afraid of him. Everyone was looking for their fifteen minutes of fame.

How was it possible that a person born into such wealth and fortune could commit such heinous crimes? What was his motivation? Had he been abused as a child? These were just some of the many questions being asked. There were no answers.

BOOK 3

63

Jake moved in to a hotel located in downtown Manhattan.

Craig Nealis vanished in to thin air. With his resources and wherewithal it was not farfetched. He had managed to stay several steps ahead of the authorities.

Jake took an indefinite leave of absence from work. The Agency understood his situation. They wanted him back at work, but realized he would be ineffective.

One evening, while he was having dinner at a

Chinese restaurant in Little Italy, a waiter walked up to Jake and handed him an envelope.

"What's this?" asked Jake

"That man said to give it to you," said the waiter as he pointed towards the entrance of the restaurant.

Jake looked towards where the waiter was pointing, but no one was there. The waiter shrugged and walked away.

The envelope was sealed. Jake looked at both sides to see if it was addressed to him. There was no writing on it. He looked around the restaurant to see if he recognized anyone, but didn't see any familiar faces. He opened the envelope cautiously. Inside, there was a typewritten note and a second envelope. The note which was addressed to him:

Hello Jake,

I hope you didn't think I had forgotten about you. I want you to know that I am constantly thinking of you. My life has taken a turn in a most unexpected way since I took your daughter and killed your wife.

I can't say that I am disappointed. It has added meaning to my life. I can even say that I'm beginning to fall in love in a way I never expected. I have you to thank for that. You can take pride in this fact. I owe you. Consider the fact that you are still alive as sort of payment. I do want you to know that I can kill you at anytime. If you are still looking for me, let me tell you that it is of no use. Neither you, nor anyone else will ever find me. No one is ever going to take the things I take pleasure in away from me. Before you get back to dinner, I'd suggest you open the second envelope. I have enclosed a few photographs to rest you assured that your loved ones are doing well and are safe with me.

Yours truly

Jake opened the second envelope, and pulled out its contents. There were five photographs inside the envelope. He looked at the back of the stack. He was fearful of what he was going to see when he turned it around to the front. The thought of not

looking at the photographs crossed his mind, but unfortunately that wasn't a matter of choice for him. He would have to look at them regardless of what he was going to see. He looked at each one. He could sense Craig Nealis, present in the room, laughing at him. Three photographs were of Agent Clarkson and two were of Jenny.

The three with Agent Clarkson were of Nealis performing various sexual acts with her. She was naked in all three. The two with Jenny tore Jake from the inside. He clenched his fists, and began pounding the table. Everyone at the restaurant froze and stared at him. He didn't look back at them. He crumbled the photographs in his hands.

Jake took cash out of his wallet, placed it on the table, and left the restaurant with his head hung low. He stated down at the sidewalk, but it may as well have been the sky above. When Pedestrians saw him staring at the sidewalk, they looked down as well to help him find whatever it was he had lost. They didn't know that he had lost sense of self, of reality…of life itself.

Jake couldn't shake the image of Jenny in the

photographs from his mind. He was incensed. Suddenly he stopped, looked up at the sky, and let out a howling scream. He screamed again before he fell down to his knees.

People, mostly tourists, stopped to look at the deranged New Yorker. These were the stories they had heard about the city. They had heard about lunatics walking the streets. Parents took their children by their hands. They protected them from the crazy man who was looking up at the moon, howling like a wolf, while kneeling down on his knees. They would have a story to tell when they got back to wherever they had come from. Some people snapped pictures of Jake with their cell phones while others shot videos to post on the Internet.

"I'm going to find you! I'm going to kill you!" yelled Jake, as he looked up at the starless night sky, above the bright lights of New York City.

64

Detective Jones had left urgent messages for Jake to call him back. It wasn't like him not to return a call. Something was wrong. Jones, along with his partner Detective O'Brian, decided to pay Jake a visit at the hotel. Over the course of his ordeal the detectives had gotten to know Jake well. They had become friendly with him. Both were equally concerned when he didn't return the calls.

They flashed their shields as they entered the hotel. The receptionist looked up at the two detectives and nodded. This was nothing out of the

ordinary in New York.

O'Brian pressed the elevator button. They waited as the floor numbers flashed in descending order.

"I hate elevators," said O'Brian.

"I never knew that, and we've been partners for ten years," said Jones with a surprised look.

"Yeah, I've never told anyone before. It's embarrassing to confess to being afraid of elevators when you are a detective," he said as the elevator doors opened.

"You are a strange motherfucker. Next, you are going to tell me you are afraid of clowns," said Jones as they entered the elevator.

The elevator stopped on the eleventh floor. The detectives stepped out and walked to Jake's room. There was a Do Not Disturb sign hanging on the handle. Jones knocked on the door. There was no response. He knocked again the second time a bit louder than before.

"Jake, open the door," shouted Jones.

"I didn't order anything," yelled Jake.

"Jake, open up, it's us," said Jones.

Jake recognized the detective's voice. He got up to open the door. He was drunk. From the way he looked, it appeared as though he hadn't slept for days.

"You look like shit," said O'Brian as Jake opened the door.

"Come in," said Jake.

"You look like shit," repeated O'Brian.

"You guys wanna drink?" asked Jake. He looked at the detectives before continuing, "Oh, of course not, you are on the job."

"You don't check your messages anymore?" asked Jones.

"As you can see, I'm not doing too well." Jake poured a drink for himself before sitting down on the couch.

Jones was not amused by Jake's behavior. His facial expression expressed exactly how he felt. He took the drink out of Jake's hand, walked to the sink, and poured it out.

"We like you Jake. That's the only reason why we are here. There are a lot of cases of kidnapped children, and murdered spouses, but after they go

unsolved they are usually forgotten. I haven't forgotten you my friend. I didn't take you as someone who would give up so easily. I had you figured wrong. The only reason you have been part of the investigation is because of Agent Clarkson. I don't know what the two of you had going on, but whatever it was, she kept you involved. Then, she vanished…"

"Are you implying that I had something to do with that?" interrupted Jake.

Jones looked Jake in the eyes. He was trying to figure him out. "She vanished and you're sitting here drinking away your sorrows."

Jake looked down at the carpet. He was ashamed. He looked up at the detective apologetically.

Jones saw that Jake was having difficulty forming the right words, "Forget about it. Get your shit together."

Jake picked up the envelope the waiter at the Chinese restaurant had given him. He pulled out the photographs, looked at them briefly, and without saying a word placed them on the table.

Jones picked up the photographs. He went through each one as O'Brian looked over his shoulder. They were both shocked and sickened.

"Jesus Christ," said O'Brian.

"Where did you get these? How long have you been holding on to them?" asked Jones.

Jake told the detectives about what happened at the restaurant.

"I swear to God I am going to find this motherfucker," said Jones as he looked at the photographs again. His eyes were glaring with anger.

Jones felt what Jake had been feeling. He walked to the cabinet and poured a drink; he took a quick shot and poured another.

Jake still hadn't told the detectives about the call from Nealis. He hadn't told them about the e-mail either. He couldn't bring himself around to it. He thought about telling them about it then, but couldn't find the strength. It was too painful to watch. He was depressed. He didn't want the video to be seen by anyone. He couldn't cope with the thought of anyone seeing Jenny and Agent Clarkson

like that, being molested and raped.

The two detectives left Jake alone in the hotel room. Before walking out of the room, Jones turned around and said, "You have my word. I'm not going to give up on you."

Jake remained on the couch. He didn't look up at the detectives as they left. His eyes were focused on the photographs that were staring back at him in the face. He could feel Nealis laughing at him as he sat there helplessly.

Jake had lost the energy to scream.

65

Jake listed the house on Long Island for sale. The property values had risen again and stabilized. If he didn't sell the house his neighbors would always live in fear for themselves and their families. It had been a difficult decision for him. He had hoped that one day Jenny would return home. But even if she did, she would always be afraid to live in the house with so many bad memories.

At first it was difficult to get real estate agencies to take the listing. They were hesitant to have their agents, who were mostly women, do

open houses. They didn't want to let complete strangers into the house. A couple of local firms did agree to take the listing, but at the highest commission rate. It was always about the money.

The house was listed as an exclusive. Anyone who was interested in seeing it was required to make an appointment with the listing agent. At first there were no inquiries, but over time there was some interest from potential buyers. However, unbeknownst to the real estate agents, the interest was mostly from people who were curious to look inside the house where two murders had occurred.

It was as though they were looking inside a haunted house. Potential buyers would whisper amongst each other as they walked from the living room, through the kitchen, to the backyard. They had read the news articles, and knew the exact locations of where the murders had taken place.

Due to lack of interest, Jake relisted the house with a real estate firm in Flushing, Queens. He did it at the suggestion of one of his neighbors. Within weeks there was a steady flow of potential buyers coming in to look at the property. These were

serious buyers, not curious onlookers.

The house was sold, above the listing price, to an Asian family within three months of the listing. The Asian population in Nassau County of Long Island had started to grow at a fast pace. As they migrated east of New York City to Long Island, they looked for homes in good school districts for their children.

Jake insisted on meeting potential buyers. He wanted to make sure they knew the history of what happened in the house. The real estate agency did their best to convince Jake not to speak to the buyers. They felt it would deter them from purchasing the house. Jake was adamant, and said he wouldn't sell it otherwise.

The young Asian couple who were interested in buying the house had two children, a boy and a girl. Both children were close to Jenny's age. Jake wanted to ensure them the house and the neighborhood was safe. He wanted to let them know that what happened to his family was a matter of chance.

The real estate agent bit her teeth as Jake spoke

to the buyers. She was a recent immigrant from China and had an accent. Her pupils moved back and forth, from the buyer to the seller, as though she was watching a tennis match from a distance. She hoped the buyers wouldn't back out of the deal.

When Jake talked about the murders, the real estate agent laughed nervously, and said to the buyers, "You no worry. This is good house. Ah, schools very good for children. You get good price. Very good. Very good."

When Jake spoke about Jenny, the real estate agent cut in again with an anxious laugh, "Ah, you no worry. Lot of children in the neighborhood. Best area on Long Island. Good school. You going to love it…very safe…very safe."

The real estate agent was relieved when the meeting was over. She looked at the buyers to try to figure out if they had changed their mind about purchasing the house. She was certain they had. She was afraid that she had lost the commission. She was already planning on telling her boss to drop the listing. She thought it was going to be impossible to sell that house because the owner was

crazy.

The buyers thanked Jake for meeting with them. They said they were still interested in buying the house. The real estate agent let out another nervous laugh, which sounded like a sigh of relief, and said, "Good, good, you're making very good decision. This is very good neighborhood and it's going to bring you good luck."

66

Time stood still for Jake. He spent most of the day locked up in the hotel room. When he wasn't at the hotel, he roamed city streets. He was deeply depressed. He gave up cigars, and began chain smoking cigarettes. A cigar required time. Cigarettes were a quicker fix.

Jake had lost contact with most of his friends when he accepted the job with the CIA. It was one of the many sacrifices he had made to serve his country. He thought about visiting old friends, but didn't. He wouldn't know what to say to them.

"Hey, it's Jake, remember me? My wife was murdered and my daughter kidnapped and now that I need somebody to talk to, here I am. I even managed to start a new relationship with a FBI agent. I wish I could introduce you to her. But wait, she was kidnapped and raped by the same man who took my wife and daughter from me. Am I not a treat? Let me in and I'll tell you all about it. Oh, by the way I am also a CIA agent. Boy, I've got stories to tell you," Jake chuckled at the thought.

Usually, by the end of the day when he was about to go to sleep, his mind would drift from thinking about Nadine to Jenny to Agent Clarkson. He also thought about the other poor souls, the young girls, who had been kidnapped, molested, raped and murdered by Nealis.

The image that was the hardest to shake from his mind was that of Nealis himself. Jake had regular nightmares where he would be at a park or the beach with Nadine and Jenny, or at other times with Agent Clarkson, and with a sudden shift or a blink they would be gone. They would reappear in a dungeon or in hell with the devil laughing in the

background. Nealis was the devil. The sound of laughter would increase incrementally as Jake stood by and watched them from the outside unable to help. His heart rate would increase and pupils shift behind closed eyelids, in REM sleep, to the point where he would wake up with his face drenched in sweat, and body in a cold shiver.

67

Craig Nealis had taken a liking to Agent Clarkson. She reminded him of his late mother. He would curl up, sit on her lap, and suckle her breasts while making baby sounds, "Goo-goo…ga-ga…goo-goo…ga-ga." He would pretend as though he was a baby breastfeeding on his mother.

From time to time he would bring all of his little dolls into the room to watch him breastfeed. He would have one of the girls sit nude on Agent Clarkson's lap to suckle her left breast while he suckled the other. The little girls knew better than

to resist. If they disobeyed, he punished them.

"She's our mommy," Nealis would say. "She's our mommy, and she loves us very much."

Tears would pour out of Agent Clarkson's eyes and fall on the face of the girl who was suckling her breast at the time. She would run her fingers through the girls' hairs, and say, "Everything will be all right. Everything will be all right."

When any of the little girls cried, Agent Clarkson would begin to hum. She would sing them a lullaby: *Hush-a-bye, don't you cry, go to sleep you little baby. When you wake you shall have all the pretty little horses. Dapples and greys, pintos and bays, all the pretty little horses…Hush-a-bye, don't you cry, go to sleep you little baby.*

Some of the girls began calling Agent Clarkson "Mommy." It gave them comfort to see and be with her.

Agent Clarkson was too sedated to do anything. She had gotten addicted to every drug Nealis pumped into her. Her weight steadily decreased. Her skin became pale. Her face looked as though it had aged ten years. Both of her arms were covered

with needle marks. She would sleep on the bed curled up in a fetal position.

"You want it, don't you?" Nealis would ask. "Tell me you want it, and I may give it to you."

"Yes, yes, yes, I want it. I want it. I want it. Just give it to me and I'll do anything you want. Please let me have it. Oh God. Oh God, please let me have just one more hit," Agent Clarkson would respond. This is what Nealis wanted to hear. It made him happy. He gave her the drugs she craved.

He forced her to say the same words repeatedly. At first she had refused. But once she got hooked to the drugs, she was willing to say anything. She was willing to do anything. She would even kill if he asked her to.

68

Jenny had grown up fast. She still had a small body, but had matured mentally beyond her age. She stopped playing with dolls. She also stopped crying herself to sleep every night. She spent most of her time thinking about her mother and father. The helplessness had turned into hope. She knew her father would find her. She could feel it. And if he was angry, he would forgive her.

Jenny felt sorry for all of Nealis' little dolls. The person she felt sorry for the most was Agent Clarkson. She wanted to help her, only if she could.

Jenny would close her eyes, and imagine meadows and ponies. The thoughts made her feel clean. She imagined herself flying across the field with butterflies. She couldn't remember when she had last seen one. It must've been when she was with her mother, she thought.

69

Detective Jones walked into the precinct. He was always the first one in. As he entered the precinct he noticed the office lights were on. He looked around but didn't see anybody. He was certain when he left the night before he had turned them off.

"I must be going senile," said Jones.

As Jones walked into the office, he saw the back of O'Brian's head. "Get in to a fight with the girlfriend?" asked Jones.

Detective O'Brian was startled by his partner's

voice. He nearly fell off the chair.

"Jesus Christ," said O'Brian trying to compose himself.

"What the fuck are you doing here this early? Did she let you go to bed at a reasonable hour for a change?" asked Jones jokingly. "She must've been sore from the night before."

"Take it easy," warned O'Brian.

"Man, you must have a huge dick...is it more than 8 inches?"

"What's in that coffee you are drinking? You're wired up this morning," said O'Brian.

"I gotta stop drinking this shit. I already drank a large cup before this one. Starbucks is probably making a platinum card just for me. Half of my paycheck goes to them."

"10" said O'Brian.

"10 what?" asked Jones.

"10 inches," replied O'Brian.

Jones looked at his partner's face and saw that he was serious, "Get the fuck outta here...Oh, shit, you really aren't shitting me, are you? Come on, man."

O'Brian stood up, and began to untie his belt.

"What the fuck are you doing? Keep your pants on. I don't need to see your shit," said Jones. He looked at his partner and shook his head in disbelief. "I'm the black guy. My shit is supposed to be bigger than yours."

"You really are taking this seriously," said O'Brian. "Forgettaboutit."

"That's easy for you to say," said Jones. "Really?" He held his hands apart about a foot from each other. "Did you have a surgical procedure to have your shit extended?"

O'Brian realized that his partner was taken aback by the revelation. He had to change the subject, or the conversation would go on. The opportunity presented itself when two female police officers walked into the office.

"We are headed out to Dunkin Donuts. You guys want coffee?" asked one of the female officers.

Both detectives said they would take a cup.

"You guys alright?" said the other female officer as she gave the detectives a quizzical look.

"Did we interrupt something here?"

"Yeah…I mean no, everything's cool," replied Jones.

The two female officers walked out of the office leaving the detectives to continue their conversation.

"I couldn't sleep last night. I kept thinking about the sex videos. I was thinking there had to be something in them, some clues that everyone else had missed. That's why I came in early this morning. I've been going through the videos. As difficult as it is to do, I had to," said O'Brian. He leaned back in the chair, and looked up at Jones who was standing up across from him. After a brief pause he continued, "Come around…take a look at this."

Jones walked around the desk towards his partner who had a video cued up on the monitor. O'Brian hit the play button. They watched the video together. Then O'Brian played another, more recent, video.

"Did you notice anything different?" asked O'Brian.

"I've seen that video a hundred times for clues, but haven't noticed anything that would give up the location of where it was shot. Why, is there something you see that I'm missing?" asked Jones.

"Well, take a look at the first video again. Look at the size of the window with the curtain in the background. Pay attention to the size in proportion to everything else in the room, and then look at the second video for consistency." O'Brian hit the play button, and both detectives watched the videos again.

"Oh, shit. How could we've missed that?" asked Jones rhetorically.

The size of the windows hidden behind curtains was different in both videos. The window in the older video was smaller than the one in the newer video. It was easy to miss the fine detail.

"What do you think it means?" asked O'Brian.

"Either he's trying to outsmart us, or he has switched locations."

"If he has changed locations, then the size of the window suggests that he's in a church, a school, or possibly even a commercial building," speculated

O'Brian.

Both detectives felt they were on to something big. They just needed to figure out what it was, and how they were going to pursue it. Regardless of where the videos had been made, they needed to know an address where to begin the new search. Every lead they had pursued thus far had led them to a dead end. This time it would be different, at least that's what they hoped.

Detective Jones' cell phone rang. The ringtone was set to a song by a young singer. He rushed to answer it. He only said two words before ending the call. It was the same word repeated twice after short intervals, "Yes."

"Let's go," said Jones.

The detectives rushed out of the precinct to their car. Jones took the driver's seat. They were on the road within seconds.

"Is that why you are letting your hair grow out?" asked O'Brian.

"What? What are you talking about?" asked Jones. He was speeding down the Cross Island Parkway.

"You know…the haircut."

"What are you talking about?"

"Hey, you have the ringtone, so might as well have the haircut to go along with it. I'm just saying," said O'Brian.

"Jesus Christ, my son must've put it on there. He was playing around with my phone last night," said Jones. He was either very embarrassed or extremely irritated.

"Uh, huh"

"What's that supposed to mean?"

"Nothing, I believe you. It's just kind of weird for a grown black man to be listening to young white boy."

"Drop it," warned Jones as he pressed the accelerator.

Jones was thinking about the phone call he had received at the precinct. Chances were that this was going to be yet another wild goose chase. The town in New Jersey they were headed to was considered to be among the wealthiest in the nation.

Jones called Jake, gave him the address of the house, and asked him to meet him there.

70

A description of the rooms in the sex videos had been sent to every police department in the northeast. They had been instructed to contact Detective Jones if there was anything that even slightly appeared suspicious.

The Alpine Police Department had received a call from a woman. She called to complain about an unbearable stench coming from the home of one of her neighbors. The woman was notorious for calling the police every time she sensed something was wrong in the posh neighborhood. Perhaps in

another area the police would have been slow to respond, but that wasn't the case in Alpine. Considering the town's prominent residents, they were always quick to follow up.

Two police officers had taken the call. The dispatcher instructed them to be courteous to the woman who had called in with the complaint. Both officers were young, and still learning how they had to treat people in the affluent neighborhood. This wasn't taught in the academy, nor was it in any brochures. They had to learn on the job.

As they drove up to the house, they saw a woman who was waiting for them. She was holding a leash. The officers looked around for a dog. They didn't see one.

"The little guy must be hiding behind the bushes," said the police officer to his partner.

They stepped out of the car, and walked up to the woman. One of the officers nearly fell to the ground. He grabbed his gun with one hand, and his chest with other. He wanted to make sure his heart was still beating. A Great Dane had leapt out of the bushes, and rushed towards him.

"Oh, shit. That horse almost gave me a heart-attack," said the officer. He coughed and tried to regain his composure.

The dog came to a screeching halt beside its master, and stood ready waiting to receive instructions. With a ferocious look in his eyes, he appeared to be waiting for a command to attack.

"I thought those dogs were supposed to be gentle," whispered one of the officers. "He looks like he's ready to eat us."

"Hello, boys," said the woman.

"Did you call about an odor coming from a neighbor's house?" asked an officer as he kept his eyes peeled on the miniature horse.

The officer loved dogs and owned two of them himself. But the dog staring at him wasn't like any he had ever seen before. The Great Dane growled as it clenched its teeth. The officer wasn't sure if the dog was drooling or salivating.

"Yes, I did. Don't you smell it?" asked the woman who became annoyed at the officers' lack of sense of smell.

The two officers took a couple of deep breaths,

but weren't able to smell anything out of the ordinary.

"No, Ma'am," said an officer, while the other shook his head to indicate he didn't smell anything either.

"Follow me," said the woman. She walked up to the front of the house. "There, do you smell it now."

"No, Ma'am," said the officer.

He was certain the woman was crazy. There was a strong possibility that she had some of the same traits as her dog, including the sense of smell.

The woman looked as though she was going to bite the officer herself. "Well, knock on the door. There's definitely something rotting inside the house."

The officer rang the bell. There was no response. After a short wait, he rang the bell again. He took out a flashlight from his belt, and banged it on the door. The knock was loud enough to be heard down the block. If there was anyone in the house they would have heard it. Again, there was no response.

"I'm gonna take a look around the back," said an officer.

He carefully walked down the front doorsteps. He avoided coming close to the beast that appeared to have calmed down considerably. The officer didn't want to take any chances so he walked slowly making sure not to startle him.

He pointed the flashlight, and looked through a window on the side of the house. It was dark inside. The officer cleaned dust off the glass to get a better view. He didn't see anyone inside. The house was well decorated with antique furniture and old paintings. He stepped away, and continued to the back yard. As soon as he turned the corner, he smelled an odor. He looked down at the basement windows; they were all covered. He knocked on one of them with the flashlight. There was no response. He knocked again, and the glass shattered. The officer covered his mouth and nose as the stench escaped through the broken glass. He was sure it was rotting flesh. He ran back to the front of the house.

"What's the matter?" asked the second officer.

"There's something dead inside there. Call for back-up," ordered the officer. He was on the verge of passing out. He vomited right in front of the woman. The Great Dane quickly stood up, and began eating the lunch the officer had regurgitated. Seeing that, the officer puked again.

Within minutes five police cars appeared on the scene. They were followed by an ambulance and a fire truck.

"Ma'am, I'm going to have to ask you to step away from the house," instructed the officer.

The woman seemed angered by his request. "No, I want to see what's in the house."

"Ma'am, please step away for your own safety."

The officer looked at the dog who did not like the tone he was using towards his master. It was time for the beast to let his presence be known. The dog began growling at the officer.

The woman walked down the steps. From her body language, it was obvious she didn't want to go. For years she had wanted to see the inside her reclusive neighbor's house. This was her golden

opportunity.

The woman's trusted companion followed her closely. He had cleaned up the mess off the floor. He appeared to be thirsty, and was looking for water. Just before getting off the property, the Great Dane squatted down and relieved himself. As he got up to walk, he left a mound of excrement on the ground. The woman didn't bother to clean it up. If the cops weren't going to treat her with respect, she wasn't going to give them any either.

A fireman tore through the front door of the house with an axe. The police officers entered the house with caution. One of the officers switched on the lights.

Several officers went up the stairs to the second floor to search the rooms. The two officers who were the first to arrive on the scene went to open the basement door. It was locked. They looked towards the fireman who had torn open the front door. The fireman smiled. It was apparent to everyone he loved his job. With one swing he broke down the basement door. Just as the door opened the entire house became engulfed with a

dreadful odor.

"Oh, fuck…that smell…that's rotting flesh," said the fireman.

The two officers drew their guns as they descended the stairs to the basement. It was dark. One of the officers ran his fingers across the wall to search for a light switch. He located the switch and flipped it on. There was no light. Either there was no electricity in the basement, or the fuse was blown. They had to rely on their flashlights. The smell became unbearable as they approached the bottom of the staircase.

They pointed the flashlights in every direction, but didn't see anything. There were several rooms. The doors were closed. The two officers had made a silent pact to stay together as they searched the basement. Though neither one admitted to the other, they were both terrified of what they were inevitably going to find. They walked to the first door, turned the knob, and entered the room. It was vacant. They walked into the second room. It was the same as the first, empty.

"Where the fuck is that smell coming from?"

asked one of the officers.

They left the second room, and walked to the third. As an officer turned the knob, the door didn't open. It was locked. He thought about calling the jolly fireman with the axe, but decided to use his foot to break it open instead. He lifted his leg, and with all of his might kicked in the door.

"Jesus Christ, that smells bad," said the officer.

The officers flashed their lights through the room. They both stopped simultaneously as their flashlights came across what appeared to be two bodies. Both officers looked at each other.

"Down here!" they yelled.

Less than ten seconds later every police officer, EMT, and fireman descended to the basement. They made their way into the room with the two decomposing bodies.

They appeared to be corpses of two young girls. Both were nude. They were lying on a table. They were bound at their feet with legs spread eagle. Their wrists were tied to the table with arms spread apart above their heads. The table looked like a sexual contraption. Their necks had been

sliced. The floor below the table was covered with dried out blood.

One of the firemen found the circuit breaker. He searched for a switch for the basement.

"Got it," said the fireman as he flipped the switch. Every room in the basement lit up instantly.

"What the fuck?!" said an officer, as he looked around the room. It was decorated to resemble a dollhouse. "I've seen this before."

71

Jones pulled the car into the driveway. As he approached the house he flashed his badge to the police officer who was standing guard at the front door. O'Brian flashed his badge as well. Just as they were about to step inside the house, they heard a motorcycle pull into the driveway. It was Jake.

Jake kicked the stand, leaned the Harley Davidson on its side, and walked up to the front of the house. He shook hands with the detectives. The three of them entered the house which was crawling with police officers, FBI Agents, and forensics

teams.

The odor of rotting flesh had subsided. The bodies of the two young girls had been removed from the house. They had been taken for autopsies. As their hands and feet were unbound, their flesh came off with the rope. The back of their bodies had to be peeled off the table on which they were tied. It was evident both girls had been sexually abused. Both of their vaginas were covered with blood and semen.

It would take a while before DNA results and dental records confirmed the identities of the girls. Their faces had rotted beyond recognition. They could not be identified by photographs alone.

Jake walked through the rooms in the basement. Each seemed familiar. He had seen the sex videos enough times for clues that every detail of each room was etched into his memory. A part of him was relieved when he walked in to the room where Jenny had been locked up. Since she wasn't there he hoped she was alive.

Detectives Jones and O'Brian spoke to the two police officers who were the first to arrive at the

scene. The officers told the detectives they had been alerted about the odor coming from the house by a woman who lived in the neighborhood.

"We would like to speak to her," said Jones.

"I will take you to her," offered one of the officers.

Jones introduced himself, along with O'Brian and Jake, to the woman who had called the police with the complaint about her neighbor.

"My name is Mrs. Jenaskowski, and this is Charlie," said the woman as she introduced herself and her best friend, the Great Dane.

The police officer who had accompanied them to Mrs. Jenaskowski's home excused himself. Jones thanked him.

"That boy doesn't have the stomach for the job he's doing. He nearly threw up all over poor Charlie here," said Mrs. Jenaskowski.

Mrs. Jenaskowski's home was clean, and furnished with furniture from the turn of the

century. There were family photographs on the wall along with original paintings.

Charlie was passive while he was inside the house. He walked up next to O'Brian, and sat down by his feet. The detective patted the dog on his head.

"Nice doggy," said O'Brian nervously.

Mrs. Jenaskowski offered the three men drinks; which they graciously accepted. Their goal was to make the old woman feel comfortable. This would allow them to get as much information from her as possible about her neighbor who happened to be a serial kidnapper, rapist, and killer.

"I saw them taking out a body from the house. Was it that man who lived there?" asked Mrs. Jenaskowski.

"Unfortunately, it wasn't him. What can you tell us about him?" asked Jones.

"Why unfortunately? If it wasn't him, then who was it? For all I know he lived there alone. I never saw anybody go in that house or come out other than him. He was a very strange man. Not very friendly," replied Mrs. Jenaskowski.

"Can you describe what he looked like?"

Mrs. Jenaskowski described her neighbor in detail. However, her description didn't match the man they were after. This was puzzling to all of them. Jones took out a set of photographs from an envelope and set them in front of the woman.

"Do you recognize this man?" asked Jones.

Mrs. Jenaskowski picked up the photographs. She studied them closely one at a time. "No. Who is that?"

This is not what they wanted to hear. They were sure they had found Nealis hiding place.

"What kind of car did your neighbor drive?" asked Jake.

"He changed cars frequently. I don't know what he did with the old ones. I remember he had this old station wagon which I saw him driving a couple of times, and then it was gone."

Jake whispered in O'Brian's ear. O'Brian nodded, and got up off the chair. He excused himself, leaving Jake and Jones with the woman.

"Do you know if anyone else in the neighborhood knew him?" asked Jones.

"He didn't come out much in the day time. I think I was the only one who saw him on a somewhat regular basis. I go out to walk Charlie at all times of day and night. I get to catch up with most of my neighbors. Everyone is so busy these days that no one really cares to get to know who is living next door to them. I remember when I was growing up, everyone knew everyone in the neighborhood. Times sure have changed."

"Can you tell us when the last time you saw him was?" asked Jake to get the woman back on the subject of her neighbor.

"It was about two months ago or maybe a little more than that."

"Did you speak to him?"

"No, he wasn't much of a talker," replied Mrs. Jenaskowski.

"You called the police to complain about the odor, can you tell us more about that?" asked Jones.

"One day I was walking Charlie and he started barking and dragging me to that house. Whenever Charlie does that it means he senses something. He led me to the house, but I didn't notice anything

other than a light odor. It wasn't that bad at the time, but kept getting worse each day. It became unbearable, and I called the police."

Charlie had fallen asleep. After O'Brian left, he moved to lay down by Jake's feet. He was breathing heavily.

"That Charlie sure is a fast sleeper. He's all I've got. My children moved away years ago. They don't visit me much anymore. They're probably waiting for me to die, and leave them an inheritance. My husband passed away ten years ago. Now all I've got is that silly dog. And he doesn't have too much time left either. I don't want to say it, but it's all true." Mrs. Jenaskowski's eyes became tearful. She just wanted someone to talk to.

"I'm sorry Mrs. Jenaskowski. I'm sure everything will be alright," said Jones sympathetically.

Jake and Detective Jones thanked her for her time and hospitality. They told her she had been very helpful. Jones gave her a business card. He asked her to call him if she saw anything out of the ordinary. As they got up, so did Charlie. Jake ran

his hand across the dog's back.

"That's a good boy," said Jake.

Charlie appreciated the gesture. He barked. He walked to a corner, and went back to sleep.

"Where did O'Brian go?" asked Jones as he stepped out of Mrs. Jenaskowski's house.

"He went to check the garage," replied Jake.

O'Brian was waiting for them as they approached the house. He didn't have to say anything, Jake and Jones saw the Mercedes-Benz and the company car parked in the garage. This confirmed it; this is where Nealis was hiding.

"Nealis must have been wearing a disguise," said Jones. "That's why Mrs. Jenaskowski didn't recognize him."

"Why did he leave? And who were those two little girls?" asked Jake.

The questions continued to pile up. Nealis had made a mockery of the authorities. He had eluded everyone on his tail.

72

The time for slow news days in New York had come to an abrupt halt. Every newspaper, radio station, television network, cable channel, and local television station had once again become fixated on Craig Nealis. The raid on the house in Alpine had been covered by every media outlet. It was the number one trending topic of discussion on every social network.

Psychologists, psychoanalysts, and even psychics had been brought in to share their insights on what must be going through the killer's mind.

Even the way the house was decorated had been analyzed to the nth degree. After a thorough analysis, the investigation proved how a madman was the only one capable of conceiving such decorations.

The general public was eating it all up. They couldn't get enough of it. Each person felt they were going to be Craig Nealis's next victim. Increasing number of parents began to accompany their children to school. They set up code words between themselves and their children. Parents reiterated to their kids: don't talk to strangers.

In many cases it brought families together. There were more "I love you's" exchanged between family members than before. Neighborhoods came closer as a unit. People began to care for each other. Everyone looked out for suspicious activity. "If you see something, say something" directive by the police was being followed. They were sure the cold blooded killer was going to strike their quiet neighborhoods next.

The news networks began running specials on other notorious murderers and kidnappers. This

added to the hysteria. News programs became the highest watched television shows. This helped advertisement rates increase. The network executives loved every minute of it.

The networks worked at a feverish pace to add more specials to the daily program lineup. The field reporters and researchers gathered any information they could get their hands on about Nealis and his victims.

Employees of the bank, where Craig Nealis had been the president, were warned not to speak to the members of the press who were camped outside its headquarters. With the field reporters' persistence, several employees had come forward under the premise their identities would be kept confidential. The fear was they would lose their jobs if the bank's management found out they were passing information to the media, or worse they could be met with the same fate as Margaret Sama.

Employees who agreed to talk to the media were looking for their fifteen minutes of fame. They set their DVRs to record the news programs they were scheduled to appear on, and then watched

the broadcast repeatedly. They felt like celebrities. Narcissism has no boundaries.

Employees who were caught or identified speaking to the media were demoted several levels below their pay grade. This ensured the bank would not be charged with wrongful termination, and sued by the employees who had been demoted. This was a brilliant move by the bank's management. In many cases it forced the employees who were disciplined, to resign and look for work elsewhere. They couldn't manage to live on the lower salaries. Financially this was a better alternative for the bank, than the severance it was paying to those who were being laid off due to the falling stock price.

73

The DNA results confirmed the identity of the two girls who were found dead at the house in Alpine. They had been kidnapped three years earlier, from Central Park, in the heart of Manhattan. Their case was unique as they were twins. They had been kidnapped together. The investigation led the authorities to conclude they were taken by someone they knew or recognized.

Their nanny had confessed she was busy talking on the phone with her sister in Guatemala when the girls disappeared. There was a thorough

background check done her. She was a legal resident. She didn't have a criminal record. There wasn't anything that led detectives to believe she had anything to do with the twins' kidnapping.

The parents of the twin girls were both well to do. They had successful careers on Wall Street. The family was left distraught by the kidnapping. Both of the parents blamed themselves for what had happened. The girls' mother fell into a deep depression. She was forced to quit her job at a prestigious investment bank. The father did his best to keep the family together. He kept hope that one day his two angels would be found, safe and sound.

As days turned into weeks, and weeks into months, they gave up on the possibility of a ransom demand. A hefty reward was put up for anyone who provided information leading to the twins' whereabouts. Numerous leads came in, but none ever panned out.

The autopsy confirmed the girls had died two months earlier. That would have put their age at roughly eight years old. The autopsy also confirmed both girls had been sexually molested at

the time of death, and numerous times prior.

The girls' parents went to the morgue to identify their bodies. Their father did all he could to stop his wife from going, but she insisted on seeing them. She needed closure. She had to see her babies, even if it was for the last time.

Three months later, with her depression getting worse, she took a hand full of sleeping pills and went to sleep. Her husband found her on the living room floor. He fell to the ground, picked up her head, and tried to wake her up. He shook her violently and yelled, "WAKE UP! WAKE UP!" She was dead. He looked up, and asked, "God, why did you do this to my family?"

He went into the bedroom and pulled out a handgun from a safe. He walked back to the living room, picked up his wife's head, and rested it on his lap. He kissed her forehead, and stroked her hair with his fingers. He placed the barrel of the gun in his mouth and pulled the trigger. Boom.

74

Like most other people, Jake learned of the double suicide of the parents of the murdered twins the next day. Though he didn't know the family, he felt a strong connection and an unbreakable bond with them. He felt their pain. He knew what had kept them alive, for the previous three years, since their daughters had been taken from them. It was hope they would one day be found, alive.

Jake had never contemplated suicide. Perhaps, because there was hope Jenny was alive. When Agent Clarkson was abducted, it only added to his

will to live. If one day he found out they were both gone forever, then perhaps he would lose the resolve to live as well. But at that moment, it was unthinkable. Life has a funny way of changing a person's mind quickly, without warning.

Jake felt a new surge of energy. He had let himself slip into despair. He never wanted to know the feeling one must have when all hope was gone, along with the will to live. He realized that he needed to pull himself together if he was going to find the two people, Jenny and Agent Clarkson, keeping him alive, for now.

There was nothing Jake would have enjoyed more than to put both of his hands around Nealis's neck and strangle him. He thought about the joy he would feel as he saw life escape from the murderer's eyes.

Jake picked up the phone to call Jones. He needed someone to talk to, and clear his mind. He found comfort in the fact Jones hadn't given up on the investigation since the FBI was the primary law enforcement agency that had been working on the case.

Jake believed since Jones was pursuing a case that had pretty much been taken away from him, he was a good man. Why would he continue to work on it, if he didn't have the desire for justice to be brought to the perpetrator? This thought made Jake believe in Jones.

"Hello, Jake," said Jones as he answered the phone.

Jake smiled when he heard the detective's voice. "Detective, I'm sure you've heard about the suicides."

"Yes, yes I have. I heard just before the news picked up on it. I was about to call you, but you beat me to it," said Jones. "It's a fucked up world we live in."

"It is indeed," said Jake.

"What can I do for you?" asked Jones.

"If you have time, I would like to get together with you."

"Sure, is there anything on your mind you want to discuss?"

"There's nothing in particular, it would be good to grab a drink with a friend," said Jake.

Jones felt how depressed Jake sounded. The thought that Jake might be thinking about killing himself crossed the detective's mind.

"You are not going to do anything stupid are you?" asked Jones.

"Don't worry detective, I'm not going to kill myself. If I was going to do that, I would've done it a long time ago."

"Alright...when you call me out of the blue like this, you know the thoughts that are going through my head. They ain't good." said Jones. He managed a slight chuckle.

They agreed to meet at an Italian restaurant in Little Italy.

75

Florio's Restaurant, a landmark of New York City, had been established in Little Italy in 1960.

Over the following three decades, Little Italy was gobbled up by an expanding Chinatown. All that was left of the former mobster haven was little more than three blocks.

The Italians and the Chinese had their struggles as Chinatown expanded. Over time, like everything else, the violence and the quarreling abated. The Chinese prevailed. In fact, majority of the clientele of the remaining Italian restaurants were now

Chinese. Both, the Chinese and the Italians, realized that within another couple of decades the remaining Italian owned businesses would be closed. It would all be known as Chinatown.

Florio's was one of the few restaurants that allowed smoking to its loyal patrons. The New York Department of Health had been after them for years issuing summons for violating city smoking laws. The management at Florio's was vigilant and determined to keep fighting the city in the courts until they were bestowed the "grandfather clause" which would allow them to continue to function as a smoking and dining establishment.

Jake saw Detective Jones walk in to the restaurant. He stood up to greet him. It was a Wednesday night. The restaurant was relatively quiet. It was perfect for them to have a conversation without worrying about being overheard by someone at the next table.

"This place is something else," said Jones.

A waitress approached the table, "Would you like a drink?"

Jake looked up at the waitress who was in her seventies. "Aunt Paula, How are you? It's great to see you," said Jake. He kissed her on the cheek.

"At this age, you know how it is.... It's wonderful to see you too, Jake," replied the waitress.

"This is Detective Jones."

Jones shook Aunt Paula's hand, and said, "It's a pleasure. Quite a place you've got here."

Aunt Paula had been working as a waitress at Florio's for decades. She had become a fixture, just like the restaurant itself, in Little Italy. All of the regular customers knew her well. They respected her for both, her age and her wisdom.

Jones ordered a beer. Jake took out two Cuban Hoyo de Monterrey Epicure cigars from a portable humidor. He offered one to Jones. The detective looked at the cigar and admired it before pressing it under his nose to take in the aroma of the aged leaf. He picked up a cutter off the table and snipped the cigar. He lit the cigar on one end with a torch

lighter. Once the cigar was toasted, he placed it in his mouth, took a few puffs and let out a thick cloud of white smoke.

"Wow," said Jones. "I can get used to this."

They talked about various subjects. One topic they avoided was that of Craig Nealis. They wanted to enjoy dinner before bringing up the subject that was on their mind.

"Dessert, boys?" asked Aunt Paula.

"Just a coffee for me, please," said Jones.

"I'll have the same, Aunt Paula," added Jake.

The elderly lady walked away as the busboys picked up the plates from the table. By the time the table was cleared, Aunt Paula walked back with two cups of coffee.

"Just let me know if you boys need anything else. I'll make sure no one bothers you," said Aunt Paula.

Aunt Paula knew Jake was a CIA agent. Over the years he had been going to Florio's, she had somehow discovered what he did for a living. Though he never asked her if she knew, he had a good feeling she did.

"Were there any clues at the house where the twins were found as to where Nealis could be hiding?" asked Jake.

They were done with dinner. They had managed not to bring up the subject, but it needed to be discussed.

"He was methodical on how he left the house. He knows that he has already been identified so it's not of much concern to him to hide his identity by getting rid of evidence. He's toying with us now," said Jones as he blew out another cloud of white smoke.

"I think he's been toying with us for a while. He feels invincible," said Jake.

"I agree. He's bound to fuck up somewhere." Jones told Jake about the discovery his partner had made about the size of the windows.

"That's interesting. He must be hiding in a church or a school. Did you check the bank's records to see if there are any such properties listed in its real estate portfolio?" asked Jake.

"The investigators are working on it," answered Jones. "The house in Alpine was listed as a

corporate property of the bank. They hadn't looked at that detail during the initial investigation. They are now going through all of the bank's real estate holdings with a fine toothcomb. If there's anything there, they'll find it."

"That's good."

"Don't' give up Jake. We are going to get him. I promise you." Jones felt there was something on Jake's mind, something that he wanted to talk about. "What is it Jake?"

"I should've been there," said Jake. "I should have been there with Nadine and Jenny."

"Look, you are not going to undo what has already been done. There is no sense in beating yourself up over it."

"I know that, but I just can't help it."

"There is a reason why Agent Clarkson wanted you to be a part of this investigation. I'm not sure what that reason was, but I respected her wishes and have kept you involved."

"We are in love," said Jake.

Jones was taken aback by the revelation. He looked surprised. He pulled on the cigar, and held

the smoke in his mouth before letting it out.

"Jesus Christ!" said Jones.

"Please keep that between us. I wanted you to know."

"I understand, Jake. I understand."

They stood up to leave. Before Jake walked out, he thanked Aunt Paula for her hospitality and kissed her.

Jones also gave Aunt Paula a hug. He told her he would be coming back to the restaurant on a regular basis going forward. To that, Aunt Paula smiled and said, "You are always welcomed."

76

The caller ID indicated the number as 'unknown." Jake ignored it. The phone rang a second time; he answered it after the first ring.

Jake had always hoped that one day the phone would ring, and the voice on the other end would be that of his daughter. It was wishful thinking; he had become the king of it. He was aware that the odds of getting a call from Jenny were slim to nonexistent.

"Hello," said Jake. There was no response. "Hello." He thought it was another prank call.

"WHO IS THIS?"

Jake thought it was a prank call. He would've changed the phone number long ago, but it was the only one Jenny knew. It was their home number that he had transferred to a cell phone. He would never change the number; at least not until he had found Jenny.

Jake's heart sank and his eyes became heavy and filled with tears. Was he dreaming? "Jenny?" He couldn't believe it, "baby, is that really you?"

"Daddy?" said Jenny, as she cried, "I love you, daddy."

"Where are you honey? Are you okay?" Jake was thinking like a father. He was like any other parent whose child had been kidnapped. He knew that she wasn't okay. It made him feel better just to ask.

"No daddy. Please help me," cried Jenny. "He hurts me. He hurts…"

"Hello…hello…baby, are you there? Talk to me honey. Please talk to me," cried Jake.

There was no response. Jenny was gone. Jake picked up another phone from the desk and called

his friend Pat, a colleague, at the CIA.

"Pat, listen to me, Jenny just called me. I couldn't talk to her for long. The call was disconnected. Whether it was intentionally cut off or not, I can't be sure. Are you still running a trace on my phones?" asked Jake.

"Yes, give me a second," said Pat as he began to feverishly type on a laptop.

Pat had been a long-time friend of Jake's. They had begun their careers in Langley at the same time. When Jake asked him for help in finding Jenny and Nadine's killer, Pat said he would do whatever he could to help.

Jake had asked Pat to run a constant tap on his phones, and monitor the origin of every call. Each of the previous calls to Jake's phone had been tracked, but didn't lead anywhere.

The fact that the phone number Jenny had called Jake from was blocked didn't matter much to the CIA. Their tracking software was linked to the National Security Agency. The NSA had information on nearly every telephone number in the United States and abroad, regardless of whether

it was a cell phone or a land line.

"Alright, got it," said Pat. "It's a California number. But that doesn't mean the call was made from there. I'm running diagnostics on where the call originated. I'll have the results in a few minutes."

Jake held on. He was excited. He felt his body tremble. He felt proud of his daughter. It took courage to do what she had done. He wondered if Agent Clarkson was with her. He wondered if Jenny knew that she was a friend.

Jake went through a range of emotions. At one moment he felt Jenny was within reach, and the other he felt her slipping away. It was out of his power. That is a horrible feeling. It's like believing one's involuntary muscles are voluntary, but they cannot be controlled. It was impossible.

"The call came from the Northeast United States," said Pat. "That's all. The call was too short to get the exact location or the state where it originated. Just a moment more and we would've had it."

"Is there anything else that can be done to find

the location?" pleaded Jake. "Please Pat. Jenny needs my help. Please."

"I have requested further diagnostics. It may take some time. I'll keep you posted."

Jake thanked his friend before ending the call.

Jones listened as Jake told him about the call from Jenny. He heard Jake's voice shaking, over the phone, as he spoke.

The detective tried to imagine the pain Jake was feeling, but couldn't. He could never feel that sorrow unless it was his own child who had been kidnapped. He could never feel that grief unless it was his wife who had been murdered.

People try to sympathize with others for their losses and tragedies; it's a human trait. Society has taught them to do that. People are puppets. In the end, no loss or tragedy is felt more by anyone than by those who have suffered it firsthand. Regardless of how much psychologists or psychiatrists try to help them, the directly affected never truly recover.

They eventually learn to put a veil over it; the veil is usually very thin.

Over the years Jones had seen his share of tragedy. He had witnessed families destroyed by drugs and violence. He had seen automobile accidents and suicides. The victims were always the families. They suffered. It wasn't as though he had become immune to it. He had learned to live with it. That's what people do; they learn to live with all they suffer through.

Jones invited Jake to his house. He felt Jake needed to be around a family. It would calm him, he thought. It wasn't much, but that's all he was able to offer to this broken down victim.

"Thank you," said Jake.

77

Craig Nealis had more time to spend with his little dolls and Agent Clarkson. His favorite was Jenny. She was growing up to be more beautiful than when he took her from her perfect little world. He gave himself credit for that. He was proud of himself. He felt special.

Nealis walked into Jenny's room. She was asleep. The only thing she had on was the blanket she was under. He had begun to make his entire collection of little dolls sleep nude. It excited him to see them lying naked on their little beds as he

walked into their rooms to play with them. Jenny had her head turned away from the door. Her eyes were open.

Jenny had memorized his schedule. She could feel Nealis approaching as she lay in bed barely able to move. She had become accustomed to what would happen after he entered the room.

In the beginning Jenny would be asleep as Nealis came in to her room. He would creepily walk to the foot of her bed. He would lift the blanket, take off his robe, and lay down next to her. He would cuddle up beside her, and kiss the top of her head. "I'm here baby. I'm here," he'd say, as he stroked her blond hair.

Jenny had learned not to scream. It made him angry. She would let herself go. She would close her eyes and dream about her mother. Nealis would spend an hour with her daily. She had stopped crying. That also made him angry. She had learned not to do anything that made the monster upset.

That day when he left her in bed, he told her, "I'm going to see your new mommy now. I am going to tell her how much fun we had together."

Jenny waited for the door to close. She heard the click which meant he had locked it. She sat up on the bed. Her legs were sticky. She wiped herself with the blanket. Regardless of how much she cleaned herself, she still felt dirty.

Jenny got off the bed. She was barely able to walk. Why did it hurt so much? She wanted the pain to stop. It never did. She looked down on the floor and noticed something. She picked it up. She had seen it clipped to Nealis's belt before. It was a phone. She was scared. She cautiously walked to the door and put her right ear against it. She listened for footsteps. He could come back at any moment to get the phone. She was terrified.

Jenny looked at the dial pad and saw the numbers. Nadine had made Jenny memorize their home phone number, and taught her how to dial the phone in case of an emergency. Jenny had been repeating the number in her head since the day she was kidnapped. This was an emergency. She needed to remember the number.

She wondered who would answer the phone when she called. Did they still remember her?

Would they even remember her voice? Were they going to be angry at her?

"I didn't do anything wrong," cried Jenny in a whisper.

One by one, she dialed the numbers which she had memorized. She heard the bell ring. It seemed to ring on forever. No one answered. She felt helpless. Tears rolled down her cheeks. She wiped them with the back of her hand.

She tried once again, and pressed the numbers on the keypad. As before, she listened to the ring.

It was her father who answered the phone and said "Hello." She remembered his voice. Not a night had passed that she hadn't dreamt of hearing it one day. At first he sounded angry, but then he said her name, "Jenny." He hadn't forgotten her. She cried as she spoke. She wanted to tell him she loved him so much.

The door abruptly opened, and Nealis entered. He was angry. He snatched the phone from Jenny's hand.

"Who were you talking to?" yelled Nealis. "Who were you talking to?"

Jenny cried. "It was daddy. I just wanted to hear his voice. I'm sorry. I won't do it again. Please don't hurt me. Please, I promise I'll be a good girl."

Nealis slapped Jenny across her face. She fell and hit her head on the floor. She looked up and covered her face with her tiny hands. She was afraid he would hit her again. He looked down at her with anger in his eyes. He turned around and stormed out of the room. He slammed the door as he left.

Jenny listened for the clicking sound of the lock. She struggled to get up off the floor. She felt the back of her head and looked at her hand. She was bleeding. She walked back to the bed to lie down. Each step felt like she was carrying a ton of weight on her back. As she put her head on the pillow, it quickly became covered with blood. She thought she was going to die. She wanted to die. Her head hurt too much. Her body became numb. She hid underneath the blanket. She was trying to hide from the world. She closed her eyes and fell asleep.

She dreamt about her mother again. She dreamt she was an angel with white wings. She dreamt she was flying. She was free. It was beautiful. She was beautiful.

78

Jake pulled up on his motorcycle in front of the Jones' house. He took off the helmet and gloves. He hung the helmet on the rearview mirror and shoved the gloves in the side pocket of his jacket.

The Joneses lived near Jake's old home. They lived in Westbury, two blocks south of Jericho Turnpike on Post Avenue. The neighborhood was predominantly African American, Portuguese, and Hispanic.

As Jake walked up the front steps, a little boy opened the door. Next to the boy was a large dog.

It was a mix between a Doberman and a couple of other breeds. From the look on its face, the dog meant business.

"Are you Uncle Jake?" asked the young boy.

"Yes, I am. And you must be James," replied Jake, as he held out his hand. James accepted the offer and shook his hand. "And who is your friend next to you?"

"This is Gozee. That's short for Godzilla," answered James with a big smile.

The dog was appropriately named, thought Jake. Gozee stood on all fours ready to attack on any wrong move made by the stranger at the door. Jake put out his hand to let the beast smell it. Gozee relaxed. He sat down after taking a good sniff of the stranger's hand.

"Come on in Jake," said Jones, as he approached the door. "Gozee go to the living room." The hulk like animal immediately got up, and walked in to the living room. He lay down directly in front of the large screen television.

Jake walked in to the house, and followed Jones to the living room. A woman peeked out from

the kitchen.

"That's my wife, Janet," said Jones.

"I'll be right out," said Janet. She went back into the kitchen.

"Whatever it is, it smells great," said Jake.

James made a spot for himself next to Jake and sat down. "Do you want to watch cartoons with me?" asked James as he tilted his head up and looked at Jake with his big eyes.

"I'd love to," replied Jake.

James took the control off the coffee table and pressed several buttons. "Have you seen this one? It's Dumbo."

"Yes, I have," replied Jake.

Jake had watched the Disney movie with Jenny many times. It was one of her favorites. He looked at James and smiled.

Janet brought out the food, and placed it on the dining table. Jones helped her, while his son and Jake sat together and watched the Disney classic. Gozee moved from under the television. He parked himself by Jake's feet. The beast that Jake had seen at the door was now acting like a pussycat.

"Dinner's ready," said Janet.

Jake and James walked to the dining table and took their seats.

"Please say grace, James," said Jones.

James clasped his hands and said grace. "Thank you Jesus for everything you have blessed us with. Amen."

"Let's eat," said Jones.

Janet had cooked a large meal that was for more than just four people. Gozee crawled under the dining table. He lay there patiently.

The three adults chatted about random subjects as they ate dinner. Jones and Janet avoided the topic of Jake's family. They talked about Long Island, Nassau County in particular, and its diversity. They talked about restaurants they liked, and the movie theaters they frequented. They talked about the never ending traffic on the Long Island Expressway, and the high property taxes; the usual topics among Long Islanders.

This was as normal as Jake had been in a long time. He appreciated the Joneses gesture of asking him to join them for dinner. It meant more to him

than they would ever know. He was thinking about Jenny. The call he had received from her still felt like a dream. He wondered if Pat had been able to narrow down the location of where she had called from.

After they finished having dinner, Jones and Jake accompanied by Gozee went into the backyard. James knew better than to ask if he could go out as well.

"I guess I'll go brush my teeth and go to bed," said James.

Everyone laughed.

Jones snapped open a bottle of beer and handed it to Jake.

"Thank you." Jake took a sip from the bottle. "Thank you for everything."

"It was our pleasure…it's been a while since we had company. I'm glad you were able to join us. There's always room here for friends," said Jones.

This was a friendship born out of extreme circumstances. This was a friendship that would last a lifetime.

Jake pulled out two cigars from the inside pocket of his jacket. He handed one to his friend. They cut the cigars and lit them.

"Janet would kill me if she saw me smoking," said Jones.

"Perhaps we shouldn't," said Jake.

"It's fine. As long as she doesn't smell it in the house, she'll be okay with it. I think," said Jones and laughed. "She's a great woman. She takes good care of me and James." Gozee barked. "And yes, she takes care of you too big fella."

"He's the sensitive type," said Jake. He leaned forward and petted the dog on his head.

They puffed on their cigars. The air around them quickly became enveloped in white smoke much like a stratus cloud. It was a clear night. The temperature was in the low seventies.

"There's something important I have to tell you. It's more like a confession than anything else," said Jake.

Jones looked at Jake and waited for the revelation. He knew it was something big.

Jake paused before he spoke. He looked as

though he was rethinking if he should tell the detective his true identity.

"I'm not an accountant," said Jake. He waited for a reaction from Jones, but there was none. "I work for the CIA."

Jones nodded, and accepted Jake's revelation. He was speechless. It all made sense now. The thought that Jake wasn't an accountant had never crossed his mind. It didn't seem important to him. During the initial investigations of Jake's background everything had checked out. The accounting firm he told the detectives he worked for had confirmed his employment.

"I never thought this was going to happen to me. I thought my family was protected. I travel to some of the most dangerous places around the world, but I forgot about the dangers here. When I found out about Nadine and Jenny, I wanted revenge. I wanted whoever did it to pay. I emptied out my arsenal of weapons. I was ready to tear down walls to find that son-of-a-bitch and blow him up to pieces. You know, as much intelligence as we have on our enemies abroad, we know very little

about the scum that is in our own backyard." Jake pulled on the cigar, and let out a thin stream of smoke. "As much power as we may think we have, we become helpless once our families are involved. We're just like any other citizen." Jake pulled on the cigar again before continuing, "I have all of CIA's resources available to me, but that hasn't helped in finding Jenny and the scumbag who took her."

"Did Agent Clarkson know? Did she know you were a spy?" asked Jones. "Is that why she wanted you to be there whenever we had a lead on Nealis?"

"Yes, she knew. I figured it would be impossible for me to stay involved with the case unless someone who was part of the investigation kept me in the loop." Jake looked up at the sky.

"Are you going back once this is over?" asked Jones.

"I don't know. I don't think so. My career as an agent is over. I don't think I'll be effective in the field and I'm not the type to sit behind a desk either. Maybe I'll become a cop."

Both men laughed. Jones picked up a bottle of beer and snapped it against Jake's bottle. "Cheers."

They sat in the backyard for several hours. They talked about their childhoods and their families. They revealed things to each other they had never told anyone else before.

As they finished smoking the cigars, Jake said he had to head back in to the city. Jones offered him to stay the night. Jake thanked him, but said he had already done enough by inviting him to his house.

Jones walked with Jake around the backyard to the driveway. Gozee followed them closely behind.

"Please thank Janet for me. Tell her I said the dinner was delicious, and that she's a wonderful cook. Give James a hug for me too. He's a great kid. You are a lucky man," said Jake.

The two friends shook hands and hugged. Jake bent down to pet Gozee. The dog stood still as he wagged his tail.

79

It had to be important considering it was well past midnight; Pat wouldn't have called otherwise.

"Jake, let me get to the point."

Pat wasn't the type of person to beat around the bush. That is exactly what Jake liked about him. If there was anyone that he trusted more than Nadine, it was Pat.

"The call from Jenny originated in Rhode Island. Our friends at the NSA came through. They narrowed the location to Newport."

"I don't know what to say…thank you," said

Jake.

"Not yet, we don't have the precise location. From what we know the call didn't end at the same location where it began. There's a possibility she made the call from a bus, truck, or even a boat. There's absolutely no way of knowing."

"How about aerial shots of the location at the time of the call?" asked Jake.

"Unfortunately, there is limited satellite coverage in that area," said Pat.

Newport, along with many other cities, wasn't considered to be a target for terrorist attacks. Surveillance satellites were all dedicated to cities that were at risk.

"What do we do now? Should we set up road blocks? Search every bus and truck? Do we alert the Coast Guard, and have them search boats?"

"I've alerted the Coast Guard. As far as road blocks are concerned, that may be more of a challenge to pull off. Newport doesn't have enough resources to search every vehicle that comes in and leaves the city. I have notified the police department there to stop and search all suspicious vehicles."

"Okay, I'm going to head out there now. Pat, thanks for doing this," said Jake.

"I'm taking the next flight out of Virginia to Newport. I'll see you there. Several other agents are coming with me as well. We are going to find her Jake. I promise you this is going to be over soon." Pat ended the call.

Jake took a deep breath. It was a sigh of relief. He felt as though a major weight was slowly being lifted off his shoulders. However, it was too early to celebrate.

Jake wanted as many resources as possible to be involved in the search. The first call he made was to Jones. He brought the detective up to date on the new developments. Jones said he would coordinate with the FBI.

"Go to the helipad near Wall Street. I will alert the NYPD to pick you up from there. A helicopter will be waiting for you. It's the quickest way to get to Newport," said Jones.

"I'm on my way."

Jake threw a few essentials in a bag, and left the hotel. He hailed a cab, and told the driver to

step on the gas. Adrenaline was rushing through his body.

Ten minutes later Jake was at the helipad. There was a NYPD helicopter waiting there for him. He paid the driver, got out of the cab, and sprinted towards the aircraft.

"Jake Burke?" asked the pilot.

"Yes, I'm Jake Burke."

"We are going to Long Island to pick up Detectives Jones and O'Brian. From there we'll fly to Newport," said the pilot as he shook hands with Jake.

Less than two minutes later the helicopter was in the air. It was a clear night. The city looked stunning from above. Jake had traveled aboard helicopters numerous times before, but the thrill of flying over Manhattan was unique. It was exhilarating.

The flight to Long Island was short. The pilot landed the helicopter. Detectives Jones and O'Brian were waiting at the helipad. They boarded as soon as the helicopter touched the ground.

"These things scare the shit out of me," said

O'Brian.

Both detectives shook hands with Jake and the pilot. The helicopter was back in the air within minutes.

"We'll land in Newport in approximately ninety minutes," said the pilot.

The detectives and Jake discussed their plan on how to tackle the task of searching vehicles and camping grounds. They couldn't assume anything. Every rock would have to be turned. Chances were, if the information from the NSA was correct, Nealis was still in Newport. The probability he had accomplices in the police departments of New York, New Jersey or Rhode Island were slim to none. This wasn't a Hollywood movie. This was real life.

It became increasingly difficult to keep the fact that Jake was a CIA agent from Detective O'Brian. When Jake advised him of the fact, he didn't seem surprised. In fact, the expression on his face indicated he expected it.

"It was tough to believe you were an accountant even though your story checked out. I

don't mean to offend accountants, but they are not exactly built like you. They're not the Harley types - nor do you look like a pencil pusher, know what I mean?" said O'Brian. "I'm just saying."

All three chuckled. It was a much needed laugh under a stressful situation.

"CIA agents will be assisting us in the search. We can use as many bodies as possible," said Jake.

"There's no way that motherfucker Nealis is going to escape this time," added Jones.

The helicopter landed in Newport. The flight lasted exactly ninety minutes as the pilot had indicated. They were greeted by officers from the City of Newport Police Department.

One of the police officers introduced himself as, "Detective Kevin Arnold." He was six foot-six and appeared as though he weighed three hundred and fifty pounds. He looked more like a NFL linebacker than a detective.

"Whatever you are thinking is right," said Detective Arnold.

"As long as it wasn't the New England Patriots, you are okay," said O'Brian.

"The Jets," said Detective Arnold.

"My man!" said Jones. "That's right you were injured during preseason before your rookie year."

"I suffered a concussion and that was it," said Detective Arnold as he reflected. "Anyway, that was another lifetime." The detective paused for a moment, and then continued, "We have two cars for you and have booked three rooms at the hotel on Goat Island." Detective Arnold handed a set of car keys to each of them along with his card. "If there's anything you need, don't hesitate to call me."

Detective Arnold walked up to Jake and said, "We know the asshole we are tracking has your daughter. If she's in Newport, we're going to find her. You can count on that."

Jake thanked the detective.

80

Jake met Detectives Jones and O'Brian in the lobby of the hotel on Goat Island. A conference was being held at the hotel for pharmaceutical companies. The lobby was packed with sales people, mostly men, in suits with name tags pinned to their jackets. Each man had a story to tell. The testosterone level was high.

A salesman walked up to Detective O'Brian and asked, "Are you with Merck or Pfizer?"

"I'm with the PD," replied O'Brian.

"Is that a local company?"

"No, we are based out of New York."

"I've never heard of them. What's your product?" asked the salesman.

"Sometimes crack and others cocaine. It depends on the demographic. Are you interested?"

The salesman let out a nervous laugh. "We might as well be pushing those ourselves. Business is tough these days with the FDA regulated drugs." The salesman looked at Jake and Jones suspiciously. He waited for the punch line, but noticed the serious looks on their faces. "Let me leave you guys alone," said the salesman, and walked away.

"You're really fucked up," said Jones.

"The guy wanted to know who I was with, and I answered him honestly. Is it my fault he's missing a few screws?"

Jake saw a man walk towards him after he entered the lobby of the hotel. It was Pat.

"Jake, it's good to see you."

Jake introduced the two detectives to Pat. They all shook hands.

"The team is waiting outside," said Pat. "We

are going to find this madman."

The traffic in Newport came to a standstill as trucks and busses were searched at roadblocks. The Newport Police Department made random traffic stops to search vehicles. This was anything but normal for the small city.

The local media reported on the traffic delays. They had been asked by the police department to keep the reason for the delays off the air. In case Nealis was still in the area, they didn't want to alert him in to escaping. He had been successful at evading capture thus far, and there was no guarantee he would be caught if he attempted to leave Newport.

There were searches under way of the mansions along the World Famous Cliff Walk and Bellevue Ave. The footage of the most recent sex videos from Nealis indicated the windows of the rooms were large. The description matched the large windows of the many mansions in Newport. Most

of the mansions had been converted to museums. The chance Nealis was hiding in one of them was low, but nothing was left to chance.

81

Jake and Pat arrived at the mansion, surrounded by police officers, on Bellevue Avenue. During the door to door search, two officers had rung the bell at the gate of a mansion that was listed as a museum. It was within walking distance from the famous Rosecliff Mansion.

It was at the Rosecliff Mansion the Nevada silver heiress, Theresa Fair Oelrichs, was known for having hosted fairy tale dinners. It was ironic as the man, Craig Nealis, authorities were hunting lived a delusional fantasy life himself.

When there was no response from inside the mansion, the officers searched city records on the computer in their car for the name of the firm that managed it. It didn't take them long to find it. One of the police officers called the management company. He was told by the firm they hadn't managed that particular mansion in over five years. The officer was told the mansion had been purchased by a bank in New York City. The local police records had not been updated to reflect the change of ownership. The officer thanked the operator, and called his sergeant. Within minutes ten marked and unmarked police cars arrived at the suspicious mansion.

The area around the grand structure was surrounded by a metal gate. The mansion could not be seen from street level. Besides the distance, it was hidden behind large trees; some of which were two hundred years old.

The last family to occupy the mansion was weary of the general public. They had purchased the mansion for its privacy. The last heir willed the mansion to the City of Newport. The property,

which had been built to keep the public away, was converted in to a museum. It attracted thousands of visitors from around the world every year.

When Jake arrived at the scene he saw Detective Arnold. "Do we have a warrant yet?" asked Jake.

"We will shortly," replied Detective Arnold.

An officer walked up to Detective Arnold, and handed him a piece of paper. "We got it," said the detective, as he held up the warrant.

A police officer approached the mansion gate with a lock cutter. With a single snap he cut the lock, and pushed open the gate. The Newport Police, FBI agents, CIA agents, and the two detectives from New York, drew their weapons as they methodically approached the Gothic Revival Style mansion.

The mansion had a romantic aura. High towers, gothic arches, and large windows surrounded the magnificent construction. Porch roofs topped off the medieval inspired grand structure.

"Move back, move back," warned an officer, as

a group of tourists gathered by the mansion gate behind police barricades. The tourists were eager to find out what was happening. Whispers could be heard among the crowd as they speculated amongst each other about the police activity.

A police officer tore down the front door. Within moments the mansion was crawling with officials. It appeared the mansion was vacant. According to public records, the building had 55-rooms and 50,000 square feet of living space. Combing through the mansion would have been a challenge for three people, but there were enough police officers, detectives, and agents to turn over the mansion in minutes. They searched the mansion room-by-room. There were several kinds of rooms on the first floor: gentlemen and ladies reception rooms, an arcade, a library, music room, morning room, dining room, and a kitchen.

The second floor revealed two master bedrooms both fit for a king. There were several smaller bedrooms on the floor as well. The third floor had an additional seven bedrooms, each with thirteen foot ceilings.

The rooms on the second floor appeared to have been used recently. Inside the smaller bedrooms, drapes were drawn over large windows. This matched the description of the rooms on the most recent videos from Craig Nealis.

Jake saw the room where Jenny had been kept. He hadn't been able to shake the images of Nealis molesting her out of his mind.

When Jake walked in to one of the master bedrooms, the image of Agent Clarkson's naked body flashed through his mind. He was in the room where she had been locked up and raped by Nealis. He walked close to the bed, and felt the sheets with his glove covered fingers. He could sense her pain and despair.

Detectives Jones and O'Brian climbed the stairs to the attic. They looked up as they entered the massive room. From its appearance, the room had been gutted, and all of the interior walls removed. It had been turned into an open loft. The windows were made of stained glass. The detectives discovered several torture devices including beds with chains and hand-cuffs along

their sides.   They also found professional video equipment.

Jake was standing in the foyer with Pat when Jones and O'Brian joined them.

"Nealis left this place in a rush," said Jake. "He knows we are close."

"I agree," added Pat.

"We have to step up the search," said Jones.

Pat's phone rang. He answered it immediately. After a brief pause, he said, "We're on our way."

82

Craig Nealis saw a group of SUVs which looked to be undercover government vehicles. He was standing by the dock at the foot of the bridge that connected to Goat Island. He was conversing with a person working on a yacht. He excused himself, and walked over the small bridge. He was wearing a baseball cap. He pulled it down to cover his face.

The CIA agents, waiting outside the hotel, didn't recognize Nealis as he sauntered past their vehicles. Besides the cap covering his face, Nealis was well disguised. He casually walked up to the

front of the hotel, opened the door, and walked inside.

There were people dressed in suits walking through out the lobby. He looked around for familiar faces. He quickly looked away after he saw Jake standing with a group of three other people. Their backs were turned against him. He couldn't make out who they were.

Nealis didn't waste any time. He hastily exited the hotel, crossed the bridge, and walked back to the dock. He approached the person he had been talking to, and handed him an envelope. The two men shook hands.

Nealis stepped inside a parked car, and reversed it out of the parking spot. He noticed the same group of government SUVs which he had seen cross the bridge, driving back. He placed the gear in drive, and drove across America's Cup Avenue. He was headed to the mansion on Bellevue Avenue. He needed to leave Newport before the authorities found him, which he realized was just a matter of time.

It would be a challenge for Nealis to vacate the

mansion quickly. It was important to him to collect his little dolls. Leaving them behind was not an option he had considered. Where he was headed, he would need them more than ever before.

The thought of killing Agent Clarkson crossed Nealis's mind. He decided against it. He was still enjoying her company. She gave him the balance he needed. He, along with his little dolls, needed a mother figure; she was perfect for the role.

83

The yacht had a crew of eight, including, the captain, chief officer, engineer, chef, two stewards, and two deck hands. Nealis handpicked all of them. The crew was paid by a company domiciled in the Bahamas. Other than the captain, they were all from various countries in South America, and none were legal residents of the United States. They spoke only a handful of English words. Nealis didn't have to bother speaking to them. If he needed to get rid of them, no one would raise an eyebrow. Not that it mattered to Nealis.

The crew, including the captain, was under strict orders by Nealis not to enter the third level of the yacht. There were hidden passageways and hatches that allowed the crew to send food to their employer. They were told he was with his family, and should not be disturbed, ever.

The large boat was a few feet short of being considered a mega-yacht. This was intentional. Since there were only a handful of mega-yachts sailing the seas around the globe, Nealis did not want the attention of being among them. He preferred to sail under the radar.

Nealis had named the yacht *Little Doll*. It was decorated with incredible furnishings. All of the knobs, including those in the bathrooms, were gold plated. A helicopter was among one of many toys onboard the floating palace.

The yacht was one hundred-fifty feet in length and thirty-five feet wide. Nealis had it built in Amsterdam to his exacting guidelines. Privacy was of the utmost importance.

The main salon was furnished with Italian furniture and a Steinway & Sons Grand Piano.

There were crystal doors, without handles, and glass walls throughout the yacht. Each door was designed to be pressed at a specific spot which enabled it to be opened. This prevented anyone from unintentionally entering a room. The only rooms with door handles were those used by the crew.

Each bedroom on the third floor, per Nealis' wishes, was designed to reflect a dollhouse. The boat builders found the request odd, but didn't question it. They were paid a hefty sum to build it. It was paid for by a company based out of the Cayman Islands. Nealis's name wasn't on the title.

84

The Coast Guard spotted the luxury yacht on its radar, and attempted to make contact. They had been ordered to stop and search all vessels leaving Newport. The captain of the yacht did not respond. The lieutenant on the Coast Guard boat attempted to make contact again. As before, there was no response from the yacht.

The captain was under strict orders from Nealis not to stop the yacht. He was told he would be fired from the job if he did. The captain became nervous when he realized he was being ordered to stop by

the Coast Guard. He informed Nealis, who was resting with his family.

"Keep moving," ordered Nealis.

"Sir, I don't think that's a good idea," said the captain.

"I paid you to captain the boat, not to think. Now, do exactly as I tell you," retorted Nealis.

The fact the yacht was not responding was enough for the Coast Guard to alert the CIA. They had orders from their superiors to do so if they spotted any suspicious activity at sea.

The Coast Guard vessel, Response Boat-Medium, was traveling at 38 knots. It was 40 nautical miles away from the yacht. The speed of the new Response Boat-Medium was a vast improvement over the Coast Guards old fleet of Utility Boats. The vessel they were pursuing was traveling at 20 knots.

85

Pat had a speedboat on standby at the pier off Goat Island. He advised the agent, who had called him while he was at the mansion, to prepare to move.

Jake, Jones, O'Brian, and Pat arrived at the pier within minutes of leaving the mansion. The engines were on, and the speedboat began moving as soon as they boarded. The boat was capable of traveling at 60 knots. They caught up to the suspicious yacht before the Coast Guard arrived. Pat attempted to make contact with the yacht. As with the Coast Guard, there was no response. The speedboat

pulled ahead of the yacht. Pat saw the captain of the large ship as he stood looking out from the control room. He turned on the megaphone, and ordered the captain to stop. The captain didn't acknowledge Pat. They pulled the speedboat next to the yacht. Pat and Jake threw ropes on its side. Jones and O'Brian watched the two CIA agents in amazement as they climbed the ropes. It was obvious to the detectives they had done it before.

Once aboard, Jake and Pat ran along the side of the yacht. They found the stairs that lead to the deck where the control room was located. With guns drawn, they entered the control room, and pointed their weapons at the captain. The thought that it was Nealis crossed Jake's mind. He was prepared to pull the trigger.

"Show me your hands, and turn around," ordered Jake.

The captain spread his arms out, and turned around. He looked dumfounded. When he accepted the envelope full of cash from Nealis, he hadn't figured this in to the equation. He thought it was a way to make some quick money. His was getting

married, and needed the cash to pay for the wedding.

"Stop the boat," ordered Pat.

It took several minutes for the yacht to come to a halt. "Why didn't you stop?" asked Jake.

"I had been ordered not to," replied the captain nervously.

"By whom?" asked Jake.

"I don't know…I don't know his name. He told me to call him, Sir," replied the captain. At the time the captain didn't think much of the request. He was just happy to get the money.

"Where is he?" asked Pat. He kept the gun pointed at the captain.

"He's on the third level."

"Stay with him, I'll check," said Jake.

Jake left the control room, and ran to the third floor. Once he got to there, he noticed the entrance was blocked by a glass wall. He looked for a handle, but didn't see one. He searched for a fire safety box, and located one off to the side of the staircase. He broke the glass of the fire safety box with the handle of his gun, and pulled out an axe.

Jake shattered the door with one swing. As he entered the floor he was puzzled by the crystal panels. They covered the length of the floor. One by one, he began to hack the panels down with the axe.

Jones and O'Brian gathered the courage to climb the ropes when they heard the sound of shattering glass. They would worry about their fears later. The Coast Guard arrived at the location, and watched the detectives climb aboard the yacht.

As each of the crystal walls fell, rooms were revealed behind them. Jake felt a sense of urgency when he noticed the rooms were decorated like dollhouses. The first two rooms were vacant. Could this be it? Are they here? thought Jake. His adrenaline pumped with each swing.

Jake lifted the axe to shatter the next wall. As it came down, he couldn't believe what he saw. A woman lay naked on a bed with her face pointed away from the door. He approached her cautiously. As he stood above her, he saw her face. It was Agent Clarkson. Her eyes were open, but her body was lifeless.

"Samantha…Samantha…can you hear me?" asked Jake.

He checked to see if she was breathing. She was alive. He covered her with a blanket. He tried to get her to move, but her body was limp. She had been drugged.

Jones entered the room, and saw Jake sitting on the bed next to a woman covered in a blanket. Her head was on his lap.

Jake looked up at Jones, and said, "It's her."

He left Agent Clarkson with Jones. Jake had to find Jenny. Coast Guard officers and O'Brian joined him in breaking down the remaining crystal doors.

"In here," yelled a Coast Guardsman.

Jake rushed to see what it was. It was a little girl, but it wasn't Jenny.

"What's your name sweetheart?" asked Jake.

"I'm Emily," replied the little girl. "Are you a prince? Jenny said a prince will rescue me."

When Jake heard the girl say his daughter's name, his body trembled. His lips shuddered as he spoke.

"Where is she? Do you know where she is sweetheart?" asked Jake. He spoke calmly. He didn't want to startle Emily, and scare her more than she already was.

"No," replied Emily. Suddenly, she looked up, and pointed her finger towards the door. "There's she is."

Time stood still for a moment. Even though it took less than a second for Jake to turn around, it felt like an eternity. He stood facing her. He felt relieved. He felt an indescribable calm across his body. He was at peace. At that moment, nothing else mattered. The way she looked, reminded Jake of Nadine. She looked up at Jake, unable to speak.

"Baby," said Jake.

"Daddy," whispered Jenny.

She ran towards Jake, and jumped into his arms. Jenny didn't cry. Jake did.

"Oh, baby, I'm so sorry…I'm so sorry," cried Jake.

"Where's mommy?" asked Jenny.

She didn't know her mother was dead. Jake would have to tell her. He'd wait.

86

The yacht was searched. There was no sign of Nealis. He had disappeared. Two other young girls were found on the ship. One was six years old, and the other was days away from her eighth birthday. She'd live to see her ninth.

When Coast Guard boat arrived at the pier, they were welcomed by all major television networks, and other media outlets. They were there to get the latest scoop. Officers from the Newport Police Department shielded the faces of the young girls as they carried them to ambulances that were on

standby.

The EMTs did their best to revive Agent Clarkson. She was unconscious. She was taken to a hospital, and listed in critical condition. She was admitted to ICU. It would be several days before she regained consciousness.

When Agent Clarkson opened her eyes, she saw Jake sitting next to her. He was asleep. She looked at him, and smiled. She wondered how long he had been sitting there next to her. She held his hand, and squeezed it. When he opened his eyes, he saw her looking at him. He leaned forward, and hugged her. "How's Jenny?" she whispered in his ear.

87

He got the idea of a mini-submarine while watching a television special about the co-founder of a large software company who had one on his boat. When Nealis had his yacht built, it was the first thing he demanded.

As soon as the captain alerted him about being contacted by the Coast Guard, Nealis rushed to the lower level of the yacht. He had an elevator installed to go from the bedroom to the lower level. The entrance to the elevator was hidden behind a glass panel inside the bedroom.

By the time authorities boarded the yacht, he was deep into the sea. He surfaced off the coast of Long Island.

Nealis had done his homework on finding countries that did not have extradition treaties with the United States. He had enough money to last several lifetimes. He vanished.

The mini-submarine was spotted at Jones Beach by a surfer a week after Nealis came ashore. The surfer told the lifeguard about the discovery. The beach was vacated, and taped off by the police.

Police boats surrounded the nearly submerged vessel. The divers approached it with caution. They tied ropes to the hooks on both sides of the mini-submarine. It was lifted out of water, and placed on the deck of a police boat. After a thorough investigation, the forensics team didn't find any evidence that indicated who it belonged to or where it had come from. The authorities were baffled.

88

Craig Nealis sat in the living room of a house on the artificial archipelago off the cost of Dubai.

He had planned his escape well. There were no miscalculations. After flying, under an alias, out of Long Island's McArthur Airport on a private jet, and a brief stay in Luxembourg to refuel, Nealis landed in Dubai. He had carefully chosen the crew of the private jet. He paid off the right people to acquire a Canadian passport.

Nealis watched as the discovery of the mini-submarine, found off the coast of Long Island, was

reported on the news.

The reporter said, "Authorities are still investigating where the mysterious vessel came from, and who it belongs to."

To add to the mystery it was reported there was a possibility the mini-submarine belonged to a drug cartel, or a covert military organization.

Nealis had the inside of the mansion, on the manmade island, decorated to resemble a doll house. He would not wait much longer to compile a new collection of little dolls. It was just a matter of how he was going to do it. He was still working out the details in his head. He was determined more than ever before.

The only thing Craig Nealis underestimated was Jake Burke's resolve to hunt him down, and make him pay for what he had done to his family.